The Eucalyptus Tree
Misitia Ravaloson

Copyright © 2025 by Misitia Ravaloson

All rights reserved.

Author's note

This novel was inspired by historical events. However, certain narrative liberties have been taken for storytelling purposes. Names, locations and specific details have been altered or fictionalised to strengthen the narrative. Although rooted in reality, this book remains a work of fiction.

To my daughter Ryja,

If I can become a writer, you too can be anything you dream of.

1

Razaf

1982

"Aleo mandà tsy handeha toy izay manaiky tsy ho lasa."
"It's better to refuse to go, than to accept not to go."

This is it. This moment is why I've been counting down the days until I'm eighteen.

Mid-August's usual airport crowds are here. It's when people go abroad to begin their school year in September. They're either really good students—and all these valuable brains leaving the country is why it will stay poor—or they're well-off, like the offspring of politicians and tycoons. I'm the latter, unfortunately. I'm one of those kids who rely entirely on their family's wealth rather than any intellectual prowess. Without a shred of shame as well.

I've trodden these same corridors for five consecutive years, bidding farewell to each of my five brothers embarking on their journeys to France. But today, I'm not here as an escort. I'm the sixth child, and it's finally my turn to go. My little brother, Dazo, is up next year. I don't know how my parents did it, but they orchestrated this perfectly: their sons jetting off one after the other at eighteen to study abroad.

I know the procedure by heart now: arrive two hours early, line up, check in with passport and plane ticket, blah, blah, blah.

It's boring, really. The two-hour early part was always confusing. The entire population of Madagascar is notorious for its tardiness. Really, we're late for everything. When a meeting is scheduled for 10 am, it's understood by all involved that nobody will actually arrive until 11 am. It's like an unspoken agreement. We even have a word for it: the *fotoan-gasy*, meaning the Malagasy time. But at the airport, everybody is early, which is kind of pathetic. We're all just itching to get out of this dump. Some get to escape; others aren't that lucky.

I thought I was one of the lucky ones. My father is a powerful man. Works in Finance (i.e. access to money, i.e. rich), always wears a suit and tie, holds a leather briefcase containing top secret files, as all briefcases do, has seven children, all boys—which appears to be an important detail to some people. Grey hair, dark skin, but—he insisted on pointing out to his children and anyone asking (not that anyone ever asked)—a *noble*. This, in Madagascar, means "black people not descended from slaves but from royals."

If his power was usually a good thing, this time, it isn't. It's simple maths: important and powerful people equal important and powerful enemies.

I sense trouble when the security guard singles out my father and me in the queue, treating us more like suspects than the esteemed guests we usually were. I mean, back when I accompanied my brothers, it was like a red-carpet treatment whenever they spotted my father and his briefcase. We'd be ushered through the line in no time. There is no red-carpet treatment for me, though.

Criminal, more like.

"The Ministry of Finance has ordered an investigation against your father regarding a suspicion of money laundering."

To say I am confused would be the understatement of the year.

Next thing I know, the security guards take my father away to one of their interrogation rooms, I presume. Before he disappears, he manages to look at me and mouths, "Everything will be okay."

I should say "Yes, don't worry, I'll take care of Mum and Dazo", seeing as I'm the man of the family at this particular moment. Instead, I choose to blurt out from the depth of my frustration and confusion: "What the fuck, dad?"

My mum, Dazo, and I stand outside the airport, looking like three lost puppies. A few minutes pass (I have no idea how many; it might have been hours, actually) before someone comes to talk to us. "I'm sorry," the security guard says, "I have to confiscate your passports. Your family is prohibited from leaving the territory until the end of the investigation."

And I didn't know it yet, but I never left to study abroad. My dad was pronounced guilty. There was no prison time, but he was prohibited from exercising his functions for the foreseeable future. That's all the expensive lawyers could do. A battle against the state is often a losing battle.

It all goes downhill from here.

We were loaded. No exaggeration. My dad bought a massive villa in the capital, Antananarivo. I mean, massive was what you needed anyway when you had seven children... and more. My parents also raised many of my cousins because their own parents lived in the countryside and couldn't afford accommodation while their children attended school in the big city.

This was in the 1970s, when the house was probably the only one within a five-mile radius in the Malaza neighbourhood. There was only one church nearby. The villa was surrounded by forests and wild vegetation, which made it stand out even more. However, what truly made the house unique was the massive eucalyptus tree situated right in the centre of the garden, with its distinctive blue-green leaves. It was not exactly practical having it there—we had to go around it every time we parked the cars, rode our bikes, or ran around with the dogs—but no one ever wanted to cut it down. So, there it stayed, just towering over everything.

The tree was so tall that it could be seen from a mile away. In fact, the bus stop a few metres from our house was nicknamed "Eucalyptus" because people would often ask to be dropped off "by the eucalyptus" when they didn't know the actual name of the stop. And since eucalyptus leaves are used as a natural remedy for colds, we'd get people knocking on our gate all the time, asking for some. Like we didn't get enough attention already, thanks to my dad's job and money.

As you explored the interior of the house, you would find a library with floor-to-ceiling bookcases filled with encyclopaedias, classic novels, and books about astronomy (only rich people had that, and they never read any of those books—at least, I never had, but then again, I was not exactly a great example of an intellectual), a marble fireplace, and a dining room with a long and yet still extendable oak table. Looking back, it's almost like we wanted to attract problems.

My dad openly supported the opposition party and occasionally worked for them. I don't know much about politics (just as much as I know about my dad's real job, so I can't actually even tell whether he's innocent). However, the current President would end up fleeing the country in the 90s after being accused of crimes against humanity, murder, and detention of any suspected political opponents. So, I guess supporting the opposition was at least one innocent thing my father had done.

We should have seen all of this coming. It wouldn't have been the first time the government had tried something against my big man of a father.

We were too comfortable in our indecently big house, so we got a call one sunny Saturday morning. "You've been assigned to a new position in Toliara," said the man on the other end of the line. When this sort of call came in, there was no way to negotiate, which is why it was never followed by the "are you happy with that?" type of question we got when consenting to the GP prescribing antibiotics.

We were to move to the South of Madagascar while our house was being transformed into a gendarmerie. Again, this was not our choice.

This, in itself, was not a big deal. We moved into a state-owned house, just a bit smaller, and the South of Madagascar has beautiful beaches. For any other teenager, moving to the opposite corner of the map would be dramatic, as it means saying goodbye to their friends. Not for me, with my army of brothers and cousins.

But, put into context, it just meant they (whoever they were) didn't want us in Antananarivo any more because we were "too big" (again, whatever that meant).

Of course, that didn't faze my dad. Starting from smaller doesn't scare a man who started from zero. He comes from a poor family and often tells us that he got where he is thanks to nothing more than a guava he'd picked from a tree. To summarise, because, believe me, you don't want to hear the whole thing: he started everything by selling fruits.

He renovated the entire house in Toliara, transforming it into yet another mansion, and opened the largest grocery store in town and a prêt-à-porter boutique for my mum to manage. The man excelled at everything. Even at church, he was greatly appreciated for being their best and most generous organist.

Yes, he's a great musician, too. My brothers and I followed in his footsteps when it came to music. All seven of us are self-taught musicians, but instead of playing liturgical music, we were into Led Zeppelin, Eric Clapton, and Elvis Presley. To add another layer of extravagance, my dad gave us a whole set of musical instruments at our beach house in Toliara, just a few days after we moved in. The delivery of the instruments was like the event of the century for the locals. In that part of the country, a cow was considered the most valuable gift to offer someone.

As you may have gathered, my family wasn't exactly subtle. We seemed to like the attention.

Three years in, I made new friends at my school, the church, the grocery store, and the boutique. Everyone in my new town recognised me—sometimes mistook me for another brother but never mind. To be fair, we all looked the same, and with only one year's difference between each, age was never an element of distinction, except maybe between the first and the last brother.

We even liked and disliked the same things. For instance, we all preferred fatty meat to lean meat, and drank our coffee black, no sugar or milk. This is odd because we were rarely all together. Dazo and I were an inseparable duo, but we were often separated from the five others.

We only ever came together when we played music. That's also when it was easier to tell us apart, as our instruments would give us away. From the eldest to the youngest, it went: number one on the percussion, number two on the piano, number three on the trumpet, number four on the solo guitar, number five on the accompanying guitar, number six—me—on the drums, and number seven on the bass guitar.

Outside of music and school, my teenage years were spent on the beach or a football field, smoking and drinking, or in the car driving my friends around town illegally, which was completely fine because the police were my parents' friends and worshipped my father. I thought that was the closest thing one could come to being a celebrity.

Life in Toliara was undoubtedly the best chapter of my teenage years—I'm certain my brothers would agree. We lived like local celebrities, enjoying popularity and friendship without any of the drama that came with actual fame. Nearly everyone in town was a friend of ours. Toliara itself is stunningly beautiful, located on the southwest coast of Madagascar, roughly 560 miles from Antananarivo. The twenty-hour drive between the capital and Toliara is long but scenic, on one of Madagascar's best roads—straight, smooth, and relatively traffic-free. Along the way, tourists often stop at Isalo National Park, an expansive 315-square-mile area of stunning plains and dramatic canyons. Close by is Ilakaka, famous for its sapphire mines. Upon arriving in Toliara, we can find breathtaking beaches and warm, welcoming locals.

And that nice life is probably why I never questioned what my father did or didn't do. As long as it paid for what I had...

Then, one day, my mother asked that all the children stay home and help because inspectors were coming (translation: trouble was on its way).

"We're going to welcome them in the best possible way, so your father gets good scores," Mum said.

The public treasury inspector—a tall and imposing figure, dressed impeccably in a dark suit and tie, with a crisp white shirt and polished shoes—was treated like a five-star hotel guest. There were unlimited vol-au-vents, canapés, and an expensive bottle of Malagasy vanilla rum. Despite his serious and formal demeanour, he laughed at my father's jokes and occasionally gave him a tap on the shoulder. It all went well...

Too well, in fact, because the inspector decided my family was now too comfortable in Toliara. And so, we were abruptly transferred back to Antananarivo. Not in our spacious home, which had to remain a gendarmerie until another base was found, but in a smaller, cramped state-owned house wedged between buildings—a deliberate move to hinder my father's ambitions. They were good at putting a spoke in my father's wheel. There was less extravagancy from here, but we still lived a fairly good life. And this was the capital; nothing new, no real adjustment to make (not that one was ever needed).

Starting in 1977, each of my five older brothers went to France for their studies when they turned eighteen.

Knowing all too well that there was zero opportunity for a musician, especially a drummer, to flourish in Madagascar, I saw this as the inevitable path for me, too.

I knew for sure that I didn't want to be anything other than a drummer. I also hated school, and the teachers didn't see much of a future in me, so there was no point. I didn't disagree with them. I made no effort. Didn't bother. With my family's affluence, studying abroad posed no obstacle.

Little did I realise that our wealth would become the very obstacle to my dreams, crushing them in the process.

Nevertheless, I meticulously followed the steps: patiently waiting to come of age, submitting my application to the Conservatory of Lille, and ultimately securing acceptance.

All of that for being rejected at the airport and being issued a prohibition from leaving the country.

Fuck this.

2

Hira

2017

"Izay adala no toan-drainy."
"Only a fool follows blindly in their father's footsteps."

This is it. The day I've dreamed of for as long as I can remember. I've just landed in London—Gatwick Airport, to be precise. It was my first-ever flight. Or rather, my first-ever flights. Getting here took twenty-two hours, three planes, and 5,600 miles. My first flight was terrifying. Less because of the flight itself and more because of the unknown ahead.

Landing at Gatwick is one of those moments that feels surreal. I have to pinch myself to believe it's actually happening. A lifelong dream finally coming true is almost too much to comprehend.

Gatwick Airport is massive. That's the only way I can describe it. I'm not used to airports being this large or having shops inside them. This place could easily be mistaken for a shopping centre, and honestly, I wouldn't mind shopping here. I'm amazed to learn that this isn't even the largest airport in London.

With Gatwick being so vast, it's hard to tell if there are many people here or just a few. Back in Antananarivo, the airport seemed so crowded, not because there were especially many people, but because the space was limited. August is usually when the airport there is the busiest, not in the middle of January. Still, it was nearly impossible to navigate with my two large suitcases without bumping into someone, while here, I can push my luggage along with plenty of space on either side.

The only catch here in London is that I have to hurry. People here don't waste time. It's the complete opposite of our *mora mora* lifestyle. *Mora mora* means "slowly slowly," but in this context, it's better translated as "take it easy." In Madagascar, we don't rush. We tend to proceed at a leisurely pace with most things. It's a culture, and we are proud of it.

***

This has always been the dream, despite not feeling like it right now.

In my dreams, I didn't picture myself in a room as big as a wardrobe. Not that the size of the room is the main problem here. It mostly feels lonely. Though not empty, the house feels lonelier with people around it.

I can hear Mel and her boyfriend in the kitchen, having coffee, eating breakfast, and getting ready for work. I don't want to join them. I want to leave them some privacy. They probably don't want me around all the time. Mel is lovely and was super welcoming, but the fact that we are not close makes it difficult to feel 100% comfortable in her house. She's the cousin of a friend of a friend... so yeah, not close. But she so generously agreed to take me in for a few days until I find a job in London.

The thing is, I applied for the course, got accepted into the school, and we even managed to scrape together enough money for the plane ticket. But the housing situation? That was an unsolvable puzzle.

Until Mel.

I was a freelance blogger for a French firm while living in Madagascar. I've always loved writing, and I've known for a while that it was what I wanted to do growing up. Naturally, I didn't aspire to write about windows and door frames for a carpentry company, but writing is writing, and most importantly, a job is a job, so I was glad to have it. Joanna was the head of communication at the company and the one who managed all the freelancers. In the seven years of working for her, we became—not exactly friends since it's difficult to be friends with your boss who lives 5,300 miles away—but closer than just employer/employee.

It was Joanna who told me her cousin had a friend in London who would happily host me for a few days after I told her about my dreams of going to London to study. To me, that was just a simple conversation. I never thought she would try to help. She told me about her dreams of going to Indonesia. I didn't exactly ask my cousins if they had friends in Indonesia. Not that any of my friends would have known anyone in Indonesia, anyway.

I know nothing about Indonesia, which is ironic because I apparently look Indonesian. I didn't realise this until I came to London. It turns out there are many similarities between Indonesia and Madagascar.

In my defence, I know nothing about any country at all. Until I was about ten, I thought the only countries in the world were Madagascar and France. I learnt about London because of a movie. I spotted the iconic red buses of London and was incredulous to see people sitting on the roof. There were actual stairs inside the bus. How cool. In my country, we don't even have "buses". We have "big taxis". Basically, a van. Usually, it's a very old Mercedes-Benz with countless mechanical problems, making you believe in God every time you get to your destination alive.

So, I made it eventually because I am here now, at Mel's place. A virtual stranger to whom I owe a debt of unending gratitude.

The first day was great. Mel and her boyfriend made crab soup, which I can only describe as a symphony of flavours dancing on my palate. When I came in, the delicious smell floated through the flat. It was quite the welcome.

We chatted casually, and they were curious about my reason for coming to London. I mentioned my pursuit of a Postgraduate Diploma at the London School of Journalism, but kept it short. I didn't want to go too crazy and tell them about my yet another unrealistic dream of becoming a well-known writer in England.

I had a wonderful first evening.

Still buzzing with adrenaline from landing in my dream city three hours earlier, nothing could have dampened my spirits.

It's like everything else, really. First times are always the best. The first time I got on the tube in London, for instance, I was fascinated by the parade of people of all ages, colours and backgrounds getting in and out of the train at each stop. All strangers, and each of them wearing the same expression of exhaustion, yet satisfaction and, I guess, determination. It's true, and I'd learn it soon enough, life in London was all about working and making money in order to afford rent, but it's so worth it because the city repays you in freedom and a wonderful feeling of belongingness.

The excitement of the first time quickly faded, though. After the tenth time, the tube just felt like being stuck in a can of sardines, except cans of sardines weren't loud.

While I was on a cloud when I first arrived, the reality check came crashing down not long after.

Well, by the second day, really.

I needed to find a job. Challenging doesn't begin to describe my job-hunting experience. First, I lack experience in most things. I was at school, then found my freelance writing job at sixteen, and that was it. That freelance job paid about three euros for an article, which was obviously too low, but it was enough to help my parents with bills and attend university. It's not uncommon for French companies to outsource some work in Madagascar because of the low rates there—a leftover dynamic from colonial times that still shapes economic relationships today.

With that experience, or the lack thereof, I knew looking for a writing job in London was pointless. But I didn't know how to do anything else, so I had little to put on my resume. I lied and exaggerated a lot there. My parents opened a street food stall, if we could call a set of homemade wobbly tables and chairs and an umbrella, that. I sometimes helped them out by making sandwiches and selling the food. In my resume, that translated to "waitress in a fast-food". I have many cousins, my dad having six brothers and my mum having four sisters, all married with more than one child. That translated to "babysitter". And that was it.

I applied for waitressing and babysitting jobs with these two fake work experiences. Needless to say, the employers were not impressed.

Plus, there was the language barrier. I have an okay level of English (at least, I thought I did). Madagascar is a French colony, so my second language is French. I learnt a bit of English as an optional language at school. But except for the basic "Good morning, how are you? My name is Hira", and the seven days of the week, I didn't learn much there. I was mostly self-taught, listening to American songs.

When I was a child, I went to a cyber cafe once a week to Google songs' lyrics and translations. It's through that unconventional method that I learnt the most.

But in England, my knowledge of the English language was reduced to non-existent. The accent was so different. Beautiful, yes. Romantic, yes. But different. It was so different that it sounded like another language entirely! Imagine looking for a job, not understanding the employer's words, and presenting a resume with barely enough info to cover half an A4 page. Not. Great.

At least, if I had a bit of self-confidence, it would have been—if not less challenging—less embarrassing. But self-confidence and I had always been incompatible. Some people got a job based on their experience and skills, others thanks to their vibrant personality (you know, in the movies, there was always one that got hired because the employer saw something special in them). I had none of that, so each job application was as painful for me as it was for the employers. I was a non-experimented, non-English-speaking introvert. By the end of my second day in London, I broke down and cried in my bed, wishing to be home with my parents. Oh, here's an interesting fact about me: I break down and cry a lot.

Of course, giving up was not an option. I owed it to myself and my parents, who were worried sick for me and still fully supported me, to get something—anything—out of this trip. Each day, I'd get ready and go from one café to the next, dropping off my resume. And each day, I became more and more aware of the differences between here and my home country.

I felt like a misplaced puzzle piece. Being a foreigner did that to you. Even the air smelt different, crisp and cold. I never noticed before getting here that the air had a smell, but it did. The air in Madagascar was warm and thick and carried the earthy aroma of the red soil.

Also, here, everybody moved with a rhythm I couldn't match. Their gestures and expressions were their own language. I was clumsy and out of sync with the rhythm of the crowd. Even my clothes seemed to be wrong. I don't know, I wore jeans, too, but they just didn't seem to be the right jeans.

But there was no room for doubt. There would be time to process everything later. My priority was finding a job, so I wore a mask of determination every morning.

I gave myself exactly one week to find a job. Arrive on Monday, find a job, then start school the following Monday. That was the plan. I secured a job on Sunday. Talk about last minute. Last minute is the story of my life. I sent my application to The London School of Journalism one day before the deadline, because I found the ad accidentally, just before applications were closing. We got the money for my flight ticket the day we were supposed to pay and confirm it. It seems like I always make it to the other side just when the doors are about to close.

So, I'll be a waitress at an Indonesian restaurant.

The Indonesian lady boss didn't care about my resume—she didn't even look at it. She just asked when I was available to start and if I had a black skirt. "Immediately, and yes." In fact, no, but I'd just have to buy that later.

My working schedule was 6 pm-11 pm on Mondays, Tuesdays, and Thursdays, and 2 pm-12 am on Saturdays. Onwards! I didn't know what the heck onwards meant at the time of the interview, so I agreed. Turns out onwards at this restaurant meant "systematically later than 12 am, that you will always be late for the last tube and will have to take the very long boring bus home".

Working here, I realised that I looked Indonesian. Very often, the customers would greet me in Indonesian or ask questions in their language, not realising I was not from there. It was weird that the language actually sounded very similar to what Malagasy sounded like. No single word was the same, but the tone was spot on.

It was also here that I realised how diverse London actually was. My boss and her husband were Indonesian, the cooks were mostly Romanian and Polish, one waiter was Portuguese, and another waitress was Italian. In fact, nobody was English. Customers were mainly Indonesians because they liked the authenticity of the food, although many of them complained that it was far from the *Nasi Goreng* or the *beef rendang* they usually had at home. And I, as the waitress, was always the one having to deal with these complaints, as if I knew anything about cooking, let alone Indonesian cuisine. But my boss didn't care much about the complaints. Whenever I reported some comments to her, she asked me to smile and nod. Her advice—or shall I say her whole management style? —was questionable.

Apart from the exigent Indonesian customers, there would be people from all over the world, from Brazil to Australia. Weirdly, nobody from Madagascar.

Actually, it's like nobody from Madagascar had ever stepped foot in London. I noticed this from day one, at the airport. When I handed my passport, the officer looked at it suspiciously, then curiously. During the whole process of him examining my passport—which I think took half a minute but felt like half an hour—I stood there, panicked that he would not let me in the country. I had a million questions going through my head. I even started wondering whether my passport was fake, or if my visa wasn't legit—knowing fully that I went through all the normal and perfectly legal procedures to get them. But it's just one of those things, like when you go through a baggage scan and suddenly wonder whether you put a gun (that you obviously don't own) in your bags. Then, the officer just smiled and said: "Madagascar? I don't think I've ever seen a passport from Madagascar". He then laughed, as if he didn't just give me a mini heart attack a few seconds before.

I found it odd that somebody who saw thousands of passports a day had never seen one from Madagascar, but I didn't think much of it. It could be that the guy was new.

But then, I ended up hearing that same sentence a lot in London. If I were given £10 every time someone said "I don't think I've ever met anyone from Madagascar before," I wouldn't be a waitress in Soho right now.

They told me that at the post office, when I collected my resident card. In the park, I was surrounded by curious strangers who couldn't for the life of them make up where I seemed to come from.

To be fair, I look different. Another thing I became self-conscious about. I am too black to be Asian, but too white to be a Black African. You also can't say I'm a light-skinned African, because my face apparently doesn't make me look like a typical African woman, whatever that's supposed to mean. I have the plump lips of an African woman, but the squinty almond-shaped eyes of an Asian woman. My hair doesn't help because it is not straight, but also not what we can call curly, never mind Afro. It's all just a bit confusing when you grow up thinking it is as straightforward as "I was born in an African country, therefore I'm African", when, actually, nobody sees you that way until you say so.

I've struggled a bit with this. I think part of my introversion comes from this uncertainty around my identity. One woman from Ghana came to the restaurant once and wore such a beautiful traditional dress, with Afro hair just as beautiful. I imagined wearing it, and it just wouldn't work. I don't know what box to put myself in. But then again, besides my unidentifiable origins, I could never put myself in any box. Not the popular girls, not the geeks, not the sports people, nothing. I've always lived in my own bubble.

***

Confusion fills me as I open my eyes. I need some time for my vision to clear. Even at 7 o'clock, the thin, white curtains only let in a small amount of light. But mostly, it takes time to realise this is not my room. I've been here for a week now, but my brain still can't adjust to the fact that I am not in my bed, room, house, city, or even country. This is London. And I have to get up to go to school.

My introversion is proving especially difficult during my first day at the London School of Journalism.

Now, trust me, it's hard enough being an introvert, but doing it in English? That's another level of hardship. You don't only need to make friends, look normal and hide your awkwardness... You do all that with poor English knowledge.

And it requires calculations. My first lesson is due to start at 9 am. Now, as an introvert, you don't want to be there too early because it's just too awkward, but too late is even worse because everybody would have already formed a group and let's face it, you would never introduce yourself to any of the groups. So I thought I'd arrive at 8:56 am. The perfect time to greet the small groups of people who are already there, and arrive at the same time as many others to sort of fit in. But my calculations are useless because when I arrive, nobody's waiting outside. Everyone must already be inside.

The London School of Journalism is small, and I mean smaller than the very many large institutions in London, but massive if we compare it with what I'm used to seeing. I'm only here for a short course. It's a six-month Postgraduate program.

It's all I could afford. And that's a stretch. I can't exactly afford it. It's just that they were nice enough to create a payment plan for me. I didn't have to pay anything the first month, and then I can pay at my own rhythm as long as it's all paid for by the end of the course. I was okay with it, because I was planning to work as much as needed and make the money (that, of course, before I realised more than half of my pay would be for rent).

In England, this school doesn't even appear on official registries of accredited academic institutions. I realised later that whenever I had to fill out administrative forms which asked for the school I attended, I could never find The London School of Journalism on the list and had to type the name in "Other". It should be right under the very prestigious London School of Economics, but it's not.

But I don't care about any of that. It may not be a prestigious school, but it is for me. The first time I lay eyes on the school, I am five years old again, opening my Christmas presents on the 24th of December. Yes, I always opened my presents on the 24th back in Madagascar because I apparently couldn't wait, and my parents gave in. It then became my normality to think that Santa Claus came to our house before anybody else's because I was very special.

The building is old, but not old *old*. Charming old. Beautiful old. The LSJ proudly announces that it has existed since 1930, although I'm not sure if it has always been located in this building in Maida Vale.

White paint covers the building, but some concrete is still visible. Again, old. But it looks like that's the effect they wanted, as I highly doubt an institution like this wouldn't have the money for a little makeover. I mean, the money I have to pay them is probably enough to paint the entire building twice with the most premium paint and the most expensive labourer.

The old effect works; it shows experience, history, and legitimacy. The building is tall enough to be seen from a few metres away. And as I approach, I am welcomed by a black gate with the writing LSJ in gold. I open the gate and am met with a dull car park; however, my eyes are fixed on the building the whole time.

As I open the antique Victorian oak door to the reception, I am welcomed by a really cosy space that looks more like a spa waiting room than a school. The only distinction is the poster ads on the wall, which don't show nails and haircuts but student accommodation, student jobs, scholarship opportunities, and so on.

While the outside is old and vintage, the inside looks like it was refurbished yesterday, with colourful bistro chairs, tables, and even an egg chair. Opening that single door makes me jump from 1930 to the present day—to the future, even. At the reception, all I have to do is give my name, and the very nice lady there gives me a badge along with some documents. She speaks impossibly fast. I don't fully understand her, but I'm pretty sure she tells me to go meet the other students in the hall until they announce which classroom we have to go to.

The school smells of success, which is weird to explain, but it's the same way hospitals smell like sickness and churches smell like peace. When you enter those places, you just know where you are and what you are about to accomplish. I smile the entire time.

My smile, however, fades rapidly.

As I cross the corridor and open yet another door that leads to the hall, I freeze for what feels like an eternity. I just feel two hundred sets of eyes on me, and I'm not imagining it. It's quiet for a second while the students look at whoever opened the door before returning to their lively conversations. It's not because they were interested in me, of course; it's only because they were expecting a professor or someone from the school office to come and make the welcome speech. When my legs can move again, i.e., when I finally feel safe and understand nobody actually cares about me, I pick a random seat.

Two minutes later, someone comes for the speeches and announces where we need to go. There are various subjects, including general journalism (which I enrolled in), creative writing (which I wanted but didn't qualify for due to my English level, considered insufficient), and web marketing, among others.

General journalism students are heading to classroom number five. As I walk down the corridor, following the wave of students all walking in the same direction before slowly spreading as they join their designated classes, I notice that a good half of the students heading to number five are foreigners. I can hear some small groups of people speaking Italian and Portuguese. I realise then that my shoulders relax for the first time since I opened that door to the hall. What a first day. What a rollercoaster of emotions. And it's only just started.

3

Razaf

1982

"Tsy misy mahery noho ny masoandro, fa rehefa sembanin-drahona dia folaka ihany."
"Nothing is stronger than the sun, yet even the sun can be concealed by clouds."

Disadvantaged people climbing the ladder and becoming well off are the stories I grew up hearing. How it worked when the opposite happened, I don't know.

With my five big brothers gone abroad, Dazo still at school, and my father not making any money, I was forced to be the breadwinner. I admit I was jealous of my brothers because they were able to escape. They didn't have to give up on their dream of becoming musicians and having a real career.

Most importantly, they didn't have to witness our father—once a powerful man feared by many—drowning, disappearing, losing himself. He was defeated, and there was nobody he could call to save him this time. We're talking about a man who "had a guy" to erase any of his problems. Lawyers, political officers, journalists. This time, they all turned their backs to avoid being the next one to sit in the ominous chair reserved for those who dared support the opposition. So my father simply accepted his defeat.

I know my jealousy was irrational. Of course, I was happy for my brothers. Anyway, it's not like they were living the dream either. They were all struggling to make ends meet, as my parents could no longer afford to finance their stay abroad. When we were on the phone, it felt like a competition to see who was in more trouble. The only competition nobody wanted to win.

"We don't have money for food today," I would tell them.

"We've only been sharing a can of beans for a week," my brothers would retort.

Luckily, we got our house back in Antananarivo. With a new gendarmerie base secured, the government was obligated to return my father's rightful property. I bet that annoyed the shit out of them.

THE EUCALYPTUS TREE

The house was in terrible condition, though—a far cry from the luxury my family had built and known. The marble table? Gone. The shiny wooden floors? Just a distant memory. What used to be a tiled lavatory had been turned into what we could only assume was a prison cell. The garden had lost its vibrant green, and the smell of freshly cut grass was long gone. Now, it was just a lifeless yard covered in red dust. The house was unrecognisable, save for the giant eucalyptus tree in the middle of the yard.

At least we didn't have to pay rent, and getting the house back was something my father wouldn't need to fight for.

However, other bills, such as food and clothing, didn't pay for themselves. Mum and I decided to sell a large amount of our furniture, including TVs, dining tables, and sofas; the big pieces sold quickly. But it was not exactly sustainable. We quickly ran out of things to sell.

Only four months later, all that was left to sell was my drums and our turntable—both irreplaceable for emotional and monetary reasons. I couldn't get rid of my drums. How could I? It would have meant the end of everything. I had to give up on my dream of becoming a famous international musician, but that didn't mean I had to stop playing music. I could still be a simple local drummer, or not even a drummer, but someone who played the drums in the basement. The only thing that mattered now is that I could play.

However, selling the turntable wasn't ideal either. We inherited it from my grandfather, my father's father —another highly respected and somewhat intimidating man. My love for music goes back as far as I can remember, and I suspect this turntable played a role. We all have a unique memory associated with this turntable, from songs that inspired us to play music to those that played during our first kiss. Everyone in this family would be devastated if I sold it.

And yet, that's what I did. I made a selfish choice, which was uncharacteristic of me. Growing up with so many brothers and cousins, I didn't know selfishness. Sharing was rather a habit than a value that needed to be taught. But this time only, I couldn't put other people's needs first. Prioritising myself, I chose guilt over sadness as the lesser of two evils. I mean, Dazo hadn't thought about selling his bass guitar. None of my five older brothers would have even considered selling their instruments, so the drums shouldn't have been on my list of potential things to sell in the first place.

I sold the turntable and got good money out of it. I didn't even make sure it went to someone who genuinely loved music and would make good use of it. I thought the quicker it was gone, the better it was. Because the quicker it would be behind me.

***

I, Razaf, have no diploma, no real prospects, and now no more dreams worth chasing. At the start of my father's mess, the struggle didn't feel real. Sure, it was a nightmare, but nightmares were supposed to be temporary. You eventually woke up from them. When you didn't, I guess that's when it turned into hell. And this is it. This is hell.

Today is Sunday. It's 5 am. The sun is not yet fully up, and I find myself on a bus with nothing but a plastic bag and an old blanket. Public transport at 5 am is nobody's idea of a good time, but the buses in Madagascar are a whole other level of miserable. They are Spartan, to say the least. Getting a seat on these buses should be an Olympic sport.

My business idea struck me soon after selling the turntable. I went around asking neighbours for their unwanted items: scrap metal, shoes, pots, tools, radios. They were glad to get rid of the junk. I fixed what was fixable and sold them at a low price. I was apparently good at fixing random objects, but not my life.

I also recalled my dad purchasing a used hanging scale from a junk dealer at the market. It was a "fine piece of craftsmanship"—that's how my father described the old thing, and he insisted it was an excellent deal. My father was a very passionate man. Only he could make a random hanging scale sound like a treasure. I didn't have the same passion. I looked at the hanging scale, acquiesced and moved on. I ended up needing the bloody scale to weigh my suitcases before my trip to Lille, which never happened.

But the gist is that the old scale and the turntable gave me an idea: I would become a junk dealer.

That's the story behind me sitting on the bus at 5 am.

First stop: the market. The busy and popular Mahamasina market, to be exact. It's quite central, but only a half-hour bus ride from our house in Malaza. Make that one hour and a half on the way back because of the traffic and rush hour, but I was hoping that going back home with money in my pockets would make me forget about the pain of sitting in a miserable bus for a time long enough to fly from Paris to London.

I spread my old blanket on the ground and drop all my junk onto it. They make a metallic thud as they hit the surface, but nobody is paying attention because they're all busy setting their own stall.

The job is all about haggling. People come by, sometimes other curious dealers, and other times, the occasional passer-by looking for a bargain. They poke around, ask the price, and then we go back and forth until they either walk away or we shake on a deal.

I myself tour the other stalls, negotiate, and grab some bargains to sell back. With competitors around, I have to learn rapidly.

By the end of the day, I am exhausted, but I make enough money to put food on Dazo, Mum, and Dad's plates for a couple of days.

Tonight, we have dinner at the table for the first time in months. It is not the same loud table with dozens of children. When my family ran out of resources, my cousins had to return to their home in the countryside. But it's not a sad table either. It is the four of us, not worrying about tomorrow's food, and not watching the depressing news.

Because of this, I know... I know I will keep doing this for as long as I have to. Forever, even, if that's how long it takes for us to find a solution to my father's problems. That's when it becomes permanent. Hell.

But I am doing it for my family. For Dazo. For my dad. For my mum.

Oh, my mum...

Mum is what you'd call a strong woman in the 70s—and probably in every century. Elegance is the best word to describe her, with her pleated dresses and perfectly braided bun. Despite having seven children, she always managed to find time to powder her face and put on lipstick that matched her shoes. Life hadn't been easy for her. After losing her parents at a young age, she was left in the care of her older brother, who forced her to work rather than attend school. Determined, she taught herself to read and write by secretly borrowing his books. Marrying my father was her rescue; he encouraged her to attend sewing classes, not just for a hobby, but to help her find friendship and independence.

She married at sixteen, had her first child at eighteen, and was essentially pregnant for about ten years, if you do the maths. She had hoped for a little girl but wasn't lucky in that regard—or perhaps was very lucky, depending on whom you asked. Having a boy means the family name would carry on for at least one more generation, and it's considered a great achievement in Madagascar. Besides, the number seven is believed to be a blessed number. So, seven boys really are a miracle to some.

According to our ancestors, the universe consists of seven elements: three above—the Sun, the Moon, and the

Stars—and four below—the Earth, flora, fauna, and humans.

Some people also say the story behind the number seven being a blessed number actually ties to religion.

Religion and ancestral traditions significantly influence the majority of the country's beliefs and customs. For instance, in Madagascar, funerals are never held on Thursdays, as it's said to trigger an unending cycle of deaths within the family. Opening an umbrella indoors is forbidden as it invites debt. In some coastal regions, wearing a red swimsuit is strictly avoided because it is believed to anger the sea. There may be no scientific reasoning behind these customs, yet they persist. These rules are simple and harmless enough that challenging them seems pointless. After all, avoiding wearing a red swimsuit won't cost your life, but wearing one just might. The choice is easy.

I was raised Christian. I went to church every Sunday morning with my parents and brothers, attended Sunday school, said a prayer before eating, and listened to Mum reading Bible verses before bed. But that wasn't enough to make me grow up as a "Christian"—whatever that means. It's not that I don't believe in God. Whenever I contemplate the colours of the sunset or the beauty of a sky full of stars, I am convinced there has to be a divine Creator beyond human power. It's just that I am angry.

God doesn't seem fair to everyone, with all the diseases, wars, and poverty in the world.

Well, God's fairness to me alone is questionable. I'm the shortest of the brothers, which seems unimportant, but is significant to me. Why am I the shortest of the seven brothers sharing the same parents?

For a long time, I wanted to play the piano, but people mocked me for having fat and short fingers. Whenever my dad had guests at home, I was asked to play the piano, not because of my talent, but because they found my fingers "adorable" and "amusing." My brothers didn't spare me either. Every time that happened, they found it hilarious. There was no pity among us. Anyone who was grounded or humiliated became the target of the others' laughter. It's all part of the brotherhood. Of course, there's also immense affection, even though we don't voice it.

It's mainly through helping each other out that we show that. One morning, I got home completely wasted from a night out with friends and threw up all over the living room. When Mum saw the mess, one of my older brothers told her that we had gone running early in the morning without breakfast. I felt faint and got sick, so he had to bring me back home. He said I just needed some food and rest, which was the only truth in his story. Unaware of her sons' occasional poor behaviour, Mum made me tea, bread and butter.

Other than my brothers always having my back, I had little faith in general. The incident at the airport was just the last straw that broke the camel's back. As I said, not great, not fair.

I follow the same gruelling routine every day, seven days a week, and twelve hours a day. Rising before the sun, taking the miserable, crowded bus, haggling, negotiating. I adapted to it fairly quickly. Having made new friends eased the long hours and lessened the fatigue. I also discovered my talent for identifying hidden value in seemingly worthless items. I often found jewellery, particularly necklaces, to be lucky finds, as they were always hopelessly tangled and often ignored. While mostly plastic or faux gold, real gems could unexpectedly be found within the mix. When that happened, I allowed myself to buy a more luxurious dinner for Mum, Dad and Dazo. Fish was my mum's favourite, but also the most expensive kind of food in the market.

Unfortunately, it isn't a lucrative business despite the occasional lucky discovery. But a business, nonetheless—one that I would end up doing for four interminable years!

4

Hira

2017

"Raha monina an'osy, lavitra olon-kiresa-hana."
"To live on an island is to live far from voices, far from company."

In classroom number five, the lecturer walks in and introduces himself: Mr Andrew, teaching Law and Media. It feels ambitious for the first day, but I appreciate diving straight in.

The classroom looks like something straight out of a movie: spacious and bright, with large windows inviting abundant daylight. Desks curve gently in a semi-circle, each one surprisingly equipped with power outlets. Inspirational posters line the walls, and a giant whiteboard stretches prominently across the front, framed by high-tech screens and a sleek projector.

Something else catches my attention: every other student has an iPad or MacBook ready to take notes. Pens and paper seem like relics here. Another stark reminder that I'm out of sync. Though, truthfully, even if I'd known, I couldn't have afforded a MacBook anyway.

But the real challenge of my first lecture isn't the technology; it's Mr Andrew's accent. His British English is like a foreign language to me, and I struggle to follow. I pretend to understand, nodding at intervals and laughing slightly after everyone else, desperately hoping my confusion isn't obvious. Two hours passed in tense discomfort, every minute feeling like an eternity.

The second lecture is just like the first in every agonising detail, until I notice someone else struggling too. Her face mirrors my confusion, which makes the class somewhat more bearable.

Her name is Gia, and she's Italian. At lunchtime, as groups form and scatter to various lunch spots, Gia remains at her desk, patiently waiting until everyone else has left. I linger intentionally, and when our eyes meet, I quickly speak before the silence turns awkward.

"Hi, I'm Hira," I say, forcing a confident smile.

"Gia," she replies softly, returning the smile.

"Did you... Understand any of that?"

Gia bursts into laughter, and the tension I've carried since the first lecture dissipates instantly. Her laugh confirms that I'm not alone in this.

In that simple exchange, I know we'll be friends.

Our conversation reveals a comforting number of shared interests. Simple things like music, food, movies, books, but also more meaningful aspects of life. Gia understands struggle, too, though hers is different from mine. My childhood was filled with love but strained by financial hardship. Gia, conversely, grew up comfortably in a home shadowed by her parents' silence and emotional distance.

Gia is striking, tall and slender, with short curly hair framing a face defined by high cheekbones and a gentle, pointed chin. Her clear, amber-brown eyes frequently drift downward, as if she's lost in thought. She quickly becomes my first true friend, something I never experienced back in Madagascar. Yes, I had acquaintances there, people I'd text occasionally, but never anyone I could truly trust. High school back home was a game of gossip and hidden betrayals, where friendships seemed fragile and superficial.

Gia is different. Maybe it's London, maybe it's because we're older now, but something about her makes me feel safe enough to show vulnerability. And thankfully, she does the same.

We decide to have lunch at Gia's apartment, just five minutes away from school in Maida Vale. I'm momentarily surprised. This is London Zone Two, notorious for high rents. Gia quickly clarifies that she's on a scholarship and shares the modest space with five other students.

After lunch, returning to class feels lighter and easier, even though I still anticipate not fully understanding the lecture. Gia's presence beside me, equally puzzled but quietly supportive, fills me with a newfound confidence. When school ends, I'm smiling.

It's safe to say my first day at school is a success. Not perfect, but solid enough.

Now, on to the next challenge: making it through my two-week probation period at work. I desperately need this job. I'm already dreaming of finding my own apartment and moving out of Mel's place. Mel and her boyfriend have been incredibly kind, but I can sense the invisible timer ticking down on their hospitality. Eventually, they'll need their privacy back, and I'll need my independence.

School finishes at 3 pm, and my shift doesn't begin until 6, giving me a precious gap of free time. It's too short to justify the long commute back to Mel's flat in Barking, so instead, I find refuge at The Paper Lantern on Tottenham Court Road, easily the best bookshop in the world. Granted, I haven't explored many others yet, but I can't imagine any surpassing this one. Bookshops are my favourite places on earth, comforting sanctuaries filled with quiet possibilities. Back in Madagascar, they're not nearly as common. Why would they be, when the demand is so low?

I love that bookshops in London are often on a busy street, but there's only peace and quiet as soon as we open the door. Walking into a cosy bookshop feels like entering a haven from the bustle of daily life. I don't know if it's the mere presence of books, the ambient lighting or the delicious smell of coffee (and I don't even drink coffee), but there's something about bookshops that make me feel like I'm in a safe place, a place where I can be anyone I want to be. And The Paper Lantern is another level of enchantment.

For one, the staff is lovely. This is a dreamy workplace, so I can understand why they'd smile so much all the time. Upstairs is a classic bookshop with wooden shelves filled with books of all sorts, and attractive goodies that you always feel that you need, but really, you don't. Like the tote bags with really pretty images or quotes, the bookmarks with black cats on them, the donut cushions, and the cute water bottles. The downstairs area is bustling with students, artists, and workers, each absorbed in their laptops, books, or headphones. I am unsure of their exact work, but it appears magical. The only sounds are pages turning, keys tapping, and a coffee machine brewing.

It's a place of creation, learning, and invention, topped off by an unbeatable offer: a hot drink and cake for £3. Spending three peaceful hours here, tackling homework and assignments while savouring a hot drink and a delicious cake, what more could I ask for? My first combination is peppermint tea and walnut cake. Real tea is something entirely new to me; growing up, my mum's version of "tea" whenever I was ill consisted of hot water stirred with two generous spoonfuls of sugar—an idea that would surely horrify any Brit. Perhaps I'll use my afternoons here to sample every type of tea they offer, steadily transforming myself into a tea connoisseur, at least by the time I find the confidence to chat with someone who isn't Gia.

Just one week after landing in that scary, massive airport, I can see my routine in London: school, lunchtime at Gia's place, the bookshop and work. I will become the people I admire on the tube, engrossed in my books or phone and constantly in a rush. Just the thought of it fills me with joy and excitement.

Work, I realise, will be the only downside of that routine. Then again, it is for the majority of people. However, I particularly dislike my waitressing job. I know that from day one. I feel exploited. Right off the bat, I notice that there aren't any chairs for the staff. Not a single one. We're on our feet for the whole shift. We're forced to feign bathroom trips for a single minute of rest. We also have to clean the toilets multiple times. And by "we", I mostly mean me. I'm the new girl, so I do the dirty job nobody else wants to do.

I honestly didn't think a waitress job involved anything more than greeting customers, offering a smile, asking for their orders, sending said orders to the kitchen, bringing the food, occasionally asking if everything's fine (but not caring whether it is or not), then cleaning the table and setting it for the next customers. Doesn't that sound like a lot already? I expected the worst part of the job would be to deal with unhappy customers (and yes, I do that a lot), but really, with a bit of practice and a perfectly rehearsed sorry speech, that turns out to be very manageable. Cleaning the toilets (female and male), wiping the floor, and restocking the fridge (i.e., heavy lifting) are the worst. They make dealing with unhappy customers feel like a breeze.

After my first eight-hour shift of non-stop sprinting between customers' tables and the kitchen, and making countless trips down to the basement bathroom (because the bloody bathroom had to be downstairs), my feet feel like they have been hammered by tiny nails. Every step sends a sharp pain shooting up my legs, and the soles of my shoes seem to have melted into the burning ache beneath my skin. By the end of the night, even the idea of standing still is unbearable; all I want is to take my shoes off and collapse. On the bus ride home, I dream about my bed and blanket at Mel's place. I have a tiny cupboard room there, but a cardboard box would do at this point.

At least there is a silver lining: my first day was a success. My boss, notoriously hard to impress, didn't seem terribly disappointed.

Two weeks later, I pass my probation period with flying colours. My reaction swings between "Yay, I got the job!" and a brief disgust of "Oh crap, I actually got the job." But mostly, it's excitement: soon I'll finally have a place of my own.

My new room key is given to me on February 14th. When people are out celebrating their love life, I celebrate having a normal-sized room, a double bed and... a window! Finding a place to stay proved to be far more challenging than I had expected. Being 23, and without a boyfriend for Valentine's Day—or ever, really—I figured I'd find love before a decent place to live. That's how tough the search was, and that's why holding this set of keys in my hand feels so incredibly satisfying.

To begin with, I struggled with the choice between expensive rent near my school and work or cheaper rent further away with higher transport costs. That's London for you. After multiple research and calculations, I looked for places in Zones 4 and 5 with good public transport connections.

The second challenge was the deposit. Paying a deposit equivalent to two to three months of rent was impossible. Gia recommended Airbnb.

I admit, I wasn't thrilled with the idea of living in someone's spare room. From where I come from, we do not trust people so easily. I was taught not to talk to strangers, and my mum scared me with the most traumatising stories about murders and kidnappings. The irony is that, at only 23, she married a stranger she'd got into a car with.

Before going to a birthday party, I had to ask for permission two months in advance with a list of the other children who would be there. Sleepovers were a big no. I never even dared to pronounce the word. But it was apparently not a big deal in Europe, and many people slept at other people's houses.

And it's not like I had many choices. After receiving my first fortnightly pay cheque, I spent hours researching and contacting over a dozen landlords. Before contacting them, I scoured their online profiles and dug into their backgrounds like a madwoman stalking an ex.

My choice was going to be the first person to schedule a viewing. I was ready to say yes to anything, as long as there was a bed and no obvious sign that I might be murdered.

It was a flat in Wembley. Third floor. Double bedroom. Two flatmates. Catherine, the owner, occupies the master bedroom; Eli rents one of the other two spare rooms. Catherine works as a nurse at Wembley Hospital, while Eli is a student.

Well, so far, so good.

Catherine messaged back and arranged a viewing for the very next day, February 13th. It ended up being the quickest flat viewing in the history of flat viewings. I walked in at 2 pm, and by 2:10 pm, I walked out with a big smile on my face. We'd agreed the place was mine. £400 per month. I would have moved in right then and there if I could, but I didn't want to seem too desperate. Plus, I owed Mel a proper goodbye and a "Thank You". After all, even though we never got to bond (partly because of her busy job as a nurse, and partly because I'm a stupid introvert who doesn't know how to make friends), she is the reason I had a roof over my head in London for a month.

So, I moved in the next day. I was relieved Catherine could fit me in. On a day she should be doing nothing but celebrating love with her partner—if she had one—or indulging in some well-deserved self-care if she didn't.

To most people, the room wouldn't seem like anything special. But I'm seeing it through eyes that have witnessed cockroaches in bedrooms, bare cement floors and walls in living rooms, and bathrooms with no running water.

Our house is more than decent—it was purchased by my grandfather when he was wealthy. The family did everything they could to hold onto it, knowing it was our only tangible legacy.

But I've seen where others live, friends' homes, and villages across Madagascar. I know what reality is like for the majority.

We technically had running water. But can you really call it "running water" when it only flows from 4 am to 7 am and again from 12 pm to 3 pm?

Madagascar's water distribution infrastructure is entirely outdated. Most of the pipes still in use date back to when the national water service was called *Eau et Électricité de Madagascar*—a name that harks back to the colonial era. The company may have been renamed *Jiro Sy Rano Malagasy*, but the pipes have remained unchanged. They're broken and rusted underground and have barely been maintained.

With the bar being pretty low, this room is nothing short of exceptional. It's about fifteen square meters, with a double bed positioned right in the centre. The bare white walls give it a clean, minimalist feel. That's fine. I don't care about plants and art on the walls.

One entire wall is dominated by a massive wardrobe with sliding mirror doors, reflecting the room back at me and making the space feel a little larger than it is. The window, while not offering the best view—just a glimpse of the car park below—still lets in plenty of natural light, which I love. As a bonus, a smart TV hangs on the opposite wall.

A smart TV!

I would have been happy with an old radio or some magazines, let alone a whole 32-inch TV that works with Wi-Fi. Right now, all the doubts I had before coming to London? Gone. The little voice in my head that said I was crazy to leave? That also vanished, replaced by a kinder voice exclaiming, "You did it!"

5

Razaf

1986

"Raha marary aza ny tànana, jereo aloha ny kibo tsy misy hanina."
"When your hands ache from work, remember it's your empty stomach that matters most."

I'm 22 years old, and my job is to sell a bunch of random objects to passersby. I have no girlfriend, no career, and no real direction. I suppose you could call me a loser. The worst part is, I'm stuck with no solution in sight. I don't see a better future at all. My story will forever be that of missed opportunities.

The boy who could have been.

My music degree could have been completed by now. I could have played my first concert as the leader of my band.

It's rare to have the drummer as the leader of a band, so my band would have been cool and original. I could have made something of my life. It could have been better, really. Of course, it could also be worse. I could be homeless, I could be lonely, I could be sick, I could sell drugs... But I mean, do we always have to be grateful for the bare minimum?

Now here I am. I'm in a business I didn't choose and hate, and it's no longer generating a profit. I got up every morning to sell junk because it kept my family from starving. Without the money, it's just a pointless struggle. Over the last four years, the number of people buying from me has decreased dramatically. A major reason for this is the rise of shops selling the same products I do, but at significantly lower prices. I used to find joy in selling the most valuable pieces. Of course, there were always worthless objects that cost nothing, but once in a while, there were precious classic vinyl records, beautiful retro electronics, or vintage jewellery. The vintage charm has faded, and now people can get a replica for a fraction of the cost.

Two years in, when my business started showing signs of trouble, Dazo quit school and became a junk seller too. He set up his own stall in Analakely, another bustling market area, to double our chances of making ends meet. I hated that he'd given up on school, but Dazo was no fool; he was simply doing what was necessary.

We both dreamed of studying at the conservatory and becoming respected musicians, maybe even performing together in the same band. Dazo would have happily let me take the lead, content to stay in the background, effortlessly strumming his bass.

Now we both know that our musical dreams have slipped away.

***

Today, four years after I started, and for what's probably the 30th consecutive day, I make just enough money to buy myself a bus ticket to return home. Dazo is already waiting for me at the bus station. He rides the bus from Analakely to Mahamasina every day, and then we go home together.

He didn't have much luck either.

For several days now, we've had very little food: a can of sardines that we share between the four of us, one fried egg that my mum tries to share in four equal parts, or a can of beans.

Thankfully, we have rice.

Madagascar's staple food is rice, known as *vary* locally. Cassava, potatoes, and corn are also widely cultivated in Madagascar, but rice has somehow become the centre of our food culture. Only in the dry regions in the South can we find people having to alternate rice with other food because the weather conditions there make it hard—if not impossible—to cultivate rice. Otherwise, most Malagasy people eat rice three times a day, for breakfast, lunch and dinner, all year round. A meal consists of rice and your choice of side dishes. It can be meat, vegetables, sugar, or peanuts. You get more creative the less money you have.

There's more to rice than just food. It's really anchored in our traditions. We eat rice with oil during funerals. It's rice and turkey or chicken on Christmas Day. I know about twenty-five proverbs that contain the word *vary*. One is about rice and water being inseparable, so it is often used at weddings. Basically, wishing the couple to be like rice and water.

Some people say our consumption of rice dates back as far as the mid-first millennium AD, when the country was first settled by Austronesian people arriving from Indonesia in outrigger canoes. It is believed that these people were the first to introduce their knowledge of rice cultivation to Madagascar. This is funny because it means rice is not historically endemic to Madagascar. Rice was first cultivated in Asia, with the first written record of rice cultivation issued by the Chinese Emperor in 2800 BC. And today, people in Madagascar consume significantly more rice than any country in Asia. How the love story between Madagascar and rice really started, nobody really knows.

Legend has it that rice was once considered a food reserved solely for the gods, cultivated exclusively in the heavenly fields. Everything changed when the daughter of God married a mortal and descended to live among humans. Accustomed to the divine taste of rice, she found human food unbearable. She pleaded with her father to share rice with humankind, but he refused. Undeterred, she took matters into her own hands, sneaking back to heaven, stealing rice grains, and secretly planting them on earth. From that day onward, rice became sacred, a gift from heaven itself to humanity.

Countless legends surround rice, each more captivating than the last. One tells of the Rice Goddess, a powerful figure who once dared to challenge Buddha himself. However, no grand confrontation took place on the day of their duel. Instead, the goddess simply disappeared. Her absence caused rice to vanish instantly from the earth, plunging people into starvation. No rice meant no life—a truth I wholeheartedly understand. While myths and legends may be hard to believe, the reality that rice sustains us, preventing starvation, is undeniable. At least, that's always been our reality.

The money problem isn't just about food, though. There are bills. We're clearly living beyond our means in this massive villa. It's our only significant possession, so selling is not an option. But, fucking hell, maintaining it feels as hard as trying to fill a bucket full of holes.

Every month, I put money away in envelopes for electricity bills, water bills, and property taxes. And every month, I've had to take from the envelopes for something else. There have been times when we've decided to simply turn off the electric meter. It's not a big deal here. Since it's almost never below fifteen degrees, we don't need heating (and couldn't afford one even if we wanted to). There is no washing machine, dishwasher or microwave. The fridge, TV, and lights are the only reasons we need electricity, but even for those, there are ways to get around. We don't need the fridge on as there is barely any food to store. We can survive without watching TV and use candles for light. That's what we do when times are really hard. Candles are common in Madagascar, anyway. The majority of small villages here do not have access to electricity at all, so we're not exactly in a position to play the privileged ones at this time.

Though tonight's dinner is silent, the truth speaks volumes. We all know that we need an additional source of income, sooner rather than later.

At least the three of us know this. I am not sure about my father. I no longer recognise him, and frankly, it makes me angry. I was hoping time would do its magic, and he would eventually get through this. If not for himself, then at least for his family. There is so much power in this man, yet no resilience.

Days, months and years have passed, and he only worsened. He hasn't spoken much in a while. He used to tell us stories all the time, about the moon or the war, whatever. His knowledge had no limits, so he could talk about anything and everything with so much passion. My mum would tell the story of my birth, and he would add something interesting about how the moon behaved that night and what it meant. That's just how he was. You couldn't sit near him without him telling a story or sharing an interesting fact, because he had lived a million lives. I can't believe we used to get bored with these stories. I would give him anything to tell me one right now, at this quiet table. But one can only dream.

He has been completely absent for years. I also noticed his drinking. We all had, but talking about it would make it too real, so we decided via an unspoken agreement to ignore it. One less problem to think about. I had some hope that alcohol might help him. Some people do get fun when they're drunk, don't they? Of course, that was delusional.

On days like today, especially, it's harder to pretend. The smell of alcohol fills the room. He can hardly put a spoon in his mouth without dropping half the food back onto his plate... and some out of it. His eyes are red, I think—if only he could keep them open. He appears a decade older than his actual age. What he gained in years, he's lost in weight. He was the stereotype of a rich businessman with a big belly. He's skin and bones now. And not an ounce of joy. It's hard to watch.

After dinner, I follow my dad to his bedroom to make sure he makes it there in one piece. I do this every evening, and he never acknowledges me. I'm not sure he realises I'm walking behind him to catch him should he fall. I don't know if he knows I have been catching his fall for the last four years. He never asked where I was headed every morning, where the food on the table came from and where half the furniture had gone. Like I said, not much talking. Today is no different. He lay absentmindedly in his bed, and I leave the room without a word.

I then join Dazo in the basement, where we keep our instruments. It's the opposite of our massive luxurious musical room in Toliara, but it became our refuge. It's dark here, with only a dim light bulb hanging from the ceiling, giving off a feeble, yellowish glow that barely lights up the place. We've covered the walls in egg cartons in an attempt to soundproof the room. Our brothers have since told us that egg cartons don't really do much for acoustics, but we didn't bother taking them down. The walls needed some kind of cover anyway, for aesthetics. Besides, with or without soundproofing, the space already feels isolated. Dazo and I spend hours here playing music without holding back. It feels like nobody can hear us, and we definitely can't hear the outside world.

We've become huge fans of jazz, especially the duet between Jaco Pastorius and Dave Weck. We're no longer the big band of seven; it's just a drum-and-bass duet now, so we had to adapt. When we start a song, it's just us and the music. We don't think about money problems or our dad's drinking. It's the only time I truly feel alive. Probably the only reason I'm still alive, if I'm honest.

Playing music isn't just something I enjoy; it's the one thing I know I'm good at. I believe I would have been one of those legendary drummers if I'd had the right training, but even as a self-taught musician, I know I'm already pretty damn good. I don't usually boast about myself, so if I'm saying this, you know it's true.

Song after song, we just play and don't exist for anything else. And when we stop, the room falls silent for a few minutes before I finally speak.

"Dad drinks too much," I say.

Considering everything else we could talk about, I'm surprised that's what I start with.

"I noticed," Dazo states plainly.

"I don't want to go to the market tomorrow," I add, with no transition whatsoever.

"Same here," he adds in agreement.

And we're silent again.

"So what do we do?" He comments after a pause.

"I don't know," is all I can say.

It's like having a conversation with myself. Nothing constructive will come out of it. I know we will still wake up tomorrow, take the bus with our backpacks full of junk and go to work.

And that's exactly what we do: put one foot in front of the other, the next step heavier than the last. Because what else?

***

When we return home, however, the dynamic is different. My mum is... smiling? Wonderful, of course, but every bit suspicious.

"What's up? Spill the beans already!" I demand the moment I step inside.

"Well, how about a 'Hello, Mum, how are you?'" she teases.

"Hello, Mum. How are you? Spill the beans already," Dazo says with a grin.

A smile, one that reaches her eyes, accompanies her answer: "I have good news."

"We figured," I say, mirroring her smile—it's impossible not to. At this point, I don't even care what the news is. Just seeing her this happy is enough for me.

"I've found... some work," she announces.

My smiling face is quickly overtaken by surprise. I didn't see that coming. And what does "some work" even mean? She didn't say she found a job, just "some work."

When was she even looking? Why didn't she tell us? My mum has never had a job. Sure, she's worked her whole life, raising seven biological children, plus who knows how many others, but she's never gone *out* to work. She doesn't exactly have an academic background. She married my dad at sixteen. We had a traditional family setup: Dad was the breadwinner, Mum was a homemaker. She never complained or showed any interest in working. I'm speechless.

In every possible scenario, guilt weighs heavily on me. If she's always wanted to work, then I feel like a terrible son for assuming I had to step up as the man of the house, taking over Dad's role as the breadwinner. But if she doesn't want to work at all and only feels forced to because of our situation, then I've failed in that role, anyway.

Sensing my unease, she carries on, attempting to clarify.

"I went to see Mrs Bako today. She has a big order but is falling behind, so she needs an extra pair of hands."

Mrs Bako is our neighbour. Her husband died when she was only 26, so she had to find a way to support herself. She became the neighbourhood seamstress. She's also a close friend of my mum as they're the same age.

"I said I would do it. As you know, I sew very well. I believe I'll like this, plus the pay is quite good. You two boys can stop getting up so early and struggling so much now," she adds.

It's true. Mum is great at sewing. She made all the curtains in the house, along with our pillowcases and bed sheets. I have no doubt about her skills, but I still have a million questions.

"And after this order, what then?" I ask.

"Mrs Bako says she has a couple more orders lined up and she'll need my help with those, too. And who knows, maybe I can even start getting my own clients."

"I don't know, Mum. What do you think, Dad? Any thoughts?" I ask, annoyed by his silence. I look over my mum's shoulder to where he sits on the sofa.

He just shrugs me off, like it's nothing.

"I'm not asking for your permission," she says matter-of-factly. "And why are you two not happy about this?" Her gaze shifts between me and Dazo before settling on me. Dazo has yet to say a word.

"Mum, I'm not saying I'm not happy. I'm just surprised. Do it if that's what you want. But I don't think that changes anything. We still need to work."

"No, you don't. Do you not trust me? It is my role as a parent to provide for you. It should have never been the other way around."

I open my mouth to say something, but she cuts me off.

"You're going to stop working so hard, and you're going to let me take care of you. End of discussion."

I've learnt not to contradict my mum, not only because she scares me sometimes, but mainly because she is often very right. Also, this time, because I really *really* do not want to go back on the streets to sell junk.

Dazo and I go straight to the basement afterwards.

"I think it's cool," Dazo speaks up about Mum's good news for the first time, "now that I really think about it."

I'm not surprised by this. Dazo always takes his time before speaking. He's careful not to hurt feelings or be misunderstood, so he stays quiet and assesses the situation before sharing his thoughts.

"Yeah, I guess," I reply, my words lacking any better alternative.

And I do think it's cool. I feel terrible for not telling my mum how happy and proud I am of her, but I can't shake this feeling of failure.

"What's the plan now?" he asks.

"Play, sleep, and then not wake up until noon," I say, grinning. That sets us off, laughter spilling between.

"Actually, let's celebrate this properly," he says, pulling a bottle from behind his chair.

I look at the bottle and him with puzzlement. It takes a few seconds for me to put two and two together. He stole it from my dad.

6

Hira

2017

"Ny olombelona tsy ary mitovy."
"Human beings are inherently different."

Gia isn't in school today because she's unwell. If this had happened a few weeks ago, I would have gone home, unable to face a day without her here. But I'm okay now. It took a couple of months, but I can finally say that I've managed to talk to almost everyone in my class—in groups, but it counts. There are fifteen of us, though we're rarely all present at once, which makes socialising a little less daunting. Someone is always either sick, working, or travelling. I guess there's no need to justify our absences any more—as long as we respect the minimum attendance requirement—since we're apparently all adults now. Not that I feel like one.

Talking to the other girls in my class today, though, I realise they really *are* adults. They all seem to be casually "seeing" someone. What does that even mean? I've had two big crushes in my life, and I used to dream about marrying them. Not exactly casual.

As I listen to the others discuss the boys (plural) they're seeing, I feel like an outsider. I have no experience to share. I'm certainly not going to bring up my two crushes, especially since nothing crazy ever happened with either of them. We held hands and kissed a few times, which for me was a big enough deal.

Part of my late blooming is definitely due to my upbringing. My mother explicitly forbade me from having a boyfriend before I turned eighteen. Plus, I grew up genuinely believing that kissing a boy would make me pregnant. I eventually understood it didn't work like that, but I was still scared every time my periods were late that it was because I kissed a boy and God was now angry at me and would make me pregnant.

It's fascinating to hear the girls talk. They talk about boys and dating and even sex so casually, like someone would talk about the weather. I hear new words I haven't heard before (not in real life, anyway). Things like "no strings, no labels", "situationship". I feel genuinely dumb.

But then again, I'm also the girl who didn't know how to use a vacuum cleaner a couple of months ago. Catherine showed me—clearly amused—that the cord could be extended. She noticed my confused expression when I saw the cord didn't seem nearly long enough to reach the socket across the room. She was even more amused when I was done vacuuming and tried to put the cord back. She told me to press the button on the vacuum. The cord retracted, winding itself neatly back into place with a swift, smooth motion. One button, just one button, and it was like the vacuum had swallowed the cord whole, tucking it away until it was needed again. Back home, we swept our floors with brooms, letting the dust dance in the sunlight before it settled in a neat pile.

This reminds me of a story one of my teachers in Madagascar once told. A story I struggled to believe at the time, but one I now fully understand. I briefly studied Communication back in my country. You know, before dropping everything and flying to London. It lasted just a semester. The teacher, a woman whose face I vividly remember, although her name escapes me, taught us about the importance of tailoring our communication to the audience. She shared a story from a mission she had undertaken in the south, deep in a remote village. The village was poor, and the birth rate was alarmingly high. My teacher and a team of volunteers were sent there to teach the villagers how to use condoms to prevent pregnancy.

They used bottles for the demonstration, carefully explaining each step. The villagers were also given bottles to practise with. Everyone seemed pleased, nodding along, satisfied with the lesson. The team left the village, proud of the job they had done. Three months later, they returned to follow up. They were met with angry villagers, frustrated, confused... and pregnant. My teacher couldn't understand what had gone wrong until one of the women asked: "Maybe we put the bottle in the wrong place. Where are we supposed to leave it?"

It was then that they realised the problem wasn't the villagers. It was the message. These people had never even heard of a toothbrush, let alone condoms. The volunteers' way of communicating had failed. My teacher told that story beautifully, and the whole class seemed to grasp the message. But I'll admit, I thought she'd made it up. That is, until I became the villager myself. After all, who here would believe that a grown woman had never seen or used a vacuum cleaner before?

And now I'm the villager all over again, having zero experience in all things relationship.

***

Now that I'm more comfortable around my classmates, I don't rush to leave for work or go straight home after school like I used to. I was always the first one out of the gate, because if I lingered even for a moment, I knew I'd end up walking to Maida Vale station with one of my classmates—or worse, a group of them.

Besides, today is Wednesday, which means I don't have work. I hang around a little longer before finally heading out the gate.

Walking towards Maida Vale station, I notice Leo, one of my classmates, just a few metres behind me. It's an awkward distance. Too close to pretend I haven't noticed him and to suddenly speed up without looking strange. I do the sensible thing: I stop, glance back, and wait for him to catch up.

He greets me in what feels like the most British way possible. "Hey, you alright?"

I nod, aware that he's not genuinely asking about my well-being. My heart sinks slightly, knowing this is about to be my first one-on-one conversation with a British person—accent and all. After two months in London, you'd think I'd have plenty of such encounters, but London is incredibly diverse. I've mostly spoken with people from everywhere except the United Kingdom. I've read somewhere that more than 300 languages are spoken here, a testament to the city's rich history of immigration. And it shows with all the Turkish barbers, Romanian grocery stores, Polish markets, and Indian salons—every neighbourhood is a vibrant mosaic.

However, there is no Malagasy community. Madagascar was a French colony, never part of the British Empire, which means my people tend to gravitate mostly toward France. In Cachan alone, entire apartment buildings are filled with Malagasy families.

Walking beside Leo, I'm surprised to find that awkward silence actually feels safer and more comforting than forced conversation. So, I don't say anything. I wouldn't know what to say anyway.

We stroll quietly for about five minutes before he finally breaks the silence.

"So, do you like it here?" he asks, glancing sideways at me.

"Here in London? Or at school?" I reply, trying to sound casual despite the flutter of nerves in my chest.

He chuckles warmly, making me smile in return. "I don't know... both? Honestly, I didn't realise you weren't from London, so I meant school. But now, I'm curious about both."

He didn't realise I wasn't from London? I could've sworn it was written all over my face. Yet his remark fills me with unexpected pride, as if I've successfully blended into this diverse metropolis.

"I like both. Very much," I reply, my voice steadier now.

He nods thoughtfully, still looking at me. "Where are you from then, if you don't mind me asking?"

My heart flutters again; his accent is both intimidating and charming. I clear my throat softly. "I'm from Madagascar."

His eyes widen with genuine surprise—a reaction I've grown accustomed to. I know exactly what he's about to say next.

"Madagascar? Wow! I don't think I've ever met anyone from there."

There it is. I've been trained for this particular conversation. I force a smile. "I know. I hear that a lot."

"I bet! So, what's it like there?" he asks, genuinely curious.

I can't help but laugh, even though I'm a little annoyed. I've got this answer memorised. "Nothing like the movie."

He chuckles, but I'm glad he doesn't ask any more questions about my origins. It's not that I don't like to talk about Madagascar. It's just that not everyone needs to hear about it. There is so much to say about Madagascar and about my life growing up there. It's a subject more suited for a deep conversation, rather than small talk. Gia, so far, is the only person I've had real conversations about Madagascar with.

We reach the station, and I'm caught off guard when he mentions he's taking the Bakerloo Line. I am, too. I take it up to Baker Street, then switch to the Metropolitan Line up to Wembley Park. He gets off at Paddington, so it's before my stop, but that still gives us about ten minutes together, while we wait for the next train and then ride up to Paddington.

We don't talk much on the tube, which is probably for the best. It's hard enough trying to understand what he says when it's quiet; I can't imagine how it would go on this loud, rattling train. Instead, we exchange glances now and then, just to acknowledge each other's presence. It would be weird not to, given how close we're standing.

The next day, our paths cross again. This time, he's walking ahead of me. I'm just a few steps behind, close enough that he can hear me. He slows down, waiting for me, just like I did for him before. For a moment, I wonder if he's annoyed that we're sharing the same path again, but that's probably just my overthinking. He likely doesn't care either way.

"Hi again. Is this becoming a tradition?" he asks with a teasing smile.

I'm feeling a little less shy this time, so I manage to respond in the same playful tone.

"I don't know. Why do you keep following me?"

"You're the one behind me, so who's really following who?" He laughs softly.

Fair. I smile, unsure of how to keep the conversation going.

He beats me to it before I can think of something else to say.

"Do you always take this road home?" he asks, fingers running through his hair.

For the first time, I notice how blond he is. The sun hits him at just the right angle, making his hair seem lighter. I didn't see it before, mostly because I didn't care. But now that I pay attention and the sun is showing itself more often, it's obvious. His hair has this golden glow to it. I mentally slap myself for admiring his hair before getting back to the conversation.

"I always take the Bakerloo Line," I explain, "but I don't always get off at the same station. I work in Soho some days... like today. I'll get off at Oxford Circus."

I'm a little impressed with myself, and I admit I'm showing off a bit, because the London tube was a total mystery to me a few weeks ago. I downloaded the app everyone suggested to help me figure it out, but it may as well have been a diagram of the human body with all its veins and organs. Fast forward two months, and I'm practically a pro. I can match the colour and the name of all the lines. Bakerloo Line? Brown. Hammersmith and City line? Yellow. Piccadilly line? Dark blue. Victoria line? The other blue. Jubilee Line? Grey. Central Line? The worst line, red.

"Oh really? What do you do?" Leo asks, sounding genuinely curious.

"I'm a waitress at an Indonesian restaurant. Nothing exciting," I say.

"Well, it's exciting if you like Indonesian food," he replies with a grin. "And I do."

"True," I nod, grinning. "As long as you're not allergic to peanuts," I reply.

He laughs, and I can't help but laugh too.

I have to admit, food allergies just aren't a thing in my country. I'd never heard of anyone having food allergies, and there were certainly no strict rules about them, unlike here in the U.K., where restaurant menus specifically list allergens and warn about cross-contamination. Just another random fact that surprises me while living abroad. I read that more than 20% of the populations of most developed countries have allergies (be it food, drug or animal). Food allergy alone affects about 7% of children in the

U.K. I wonder why and how, in more than 20 years living in Madagascar, I've never heard of a child suffering from allergies. I've seen parents give their three-year-old coffee, so peanuts, milk and eggs were hardly a concern. The fact that Leo immediately gets my joke confirms how common allergies are here.

"So, how come we never ran into each other before? I always take the same road, too." Leo's curiosity grows bigger.

Well, there's no need to lie now...

"I kind of run away. I didn't talk to anyone at school the first days, so it was easier to leave as fast as I could to avoid running into one of you guys. Gia's my only friend, but she's just as shy as I am, and heads straight home, in the opposite direction. I've only just started feeling comfortable with the rest of the class. So, yesterday and today, I stuck around a bit longer. And here we are."

I can feel the weight of his gaze on me, but I keep my eyes fixed straight ahead. He does this a lot—glancing at me sideways while we walk. I'm just relieved we're moving because walking gives me an excuse not to face him directly. It's a few uncomfortable seconds before he finally speaks. His voice is softer than I expected. "I'm sorry we didn't make you feel more comfortable."

Wait, what? That's not what I meant at all. My chest tightens with embarrassment, and I can feel my face heating up. This is the last thing I wanted, for him to think it was their fault. I quickly jump in, desperate to fix my clumsy explanation.

"No, no, it's not like that!" I blurt out, shaking my head. "It's nobody's fault. I mean, it's not you guys. It's me. I'm the problem, really."

I sneak a glance at him, hoping he doesn't look too concerned, but his expression is still gentle. I take a deep breath, trying to find the right words. "I think I'm just... shy. It's not that I didn't want to talk to anyone. I just didn't know how. And it's even harder when I come from so far away—"

"Okay, okay," he cuts me off, now hardly holding back a laugh.

I love that he smiles and laughs so often. It makes me feel at ease. We don't talk much the rest of the way, because, you know, we're on the loud tube again.

The tube... A surprisingly good matchmaker.

At this hour, there's never a free seat, and everyone ends up standing so close that it's almost the most intimate I've been with a human being. I find I actually enjoy Leo's company more than I expected. Or maybe I just like his charming smile and handsome face. We're standing really,

really close, but there's zero physical contact. If I moved just two inches, his shirt would brush against my arm. But I don't move. Of course I don't; I've only talked to the guy for a grand total of forty minutes. Still, it doesn't stop my mind from wandering into the craziest scenarios.

Leo's taller than me, but not by much. If I hugged him now, my nose would line up perfectly with his lips. I'd just have to tilt my head ever so slightly for our lips to touch—

Oh, God. I'll be dreaming about marrying him tonight.

Leo gets off the train in Paddington, and I continue to Oxford Circus. I try to go on with my day. I go to The Paper Lantern, have my usual walnut cake and a new-flavoured tea, complete my assignments, and then work. But all this time, I have Leo in my mind, his smile and his ridiculously gorgeous blond hair. It's obvious I like him, and I know this will just make my days interesting, exciting, awkward and miserable all at once at school.

***

Friday arrives, and it's the same old London with its beautiful diversity and its ugly, congested roads, but it feels different to me. I'm anticipating the fact that I will see

Leo and will very likely walk with him again on my way home. The problem now is that I am fully aware I like him. But he should never find out. How I will manage that, I don't know. The harder I try to appear natural, the more awkward I become. So that's going to be interesting.

When I arrive at school, after crossing the parking lot, opening the door to the reception, walking down the corridor, and opening the second door to the hall, I am relieved to see Gia. I assumed she wouldn't be in until Monday.

"Oh, hey! So glad you're back. Do you feel better?" I ask her.

"Oh yes, it was nothing. Don't worry. I could have come, but I didn't feel like it." She says, and her reply saddens me.

Gia is having a hard time at school. Like me, she's now comfortable around our classmates. We pushed each other to step out of our comfort zones, and when one of us felt more confident, we'd include the other, so we progressed together in that aspect. It's with her English that she's a lot less confident. We both have a pretty basic knowledge of English, but the difference is that I've always written better than I speak. I've written songs and kept journals in English, even as a child.

Plus, since moving to London, I've started reading a lot more in English—a habit I quickly picked up from Londoners on the tube. Now, wherever I go, I carry a novel with me. I read voraciously, as if to make up for owning only one book for over twenty years. Books are incredibly affordable here too; I often find them for just £1 in charity shops, which is a crazy price.

To me, a country where books cost less than food is truly developed. A house filled with books is the ultimate sign of privilege. They are considered a luxury item in my country. A children's book costs about three euros. It's unlikely a Malagasy family earning €30-€50 per month would prioritise spending €3 on one single paperback. And that data's from 2013. I bet books now cost significantly more than they used to, while salaries haven't risen proportionally.

My dad said we used to be privileged and have a collection of encyclopaedias in our house, but they had to sell them. So the only book I had growing up was one about a penguin playing hide and seek with his brothers. He covered himself in snow so his brothers would mistake him for a snowman. When they found him, he was so cold, it was lucky their mum made hot chocolate and pancakes to warm them all up. Fascinating, I know. I've read that book a million times. I got creative with it and sometimes changed the words or the ending as I read.

Anyway, as soon as I saw that books were a lot more accessible here, I kept buying them. Some cafes even have book swap stations, which meant I could get some for free. Reading regularly has helped improve my writing, and my grades have been decent.

But Gia's experience is different. She was called to the school office after our last assignment. It was sports journalism, so we pretended to live report a football game. The teacher pointed out she had made too many basic mistakes for someone interested in a writing career. Gia was devastated. She has lost the motivation to continue. Unlike me, Gia doesn't really aspire to be an English writer, anyway. She's only here on an exchange program, so the teacher's comment felt unnecessary, if not cruel. I could see how much it hurt her.

Besides, she is an excellent writer in her native language. I've translated and read her poems in Italian.

"That bad, huh?" I ask.

"I'll be alright," she smiled, though unconvincingly.

I know she'll be fine. But I also know it will take time, and nothing I say can change how she feels.

"So, what did I miss?" she asks as an attempt to change the subject.

A change of subject I welcome very much because I've been itching to tell her about Leo.

7
Razaf
1988

"Mita be tsy lanin'ny mamba."
"In a river full of crocodiles, we are safest when we cross together."

My mum is great at what she does. She earns more in two weeks than Dazo and I did together in a month. She initially assisted Mrs Bako with pillowcase orders but soon attracted her own clientele through word of mouth. The demand is high, so there's enough work for both of them. There's no competition.

You'd be surprised how often people redecorate their homes and need new pillowcases or curtains. People also seem to need new outfits for every major event in their lives, such as baptisms, birthdays, weddings, and, of course, engagement parties.

Now, you need to understand what engagement parties are like in Madagascar. They are just as—if not more—important than actual weddings here. We call it *vodiondry*, which literally means "the sheep's butt"—possibly the worst name for a ceremony that's supposed to mark the union of two people in love. But the engagement isn't just about the couple anyway; it's about the two families joining together.

Traditionally, the groom's family would present a sheep's rump to the bride's family as a symbol of respect for the elders. Over time, this custom evolved, and they now offer money instead. Now I'm not sure if it's much better. The entire ceremony revolves around speeches, known as *Kabary*, which can last for hours. These speeches are all about praising the values and qualities of each family. Ultimately, the groom's family is trying to convince the bride's family to join them. When this is followed by a monetary gift, it can feel uncomfortably close to negotiating a price for the bride. So, in a way, the sheep's rump doesn't seem quite as appalling any more.

But the true meaning behind offering gifts during the *vodiondry* ceremony, whether it's a sheep's rump or money, is rooted in tradition. The bride is expected to leave her family after the wedding, and the gifts are a symbolic way to compensate her family for her absence. It's a bit like a reversed dowry. Over time, people have got creative with this tradition—some offer one of every note and coin in Madagascar, from Ar10 to Ar5000. This symbolises that the groom's family offers everything they have, from the smallest to the largest fortune, to the bride's family.

No couple is really married without having completed the *vodiondry* first. And that's why engagement party dresses are our biggest money-maker.

Another busy time for Mum is Madagascar's circumcision season in winter. The belief that wounds heal quickly in cooler weather leads many to choose the months of July through October for the procedure. Circumcision is a significant tradition in my country, too—a rite of passage into manhood. During the ceremony, the little boy wears what we call a *malabary*. The *malabary* is a loose-fitting, knee-length tunic made from soft, breathable fabric to keep the boy comfortable during recovery. It's often decorated with playful patterns—such as animals, toys, or nature motifs—adding a touch of joy to an otherwise solemn occasion. During this season, my mum makes dozens of *malabary* each month.

My mum's business turns out to be highly lucrative, and I've noticed that she genuinely enjoys it.

I, on the other hand, haven't done anything remotely productive in the two years since I've stopped selling junk.

You'd think I'd have used that time to focus on a career, but nope. Instead, I've been playing music in the basement and, unfortunately, drinking. I regret picking up that glass of rum Dazo stole from Dad two years ago. Back then, I had no idea it would end up owning me.

I've always drunk, but it was only for fun when I was younger. Just friends enjoying beers; nothing out of the ordinary. Now, alcohol is like an old friend who started as good company but slowly overstayed their welcome.

The truth is, right now, drinking seems to have more benefits than *not* drinking. Since I started stronger alcohol, I've been able to connect with my dad more, because we ended up drinking together. Dazo and I stopped sneaking his rum and just started sharing it with him. He didn't even blink. Just raised his glass and drank with us.

So now... we talk.

Not about anything meaningful. But I'll take it. At least, we're communicating.

Another upside to alcohol is that it helps me forget. No, it doesn't solve my problems, but it sure dulls them for a while.

So, I keep drinking, mostly in the evenings, in the basement studio with Dazo, out on the porch with my dad or alone in my bedroom. It's become a routine, like brushing my teeth.

THE EUCALYPTUS TREE

Dad spends a lot of time on that porch. The neighbours call him "the wolf of the city" because of that. The porch sits deeper inside the yard, but when he opens the gate facing the road, he has a clear view of everything outside, like a wolf watching over his territory: the cars, the buses, the pedestrians. And everyone can see him too. When they pass by, they always take a moment to stare at our house, at the huge tree in the yard, and the quiet, mysterious man sitting on the porch.

Even at night, he's still out there. Alone in the dark, with only the shadows cast by the moonlight and his thoughts. A man left alone with his thoughts—that's a dangerous thing.

No wonder he drinks until he passes out.

That said, my dad is still the intelligent man I used to know and idolise. Tonight's conversation proves that. It's just the two of us.

As I sit next to him on the cold wooden bench on the porch, a glass of white rum in my hand, I casually remind him that tomorrow is my 24th birthday. I mention how fast time has flown, how it's already been six whole years since everything changed. I don't mean to stir up painful memories, but the alcohol loosens my tongue, and it just slips out.

He offers a simple correction: "You're wrong."

For a moment, I wonder if he's lost his mind.

"You're actually entering the 25th year of your life," he adds.

I blink, confused.

"The year you were born was your first year on Earth. When you celebrate your first birthday, you're actually entering your second year. So we shouldn't celebrate that you turned one, but rather that you've completed your first year and are entering your second year... Basically, you're two on what people think is your first birthday. And so on," he explains.

Am I drunk, or does that make sense?

We stare at each other for a second, then burst into laughter. At that moment, I realise he is still so wise, not completely lost like I'd feared. Maybe he just needed someone to talk to.

***

My birthday comes, and it's just a day like any other. Even when I was younger, I never really cared about it. Back then, there were always so many of us that it felt like a party no matter what. My parents had a tradition: for our birthdays, we'd get new clothes and shoes, except on the tenth, fifteenth, and eighteenth birthdays, when we could ask for something special.

I got my first bike at the age of ten. I already knew how to ride because I'd used my brothers' bikes for years. In fact, by the time I was twelve, I could drive, thanks to my older brothers. Back in Toliara, my five big brothers would go out drinking and partying with their friends. They taught me how to drive so I could chauffeur them around. I didn't mind. I loved driving.

Sometimes we'd even organise illegal races and bet money. That was a time when we had nothing much to worry about.

Now, I'm such a different person that that version of me is long gone.

At fifteen, I didn't ask for anything. I already had my drum set, which was all I ever wanted. At eighteen, I cared even less. I'd already quit school, knowing I had other dreams to pursue. That was enough. Of course, that was before I realised those dreams wouldn't happen.

I didn't care about my birthday then, and I don't care now.

I wake up at 9 am, which is my new early time. A few years ago, 9 am would have been lunchtime. When I get to the lounge, Mum is already working on her sewing machine. It's January, so things are quieter now that the holiday rush is over, but she still has enough work to keep busy.

The lounge isn't what it used to be. The library of encyclopaedias has been replaced by a cheap cabinet with glass shelves and plates, and the massive extendable table is now just a simple table for four made of fake wood. Still, it looks decent. Mum works hard, and it shows. We've got nice curtains, a TV, a radio, and even flowers.

She smiles when she sees me and gets up from her chair. The flattened chair cushion suggests she's been sitting there quite a while. With a kiss on each cheek, she wishes me a happy birthday. She then proceeds with her typical recital of Bible verses and the standard "may God be with you" speech. She does it every year, even though she knows I haven't thought about God in a long time.

I've got an unconventional relationship with that Man (or Woman, who knows). Sometimes, I speak to God as I would to a friend; this includes swearing. Other times, I don't even believe He exists. Then there are times I believe there's a God, but I hate Him for the life He's given me. But the worst is when I just don't care, like now. That simply means I've given up completely.

Mum hasn't, though.

She keeps saying we should have faith that everything will work out because of God's plan. So here she is, this woman I admire, wishing me things I don't think will ever come true.

Mum's the only normal one left in this family. She insisted on doing something special for my birthday, but I said no. I don't feel like I deserve the attention, and honestly, I'd hate for her to make today into some big event. In the end, I agreed to a "special-ish" dinner tonight—but nothing more.

When I step onto the porch with my black coffee—no milk, no sugar—the city wolf is already there, sitting in his usual spot, quietly watching the world drift by. He glances at me briefly, murmurs a quick happy birthday, and I brush it off with a small shrug, joining him on the bench. We're both still sober, so we don't speak. Heartfelt conversations are only for drunken nights.

Dazo soon joins us, holding a steaming cup of black coffee himself. He looks at me and says, "So, how's the future?"

It's an inside joke between my brother and me. Dazo is like my shadow, always trailing behind, often not by choice. I once had a dream, but it shattered before I could grasp it, and Dazo knew the same fate awaited him. When I quit school and started selling scrap metal on the streets, Dazo followed in my footsteps shortly after. That's how the joke began. I became his future; whatever happened to me was bound to happen to him next. Every birthday, his question feels less humorous and more unsettling. I hope he'll break this cycle and do something meaningful with his life. He's smarter than me in so many ways.

The three of us sit quietly, but it's a silence filled with unspoken words—typical for this family. In our silence, we're all clearly thinking about Mum, how much of a superhero she is, and by contrast, how pathetic we are: three capable men with neither jobs nor ambitions. From here, we can hear the rhythmic whirring of her sewing machine, and each stitch tugs a little deeper at our hearts. She's the one holding this family together. Just when we think she's reached the limits of her strength and love, she surprises us again.

My brothers in France call during dinner. With the two-hour time difference between France and Madagascar in January, it's only 6 pm there. The call is short as international calls are expensive, but all five manage to squeeze in a few quick words to wish me a happy birthday. Apart from the monthly postcards and letters, we rarely hear from them, so even this brief call feels special.

We then chat about how much my brothers must have changed over the years and joke about which one of us is poorer now. Even my father cracks a smile.

The food is perfect too. Mum made *ravitoto*—crushed cassava leaves—a traditional Malagasy dish. My absolute favourite. Sure, it might look a bit like cow dung, but if "don't judge a book by its cover" was ever made into a meal, it'd definitely be *ravitoto*. The dish is a combination of deep-green crushed leaves, fluffy white rice, and a vibrant red tomato salad. Together, they echo the colours of the Malagasy flag: white, red, and green. I'm pretty sure the flag came first and inspired the dish, but honestly, I wouldn't be surprised if it turned out to be the other way around.

Food doesn't mean much to me anymore. I eat purely to fuel my body, stripped of any pleasure after years spent struggling to put meals on the table. Choosing what you want to eat feels like a luxury. A privilege. For those without choice, the only real question is whether they'll eat at all. Tonight, though, it feels good to have had a choice.

After dinner, we linger at the table, talking more openly than we have in years. It's as though all these conversations had been bottled up, and now that the seal is broken, there's no stopping them. I'm mid-laugh when my parents suddenly announce they have a surprise. My immediate reaction is mild irritation since I had made it clear I didn't want my birthday to become a big deal, but curiosity gets the better of me. I glance at Dazo, and his mischievous smile gives him away instantly.

"What's going on? What did you do?" I ask, half-annoyed but secretly amused.

"Why don't we go outside?" Mum suggests.

Now I'm even more intrigued.

We all walk out the door, across the porch and through the yard, until Dad opens the gate. So, they meant out-*out*. I'm puzzled, but it's too dark to see their expressions clearly, so I follow quietly. It's nine o'clock now, and the town is completely still. Across the road is a patch of land the nearby church uses as extra parking on Sundays. A single car sits there, which seems odd. No one should be at the church this late.

Strange, though not exactly suspicious. I mean, it's just a car... parked in a car park.

The silence becomes uncomfortable, and I wait for someone to explain. Mum is the first to speak.

"That car is yours."

"No, it's not," I chuckle, finding the suggestion absurd.

"It's your birthday gift," she insists.

I look at Dad and Dazo. Both nod reassuringly, confirming it's not a joke. I hear the words, I see the car, but my mind struggles to grasp what's happening. I'm utterly confused.

"Relax, it didn't cost much. It belonged to Mrs Bako's late husband," Mum explains.

I can't see it clearly in the dark, but I know exactly which car she's referring to. That old Simca has been parked outside Mrs Bako's house ever since her husband passed away. It hasn't moved in years, although she regularly dusts it off to keep it clean.

"For a long time, she couldn't bring herself to let it go, but she finally decided it was time to sell," Mum continues.

The car would certainly be better off driven than sitting unused outside her house, where it might deteriorate or even be stolen.

Dazo chimes in, "It's a wreck, though. It doesn't even run. It needs a new battery, and probably plenty of other parts. But it'll make a good project for us."

Apparently, Dazo had recruited some lads from the neighbourhood to help push the car uphill from Mrs Bako's place to the car park. It's a short distance, but still not easy.

Before I can respond, Mum speaks again. "I'll need your help with my business soon. I'm looking for customers in the city, so you or Dazo can drive me."

"Mum, I know what you're doing," I interrupt.

She's obviously trying to make me feel useful again. It's thoughtful, but also slightly insulting. Mum's an exceptional driver—she even won a car race in Toliara once. A real legal race. The trophy still stands proudly in our lounge cabinet. Besides, she genuinely enjoys driving. She certainly doesn't need me to drive her.

"Alright," she concedes, gently raising her hands in surrender. "I don't need you to drive me anywhere. But accept the gift and stop complaining."

I open my mouth to object again, but she quickly interjects. "Tsk tsk. If it's difficult to accept, think of it as the family's car, not just yours. Everyone can use it. Agreed?"

I relax and finally smile. That's something I can accept. A car would indeed benefit us all. Sure, it needs work, but that's even better. It'll keep Dazo and I occupied for a while.

Mum hands me the key—symbolic more than practical since the car won't start—but the gesture makes me want to cry. I feel tears welling up, which is rare. I genuinely can't recall the last time I cried (probably in toddlerhood). It's not the car that moves me; it's this moment—me, Mum, Dazo, even Dad—all standing together outside in the dark, looking at an old broken car that suddenly feels like the best thing that's happened to our family in a really, *really* long time.

***

Dazo and I spent the next month working on the car. The first thing we did was replace the old battery. That was the easy part. After that, we had to learn how an engine worked. Being self-taught musicians, we thought mechanics couldn't be that hard.

It turns out that mechanics *was* very hard.

But we were not totally unfamiliar with car trouble.

Our parents never discovered a certain incident involving their car in Toliara. They'd left us behind for a week-long trip to Antananarivo. My oldest brother, then sixteen, was responsible enough to supervise us, though we hardly needed watching. We spent our days mostly outdoors, coming home just for dinner. Cooking, laundry, gardening, and cleaning were all managed by Lala and Rado, a couple employed by our family.

To clarify, having domestic help in Madagascar doesn't necessarily mean you're wealthy—it's a common arrangement of mutual support. Lala and Rado needed employment and housing; we needed help around the house. Over time, they became family. When Dad was transferred back to Antananarivo, they moved in with us. They still take care of our home today. Lala handles the cooking and cleaning, and Rado manages the gardening and acts as our night guard.

With our parents away, we seized the opportunity for another illegal street race in Toliara and promptly crashed their car. My oldest brother was driving, but we were all equally guilty, shouting encouragement and betting enthusiastically. We only had one week to fix the car before our parents returned. We got help from the town mechanic and friends. My parents didn't suspect a thing when they returned.

Now, working on the Simca, that past incident proved surprisingly helpful.

Each drive initially revealed new issues, black smoke one day, overheating the next, and oil leaks after that. But we persevered, patching and tweaking until finally, the car stopped resisting and roared back to life.

8

Hira

2017

"Tsy misy mafy tsy laitran'ny zoto."
"There is no hardship that perseverance cannot overcome."

"It should only take about an hour from King's Cross. It's really lovely," Leo says, encouraging me to visit Cambridge as we sit together for lunch.

It's not an official date, which is honestly a relief; otherwise, I'd be much more nervous than I am now. Also, I wouldn't have worn my work uniform if I'd considered this a date. Not that I own anything particularly fancy, but I'd have chosen something else for Leo. We only ended up in this fancy Italian restaurant because our class this morning was cancelled. The teacher was ill.

Over the past weeks, walking to the tube station with Leo after school has become a daily tradition, and we've grown really close.

Today, Leo suggested we take a walk into town since he needed to buy a birthday present for his mum and wanted to show me Oxford Street. It is, after all, the world's biggest high street, stretching 1.5 miles with countless shops. I've walked on this road often on my way to work, but never paid much attention. I've avoided entering any shop because everything looked so luxurious. All I know is it's a busy street.

But with Leo, it was fun. This guy would make waiting in line at the post office fun. We just browsed and joked about what we saw. He pointed at a carrot-shaped snack container in John Lewis, and we laughed when I told him I'd put anything but carrots in it, just because. It was not even funny, but we just laughed anyway. In a movie, this scene would typically include romantic background music, followed by a moment of laughter, then silence, before culminating in a kiss.

Don't mind me, I lost my train of thought again.

Ten or more shops later (I lost count), Leo got me to go to Liberty London. From the outside, Liberty London looked like something straight out of an old English storybook. The building's black-and-white timbered facade stood tall and proud, like a grand Tudor mansion right in the heart of the city. It looked more like a historical landmark than a department store. And the inside didn't disappoint. As soon as we went in, the smell of perfume filled my nostrils.

Expensive perfume, please.

The inside of Liberty London felt like stepping into a grand, enchanted manor, with its intricate wooden beams and elegant balconies. There were luxuries everywhere: perfumes in glass bottles that looked more expensive than my rent, soft leather handbags, silk scarves in vibrant patterns, and finely crafted jewellery. Damn, the place was fancy.

I was reminded once more of London's remarkable diversity. Just fifteen minutes away lay Chinatown, a stark contrast to here, in both the smell and the appearance of its buildings. About forty minutes away was Camden Town, a place where music and vibrant nightlife replaced the fancy. Just an hour away was Brick Lane, renowned for its vibrant street art and bustling markets. It was like a giant, unsolvable puzzle—where none of the pieces seemed to fit, yet somehow, when assembled, they created a masterpiece.

In the end, Leo bought his mum wine glasses. For £60. Everything about it felt absurd to me, from the elegant wine glasses to the astonishing price. Not absurd in a bad way; it was just worlds apart from what I was used to in Madagascar. He even got her a funny birthday card that read "*Reese with a spoon*," completed with a playful illustration. People here are effortlessly cool. Meanwhile, I cringed remembering the gifts I've given my mum. They were often a strainer or a carrot grater, as though kitchen utensils were something she'd genuinely dream about. Back home, those were totally normal mum-gifts.

With our stomachs rumbling after two hours of exploring London, Leo suggested we grab some food and even casually offered to pay.

And so, here we are, sitting in a swanky Italian restaurant, sharing a completely non-date lunch, a random conversation about London tourist places and possibly the best lasagna I've ever tasted (though I doubt Gia would approve—better keep this to myself!).

"That's a good idea. But honestly, I haven't even seen Big Ben yet, so Cambridge's way down my list," I admit.

"What? How come? Not a fan of touristy places, are we?" he teases.

"No, it's not that. I just never had the time. As soon as I arrived, I was just focused on working and doing well at school. I'm too tired to do anything else if I don't do those two things. Once, after a Saturday shift, I slept until 4 pm on Sunday. I didn't even know it was humanly possible to sleep that much," I explain.

He chuckles. "You should have told me, I would have taken you there instead."

"No, I love this! Really," I reply.

And it's true. For some reason, I want to see Big Ben alone. Coming to London is a solo adventure that's both scary and exciting. Some experiences here are not meant to be shared, kind of like my routine at The Paper Lantern. That's *my* thing.

Anything else, though? Yes, please. I want to go anywhere with this guy.

Lunch with Leo is great. We were close before, but this lunch has made us even closer. I learn so much about him, such as the fact that he is taking this course to become a sports journalist and to avoid having to take over his dad's company. He also tells me many things about England I had no idea about, like the fact that accents can differ in each city, or that we shouldn't step on three-drain covers because it's bad luck.

But there is something that really bugs me. I have no idea what Leo thinks. I'm confused as to what his intentions might be. He walks with me to the station every single day of the week, buys me lunch, and decides to spend the day with me when a class is cancelled, instead of going home or going out with his other friends to do whatever super cool hobby they share. And I can tell you he has many friends *and* hobbies. Every Monday, it's one of my favourite things to listen to him talk about his weekends. He's never had a weekend doing nothing. He goes golfing, fishing, bowling, swimming... I've never done the first three, and I can't do the last, so I'm basically someone he shouldn't be having fun with.

Yet, he's here with me now.

Or maybe it's cultural. Perhaps this is how women are treated by men in Europe.

The confusion only deepens when it's time to part ways.

We walk together up to the Tottenham Court Road tube station. He's heading home, I'm off to work. As much as I'd love to spend the afternoon with him, reality pulls me back. Life isn't all about fancy Italian restaurants and romantic strolls past London's luxury shops; I have my daily struggles waiting for me. Just like Cinderella after the ball...

Before leaving, though, he looks me in the eye, and I lose all my ability to think straight.

Is he going to kiss me?

Oh God, I don't know what to do.

Suddenly, it's very hot. He's standing so close—too close to ignore, yet not quite close enough to kiss. One more step, that's all it would take to close the gap. I don't know if he's going to do it, but if he is, he'd better hurry, because my heart's about to launch itself out of my chest.

"So... that was nice," he says, still looking at me with his striking blue eyes.

"Yes, thank you for lunch," I manage to say with a steady voice.

Another interminable second of silence passes.

"Cool. Well, I'll see you tomorrow," he says, waving like we weren't just one step away from each other.

And he's gone.

What the hell?

***

When I get to work, my mind is still tangled up in thoughts of Leo. He was going to kiss me, I'm sure of it. I might not be an expert in relationships, but I can recognise the look of someone who wants to kiss.

My thoughts are interrupted by my lady boss, who looks at me with her scary eyes as soon as I open the restaurant door.

Oh shit. I know those eyes too.

She's in a bad mood.

Her natural mood is everyone's bad mood. I've genuinely never seen her smile. Her bad mood? It's a storm best avoided. She's a small woman, but everyone fears her. Something is intimidating in her eyes.

Of course, there's the fact that she has the power to pay or not pay us. So, it's probably that as well.

I rush behind the bar to join the other waitress, Maya.

"What's wrong with her?" I whisper to Maya.

"The new girl showed up in black trousers, and the boss straight-up yelled in front of everyone that they looked like pyjamas, then sent her home. The poor girl cried," Maya explains, also whispering.

Geez. She was keen on the black skirt, but honestly, black trousers would work just as well. I mean, it's still black. I strongly disagree with the boss. I often do. However, I make a note to myself to never wear anything other than a black skirt on my shifts. Can't afford a day off here.

This job has gone from bad to worse, mostly thanks to that horrible boss. I actually prefer the busier shifts now. At least then, there's no time for her to hover or nitpick. Mondays and Tuesdays are the worst. We barely get twenty customers the entire shift, and it's not like we can sit down and wait for them to show up. We have to appear busy all the time. The boss doesn't tolerate a single second of stillness.

Once, I made the mistake of checking my phone, and she immediately sent me outside to hand out flyers advertising a 10% discount on meals.

Distributing flyers is, without exaggeration, one of the hardest jobs in the world. Most people don't take them. Those who do give you that look, the one that's a mix of pity and discomfort, like you've reminded them of something they'd rather not see. I've been through this humiliating ritual three times now, but nothing compares to the time she sent me out in February.

The cold didn't just graze my skin. It carved through it, burrowing straight into my bones. My cheeks burned red, not just from the wind, but from the shame of standing there like that, vulnerable and ignored, in the middle of a restless, uncaring crowd. It felt like begging, even though I wasn't asking for anything. I was trying to give something away. Funny how that flipped something in me. I used to walk past people handing out flyers without a second thought. Now, I always take one. I can't help it. My bag's full of them.

It reminded me of my dad, the stories he told me about how he used to sell junk on the streets. He'd stand there for hours, his eyes scanning the crowd, silently pleading with people to buy something.

Breaking the cycle. I'm here to break the cycle, I remind myself.

Luckily, it's Thursday. Thursdays are like Friday eves, so they usually get busy. Leo told me it was a British tradition to go to the pub and get drunk on Thursdays, so there are many drunk corporate people around at this time. And they're hungry.

My shift is pretty monotonous. I've memorised the menu and even picked up some key Indonesian phrases now. *Nasi* is rice, and *Mi* is noodles. In short, *Nasi Goreng* is fried rice, while *Mi Goreng* is fried noodles. If I ever went to Bali, that's honestly all I'd need to say.

I take orders, clean tables, and load and unload the dishwasher. There is not a second to sit and stop. Some curious customers, as every day, would ask me where I am from. I know these conversations by heart as well. If they are Indonesian, they are surprised that I look a lot like them, and I laugh for what I imagine is long enough, so they think it's the first time I've heard that comment, and they are pleased with themselves and leave good tips.

If they're not Indonesian, the reaction is almost always the same: "Wow, I don't think I've ever met anyone from Madagascar." And I say, "Yeah, I know, I get that a lot."

Then comes the next bit: "Madagascar? That's one of my dream destinations. It must be amazing there. What are you doing here in the cold?"

That's when I have to bite my tongue to stop myself from saying what I really think—that Madagascar might be wonderful for tourists, sure. But when you're a local, it's not magical. It's not amazing. It's hell.

As usual, though, I just laugh it off. No confrontation, thanks. And also, tips, please. Lots of tips.

Now, here's something I'm not proud of: I steal some of the tips. This restaurant pools all the tips into a jar to be shared equally among the staff at the end of the week. And I hate it.

I like to think of myself as a fair person, but I don't believe we all put in the same amount of effort.

Take Mich, for example. He's a waiter I can't stand. He was the one the lady boss assigned to "train" me when I started. Mich took that as an opportunity to dump all the unpleasant jobs on me. He'd constantly tell me to "check the bathroom," which, by the way, isn't just a quick look. It always involves cleaning something grim and emptying bins full of disgusting things. At first, I didn't realise that we were supposed to check the bathroom twice per shift. For my first two weeks, Mich made me do it four times.

When I eventually realised how much he'd been taking advantage of it, I decided to take some tips as payback.

But it's not all the tips—just some, and only when I'm on shift with Mich.

Some tips feel personal anyway. Just like that time, a lovely couple came in to celebrate the adoption of their first child. They were so kind, asking about my studies and how I was managing life in London. At the end of their meal, they left a £20 note on the table and ensured I saw it. The woman gave me a little wink before disappearing. There was no way I was putting that £20 into the communal jar. It was meant for me, and I really needed it. I was paid less than the minimum wage, with two-thirds of my entire salary going towards rent and the rest towards transport. Any extra was a godsend.

Fuck Mich.

***

At the end of my shift, I head home thinking today was an okay day. I still hate my job, but the first part of the day was good enough to balance things out. No kiss, but that's fine. I'd still give that morning with Leo a solid eight out of ten.

THE EUCALYPTUS TREE

Only when I'm tucked in bed, staring at my phone screen, do I see it. And just like that, my face lights up.

9
Razaf
1990

"Atody tsy miady amam-bato."
"An egg cannot win a fight against a rock."

Working on the car was a good analogy for my life. I managed to turn something completely broken into something useful again. I like to think I can do the same for myself. Maybe, if I put in the work, I'll find a new purpose. Music will always be there. It's in my blood. But I'm beginning to see how foolish it was to cling so tightly to that dream, to think it was my only shot at a meaningful life. It was also silly to think that going abroad was the only way to succeed, or that it was a way to succeed at all. My brothers in France are not exactly living the dream. They all work several jobs while attending university, sharing a flat with who knows how many other young men in their twenties. They sometimes have gigs on the weekends, though. They're closer to the musical dream than I'll ever be, but even for them, it's a far-off goal.

Fixing the car gave me something tangible to be proud of, and it's been a huge help for Mum's business. She's expanded and now has clients in town, meaning more deliveries and money. Honestly, I don't know how she does it. Everyone loves their mum, but I'm convinced mine really is the best. She's raised so many kids, not just her own, and made each one of us feel special. She's all love, no limits.

That's why I feel like I owe it to her to make something of my life. I can't let her down.

***

I finally decided it was time to take action. I talked to Dazo, and as always, he was on board.

The neighbourhood has changed a lot over the past few years. I remember when we first moved here—there was nothing but forest and empty land as far as the eye could see. Now, new houses were springing up everywhere, along with little shops and even a school nearby. Our house still stood out as the biggest, which made people assume we were rich. If only they knew what really went on behind those walls.

Still, appearances mattered. A well-known house made for good advertising. So I painted a sign and hung it on the gate:

"DOES YOUR CAR NEED FIXING? JUST COME AND ASK."

It wasn't much, but it was a start. And taking that step, no matter how small, felt good.

So that was it. Dazo and I were going to become mechanics. It was a big deal for two boys with no degrees and more doubts than confidence.

Of course, it wasn't as easy as we had hoped. Sure, the sign caught attention, but not everyone trusted two guys with no reputation, no formal training, and no fancy garage. At first, nothing happened. We sat outside, waiting, feeling a bit foolish every time someone passed by. I started to wonder if this was another stupid idea.

About two weeks later, a neighbour finally stopped by with his old car. It made a funny noise, and he said he'd seen our sign. We took the job immediately!

Dazo and I worked on it for three days. Three long, sweaty, frustrating days. We made so many mistakes that we thought we'd broken it more than we'd fixed it at one point. But we got it done, and when the engine finally sounded like a normal engine and less like a smoker's cough on their worst day, it was one of the happiest moments of my life, as dull as it was.

He paid us—cash in hand, the best kind—and spread the word. Slowly, more people started showing up. First, a friend of that neighbour, then another guy from down the street, and eventually people we didn't even know. Apparently, car repairs were in high demand. Because there were no car manufacturers in Madagascar, all our cars were imported from Europe. Likely dumped by French people. Those were unwanted, outdated vehicles.

The more cars we fixed, the better and faster we got, and we'd become pretty good mechanics.

In just two months, I'd learned more about cars than I ever had in all my years at school. Not that it's a high bar—school was useless to me anyway.

But we weren't just fixing people's vehicles. Somehow, we were making connections. Every customer became a new friend, or at least someone sitting and chatting while we worked. For the first time, I'd found something I genuinely enjoyed and could make a bit of money doing. Our small garage had become a gathering place. Our friends would come to hang out, watch us work, maybe lend a hand now and then.

The only problem? They'd often bring booze. And that, to me, was poison.

Most nights, I'd reach for a rum bottle, each sip a strange mix of regret and relief. Now with so many friends around, drinking at night turned into day drinking. Then it became *all-day drinking*.

My daily routine as a mechanic boiled down to fixing cars, making money, hanging out, and drinking. Lots of drinking. Sometimes it was cheap beer, sometimes rum, and sometimes both. When it was rum, I took it dry. No Coke, no ice, nothing to dull the raw burn of hot liquid as it slid down my throat and hit my stomach, searing away my sorrows.

Sometimes, we'd take it to the basement, drinking and playing music. The best combination there is. And yet the absolute fucking worst, given the alcoholic I am.

Some of our friends play guitar, too. They are all self-taught, just like us. We call them the *mpitendry tamboho*, which literally means "fence players" or "guitar players on the fence." In Madagascar, access to education is limited, so music lessons are practically unheard of. People often teach themselves, typically starting with old guitars and mastering just a few basic chords.

When you hear about Madagascar, you likely envision lush jungles, diverse fauna, and exotic beaches. All of that is true, but what people tend to forget or ignore is the place music plays in the country. From the earliest days of its history, music has played a central role in Malagasy life.

Here, music and singing are woven into the fabric of life, accompanying every moment from birth to death. Someone died? Everyone gathers to sing at night, trying to fill the silence that death has left in a family. Someone's wedding? Singing and dancing all day to celebrate.

Every region and every ethnic group in Madagascar has its own unique musical identity. In the North, there's *salegy*. In the East, it's the rhythmic *bassessa*. In the centre, it's the *bagasy*. In the South, the *mangaliba*. All of them have a very specific rhythm.

Bearing in mind that 80% of the Malagasy population don't even have access to electricity, these are not played with electric instruments, but mostly with traditional Malagasy instruments, like the *valiha* (the traditional stringed instrument made from a species of local bamboo) and the *aponga* (a type of drum, or rather percussions).

Music is passed on from generation to generation without anyone having to teach it.

Guitars came later in Madagascar, likely towards the end of the 1880s. In the Malagasy-French Dictionary by R. P. Abinal and Malzac (1888), the term *gitara* appears, and the word *lagitara* is even listed under the letter L. This confirms that the guitar was present in Madagascar by the late 19th century, with certainty by 1888. However, it likely arrived several years earlier, given the lengthy process required to compile the dictionary.

The use of the term *lagitara* also provides clues about the origins of the foreigners who introduced the instrument to Madagascar. Both French and Spanish employ similar terms to describe the instrument. Given Madagascar's history with France, it is highly probable that the guitar was introduced to the island by the French over a century ago.

The *valiha* will always be Madagascar's traditional stringed instrument, but these days, many Malagasy people can also play the guitar. Most of our friends know how—even if it's just two chords, and even if they can't name them. But honestly, two chords are enough to play a surprising number of songs.

***

So, I have a job and friends. I play music, and I even have money. From the outside, this appears to be the happiest time of my life. And yet, somehow, it's the most miserable

I've ever felt. All because of a fucking stupid, meaningless liquid.

I can't blame anyone but myself here.

That's the thing about alcohol, isn't it? At first, you think you're drinking for fun. And you are. You have a lot of fun. But then one day, you realise you haven't gone a single day without it.

And before you know it, you *can't* go a day without it. I didn't want to drink anymore; I *needed* to drink. No alcoholic enjoys drinking.

I envy my friends, who still seem to enjoy it, laughing as they share bottles, carefree in a way I can't be anymore. Four months after starting this business, which isn't even an official, registered business, I've lost all enjoyment in alcohol. It's no longer about the taste or the fun, but survival. I need it as much as I need air to breathe.

Nobody notices my drinking problem because we always drink together. Nobody measures how much I had. And nobody has to see that, however much I've had, it's never enough.

I'm also very good at hiding how miserable I feel in the morning, so life seems perfectly normal to everyone else. Sometimes, I even manage to convince myself that I'm fine. But that's just foolish. There's nothing normal about losing control, about being unable to stop drinking something you know is destroying you.

Some days, I am drunk by eleven in the morning. But here's the thing: I am sober when I get to work by the afternoon, so nobody notices. It goes completely under the radar each time. Dazo and I don't start working until 2 pm most days. We don't see each other at all in the mornings. I imagine he's sleeping in while I am locked in a losing battle against my worst enemy.

The weight loss is impossible to ignore, but people assume it's because I work too hard, that I am burning through calories, fixing cars and sweating in the heat. It's almost funny how easily people fail to see that I am simply a mess... a fucking loser.

I worked, though. I still fixed the cars, I still made money, I still laughed with my friends and my brother, and I still had dinner with my family at the table at the end of the day. I also continued to play music with whoever wanted to. I would never *not* play music.

***

Three years... I did this mechanic job for three years and was miserable throughout, even though I put on a mask of happiness and productivity every day.

And then, the inevitable. The never-ending cycle.

We started losing customers. To be fair, it wasn't sustainable at all. We just kept fixing our neighbours' cars, then the cars of their friends, and those of their friends' friends. There were only so many friends' cars we could fix. We didn't do much advertising, we didn't invest in new equipment, nor in any sort of training. New garages started to open near us, with better tools and qualified staff. They also had a phone number and a name. Two very basic things a business should have, but we didn't. Eventually, our boat sank. We shut down.

Failure once again.

People always say you shouldn't let one failure define who you are, you should never give up, or bullshit like that. I would have believed them after one failure, but I'm fed up with it all after so many attempts that got me nowhere further than my starting point. I was fed up before, and even more so now. I don't know if there's a word for when you're more done than done, but that would be me. Something like *overfuckingdone*. When I think back, I realise how foolish I was to believe, even just for a second, that I could do something with my life. You'd think I had learned by now.

Visibly not.

Things calm down for a bit now that there's no garage.

The yard looks more like a yard again, no longer like a messy garage with old cars, wrecks, and black oil on the ground. Lala and Rado are starting to grow flowers and plants again.

On the other hand, I am back to my days of doing nothing. Nothing purposeful, anyway.

Driving helps me escape the house and the urge to drink, so that's what I do most of the time.

I usually just drive without a specific destination.

Today, though, I find myself driving to the church. I don't actually go inside it. In fact, I haven't been inside a church since I was fifteen, when my parents stopped forcing me to go. But I like the place. It's uphill, and I get a beautiful town view from here.

I park at the bottom of the hill and walk up the stairs to the top. The view from the summit takes my breath away more than the climb itself. Up here, things seem small and easy to handle, unlike in my overwhelming life. I watch in silence for a while.

I remind myself that I've been in this position before. I've fallen, and I've got back up. I should be able to do it again. But optimism has never been my strong suit. I'm an empty-glass kind of guy.

THE EUCALYPTUS TREE

Sometimes I'll hear someone say how lucky we are to have a big family. The seven brothers. What a blessing. To me, it feels like a curse. The more people you have, the more you stand to lose. If life follows its natural course, I'll be the sixth to go, which means saying goodbye to five brothers before it's my turn. That's not even counting my parents. It's hard to see that as a blessing. It's hard to see anything at all as a blessing, to be honest.

I'm deep in thought when the rain starts.

It begins as a light drizzle, a gentle touch against my skin. But the sky rumbles, warning of something much heavier to come. I drive back before it gets too bad.

Sure enough, just moments later, the rain roars, slamming against the roof of my car with such force that I can barely hear the radio. The wipers swing frantically, struggling to clear even a sliver of visibility. There's also the occasional flash of headlights cutting through the storm. The closer I get to town, the denser the traffic gets, and navigating the waterlogged streets becomes increasingly difficult. Leaning forward, squinting through the fogged-up windshield, I slow down to match the crawling pace of other cars.

That's when I see... her.

She's standing beside the road, completely drenched, with her thumb up in the air. Even through the blur of rain, I can see her distress. Who wouldn't be, stranded like that at seven in the evening, hitchhiking in a storm?

I pull over instantly.

"Are you alright?" I ask while my window rolls down.

She's younger than I expected, maybe in her twenties, with a scarf tied around her head and a bag slung over one shoulder. Rain streams down her face.

"Could you give me a ride? I missed the bus," she says, her voice barely cutting through the rain.

"Sure, get in," I reply.

She hesitates for a second, visibly assessing the risks. But I must pass whatever test she's running because she opens the door and slides into the passenger seat, dripping water everywhere.

I focus back on the road and start driving again, but I can feel her watching me, stealing cautious glances as though she's still trying to size me up.

"You're a nice guy," she abruptly comments, breaking the silence.

I laugh in surprise. "What makes you say that?"

"All these cars and only you stopped," she says matter-of-factly.

"Maybe it's for the best," I mumble. "You never know who might pull over."

"True," she says, flashing a quick smile. "But I've got a good radar for bad guys." She leans forward, her hand slipping into her bag. "I have a nail clipper here, just so you know. It makes a great weapon."

I glance at her, smiling despite myself. "Thanks for the warning."

A soft laugh escapes her as she relaxes. The tension eases, and the conversation flows more naturally. She tells me she'd been in town sorting out some paperwork and needs a lift to anywhere near Tanjombato. My luck. I'm heading to Malaza, which takes me right through Tanjombato.

"Oh, fantastic!" she says when I tell her it's in my way. Her enthusiasm is infectious.

It feels like ages since I've encountered such vibrancy.

The rain intensifies for the rest of the way, drowning out most of our conversation, but her presence is comforting. Even in silence, I can feel her occasional glances.

When we reach Tanjombato, she asks me to pull over near a small shop with a flickering light outside.

"Here's perfect, thank you," she says.

"I'm happy to drive you home," I offer.

She shakes her head firmly. "This is fine. Really."

Fair. It's probably not a good idea to show a stranger where she lives. I pull into the shop's tiny car park. The rain hasn't let up, and it's pitch dark now, but she seems sure of herself. She reaches into her bag and pulls out some cash, holding it out to me.

"Here," she says.

I shake my head. "No, that's okay. I was just helping out."

But she insists, pressing the money into my hand. "You earned it. Thank you for stopping. Really."

I don't argue further. I watch as she disappears into the rain, her figure swallowed by the storm.

I'm left sitting in the car, staring at the money in my hand, feeling something I haven't felt in months. *Useful*.

The drive home is quiet, but my mind is loud with thoughts. Thoughts about that interesting and mysterious woman. Regrets that I haven't even asked her name. But beyond all that, ideas start to take shape. It's small, barely a whisper, but it's there.

I know what to do next.

10

Hira

2017

"Aza miandry ny ho faly vao hitsiky fa mitsikia mba ho faly."
"Don't wait to be happy to smile; smile to be happy."

```
"That didn't go as planned. I pan-
icked. Sorry."
```

A text from Leo.

Oh my God. I knew it. He wanted it, too. I reread the message several times, just to be sure I'm not imagining things. And because every time I read it, it makes my smile grow wider. I'm smiling like an idiot now. I'm relieved, thrilled and scared all at once.

I'm not sure what to do, though. If I reply, I will wake him. We have class tomorrow, and it's past midnight.

But it's rude to leave him hanging, right? If he's anything like me, he's probably waiting. He's already seen that I've read the message, anyway. To hell with it, I'm replying.

```
"Good to know it wasn't just in my
head. Talk tomorrow."
```

That's all I can come up with. It doesn't cover half of what I feel, but I don't want to seem too eager.

Today was not an okay day after all. It turned out to be a wonderful day. I sleep like a child on Christmas Eve: warm, content, and full of anticipation.

***

When I get to school, the first thing I do is find Gia. This will cheer her up. The first time I told her about Leo, she was just as excited as I was about this possible romance.

As I tell her about lunch, the awkward moment at the station, and the text message, her eyes light up, and she can't stop smiling. If we weren't in a grown-up school, we'd probably be jumping up and down like two toddlers.

That's why I love her. Even the smallest things make us happy for one another.

But while chatting with Gia, I can't help but notice that Leo isn't here yet. Okay, I didn't just notice. I've been watching the door the whole time, hoping he'd walk in. But he hasn't.

A wave of disappointment hits me at the thought of not seeing him today. Even if we're studying my favourite lesson, Travel Writing, it's not enough to lift my mood. I try to refocus, nodding along as Gia still talks about how she imagines my future babies with Leo, but my mind keeps drifting. Maybe he's sick. Maybe he overslept. Or maybe he just didn't feel like coming. The last thought stings, and I shake it off quickly.

The professor walks in, shuffling papers, and the classroom starts settling down.

Still no Leo.

The class begins with the professor reminding us once again how important it is to describe things in a way that shows rather than tells. Like, don't just say a beach is beautiful, make people feel the sand between their toes and the sting of salt in the air. He starts with examples of "show not tell" at the beginning of each lesson. "Don't say 'The city was busy and chaotic', instead say 'Honking cars weaved through narrow streets, their drivers leaning out of windows to shout at each other'". "Don't say 'The market was lively and colourful', say 'Stalls overflowed with pyramids of oranges, their citrus scent tangling with the spice of freshly ground cinnamon'.'" Usually, I'm fascinated by his limitless inspiration, but today, my focus can't seem to leave the fricking door.

Still no Leo.

Several minutes pass. And just when I'm about to give up, the door finally creaks open. Leo steps in. He quickly apologises for being late and the professor just nods, like it's not a big deal, when it is a huge fricking deal to me. I was dying over here.

Gia nudges me with her elbow, and I bite back a laugh, trying to keep my cool. But keeping my cool seems like a mission impossible while he glances at me and raises an eyebrow, slow and deliberate. There's a teasing glint in his eyes, a quiet challenge, as if he knows exactly how much space he's taken up in my thoughts. His lips curve just enough to make my stomach flip. Then, he looks away and scans the room for a seat. He moves casually, like he isn't even slightly flustered about being late, and drops into an empty seat a few rows ahead.

I try to focus on the lecture, but my eyes keep drifting back to him. He leans back in his chair, stretching slightly before getting his laptop on the table and flipping it open. And all this time, I don't even know what's happening in the background. Was the lecture interrupted as we watched him go to his desk? Or was it just me who was watching?

Gia nudges me again. "You're staring."

I snap my attention back to my notes, cheeks warming. "I'm not."

She smirks. "Right. And I'm the Queen of England."

I roll my eyes but don't argue. Instead, I steal another glance at Leo. As if sensing it, he turns slightly, and for a split second, our eyes meet. This time, he smirks properly, a clear curve of his beautiful lips, before he looks away again.

Great. Now I'll never focus.

During the day, talking to Leo is nearly impossible. Between classes, assignments, and the constant presence of professors, there's never a real moment. The most we manage are fleeting glances or a shared smirk across the room.

A part of me is relieved. As much as I've been dying to talk to him, the nerves are just as intense. When it comes to relationships, I'm like a fish trying to climb a tree. It's a stranger's territory. I'm just waiting for Leo to lead, really. The thought of actually having to talk, to acknowledge whatever this is, makes my stomach twist. And the kiss... he will want to kiss. I want that, too, but I don't know if I can do that without completely falling apart.

When school ends, and I think my time alone with Leo has finally come, Ruth, one of our classmates, is already rallying people.

"Come on, guys, it's Friday! We haven't gone out as a class yet, so let's change that tonight. Let's go to the pub!" she says.

It actually sounds fun. And I don't work on Fridays so I can come. But before I can answer, my eyes instinctively search for Leo. If he wants to go home, if he heads straight for the tube because he can't wait to have a moment alone with me, then I'll happily walk away from the invitation. I was relieved not to have the talk too soon, but let's not push it, I still want my kiss.

However, everyone, including Leo, thinks it's a great idea, so we all go. The group spills out onto the street, laughter and chatter filling the evening air. I walk beside Gia. She keeps throwing me a sideways glance.

"You were hoping to go straight home and talk to your new boyfriend, didn't you?"

I scoff. "What? No. I wasn't. And he's not my boyfriend."

She lets out a dramatic gasp. "Oh my God, I can't believe it. You're lying. To me." She clutches her chest like I've mortally wounded her. "After all we've been through?"

I roll my eyes, but there's no stopping her now.

"You were waiting for him to say, 'Actually, Ruth, I'd rather spend the evening gazing into Hira's eyes over a romantic moonlit walk to the tube station,' weren't you?"

Though irritating, her uncanny ability to mimic romantic heroes from her beloved fantasy novels is undeniably humorous.

I push her lightly. "Shut up."

She lets out a cackle. "I should be filming this for research purposes."

I groan. "What research?"

"For my ongoing study of your dramatic love life, obviously."

"Or lack of love life, in this case, because of fricking Ruth," I retort.

"Ha, so I was right!"

I nudge her again, harder this time, but she just laughs, linking her arm through mine.

We get to the pub, and everyone heads straight for the bar to order before settling at a large table near the back. The atmosphere is warm, loud, and effortlessly fun. I order a glass of Coke, no alcohol. I hate the stuff, having grown up in a house where it did nothing but damage.

The drinks flow, the conversation buzzes, and for once, I'm not just an outsider looking in. I don't talk as much as the others, but I find myself laughing, nodding along, genuinely enjoying the energy around me. Leo sits across from me, occasionally meeting my eyes, but there's no pressure, just the quiet, magnetic pull that's always been there.

People get up, disappear to the bathroom, and come back. Nobody really pays attention; the group is too wrapped up in jokes and chatter.

That is, until someone notices that Ruth and James have been gone for a suspiciously long time.

Gia narrows her eyes. "I'm going to investigate."

She pushes herself up with a dramatic sense of purpose and wobbles slightly. Gia is funny, but the tipsy version of her is hilarious. The shy girl I met months ago has completely vanished.

She gets up, swaying a little as she makes her way toward the bathrooms. A few seconds later, just as she reaches the door, Ruth and James step out. Gia whips around and rushes back to the table, nearly tripping over herself in the process.

She plops back into her chair, wide-eyed. "Oh my God. You guys. They were totally—"

She gestures vaguely but suggestively, her expression somewhere between scandalised and delighted.

The group bursts into laughter.

Ruth, completely unfazed, just shrugs. "What? We're not the only couple here." Then she turns to me and Leo. "Look at these two. They've been flirting since day one."

I blink. "What?"

The group roars with agreement. "Oh, come on. You weren't exactly subtle."

I feel my face go hot instantly. I glance at Leo, hoping for backup, but he looks... completely unbothered. Amused, even. He leans back in his chair, raising an eyebrow as if this is all very interesting.

I, on the other hand, am dying.

Eventually, the group starts thinning out. Ruth and James leave together (obviously), and Gia dramatically announces that she wants her bed. She's the only one who lives within a five-minute walking distance. Then, Leo pushes his chair back and glances at me.

"We're leaving?"

Oh my God. We're leaving. Together.

He said it in front of everyone.

I nod, standing up as well. We step outside together, the cool night air a welcome contrast to the warmth of the pub. Without really saying anything, we fall into step, heading toward the tube. For a while, we just walk. I keep my eyes ahead, very aware of every little thing, the way our arms sometimes brush, the steady rhythm of our footsteps.

Leo, as usual, seems much more at ease. Hands in his pockets, relaxed, like this is just any other walk.

I clear my throat. "So... about yesterday—"

His lips press together, like he was expecting that. "Yeah."

A pause.

Then, with a small exhale, "I panicked."

I let out a short laugh, more out of nerves than anything. "No kidding."

He chuckles. "Yeah. Not my best moment."

I shake my head, still unsure of what the right thing to say is. "Then you texted."

He nods, eyes flickering to me. "Yeah."

I glance at him, then ahead, watching the people moving toward the tube entrance. I hate how much my heart is hammering.

"You hate texting," I say, just to end the excruciating pauses. He told me that before. He finds texting a time-wasting process compared to the immediacy of a phone call. I'm the opposite. I'm a texting person. I hate phone calls. They make me nervous.

"I do, but this was necessary," he teases.

And we walk in silence until we're at the platform.

The train screeches into the station, sending a rush of warm air past us. We step inside, squeezing into the packed carriage. It's crowded, bodies pressed together, nowhere to move. I end up right in front of him. It was just like this the first time we rode the tube together. But, back then, we were strangers. I remember it so clearly: the awkwardness of standing next to him, the polite small talk, the way I was hyper-aware of every glance.

And now, here we are. In the same crowded carriage, the same impossible closeness.

But this time, it's different. It's a thousand times more intense.

The train lurches forward, and I shift slightly, adjusting my grip on the pole. Leo is so close that I can sense the heat radiating from his body. His hand grips the same pole just behind me, his arm brushing mine.

I glance up at him just as he looks at me. It's barely a second, but something in his gaze makes my breath hitch. The background noise of the train, the conversations around us, the fricking "Mind the gap"—it all fades. There's only the space between us, shrinking by the second.

The carriage rocks again, pressing me closer. He doesn't move away. Neither do I.

His grip on the pole tightens slightly, like he's steadying himself. His eyes flicker to my lips, just briefly, but enough for my pulse to stutter. My fingers tighten on the strap of my bag.

And then, he leans in.

It's slow, unhurried, giving me the chance to stop it if I want to. But I don't.

His lips meet mine, warm, certain, and for a moment, everything stops.

My first kiss in London is on the tube.

It doesn't get more London than that.

11
Razaf
1993

"Aleo sakafo anana ampian-tsetsetra, toy izay omby mifahy asian-dromoromo."
"Better a small meal with joy than a big meal with sorrow."

So begins my journey as a taxi driver.

Madagascar's transport system is far from ideal. The buses are always packed, with never enough seats for everyone. People, desperate and running late for work, often resort to sharing taxis. They come running as soon as I pull out with my taxi lantern glowing on the roof. I take them into town, then spend the rest of the day working around the city before heading home at six in the evening.

It's an easy enough job.

And when it comes to negotiating fares, I'm an expert. Years of selling junk and making garbage look like treasure have made sure of that. I work long hours, usually from 6 am to 6 pm, but I just sit in my car all day with no effort necessary, so it's fine with me. I do this every single day, Monday to Sunday. The money isn't terrible. No complaints here.

Most days follow the same rhythm. The morning rush begins as soon as the sun is up in the sky, a blur of people hurrying to work or the market. By mid-morning, things slow down, giving me a chance to breathe before lunchtime brings another wave of customers. Then comes the evening rush, one last burst of movement before the city settles for the night. It's predictable, repetitive. I could do it half asleep.

This morning starts like any other. I'm out by six. The first few hours are steady. One trip to the main road, another into town, then a few short rides back and forth between neighbourhoods. By nine, I've already done five fares.

Not bad.

But then things quieten down. It's often like that in the last few days of the month, as people just don't have any money left until payday.

Just as I'm considering heading home, a customer waves me down, asking for a ride to the Tanjombato supermarket. Perfect. It's on the way home, which means I can drop them off and call it a day.

I pull into the supermarket car park and let the customer out. They hand me the fare, thank me, and disappear inside. Seeing the long line of taxis waiting to pick up the next customers, I stick to my plan and decide to go home. There's no need to wait around. I turn onto the main road and start the drive back. Traffic slows me down as I near the bus stop in Tanjombato. Buses in Madagascar don't have designated lanes, so whenever one pulls over, the flow of cars behind naturally has to adjust. We just have to wait there until the passengers climb out and another wave gets in, while the *receiver* calls out the next destination, trying to fill the last empty seats.

The *receiver* is what we call the person who works on the bus alongside the driver. Their job is to stand at the back of the bus, open the door when it stops (yes, passengers enter through the back door), close it when it's ready to depart, and collect fares. There's no card reader or ticket machine here. Everything's done manually. It's impressive how well they manage it. *Receivers* brilliantly keep track of who have paid, who haven't, and how much change to give when people don't have the exact fare.

I ease off the accelerator, ready to wait it out.

That's when I see her... again.

I didn't get a good look at her last time, but I'm almost certain it's her, if only because of the way she makes me feel now. I don't usually buy into the clichéd way people describe meeting the love of their life, like being struck by a lightning bolt. That's very unrealistic. I'm sure the number of people who can tell what it actually feels like to be struck by a lightning bolt can be counted on my fingers. But now, seeing this beautiful woman running in my direction, I think I can understand it a little. And it fits the situation, considering how we first met.

Okay, she's not exactly running towards me. She hasn't even noticed me yet.

She's chasing the bus.

And from the looks of it, she's about to miss it. Again.

Mystery Girl is still twenty steps away as the *receiver* begins closing the door. Really, the bus could have waited for her. Not very nice of the *receiver* to shut the door.

Though I can't make out her words from where I am, her lip movements and frustrated expression clearly suggest she's swearing. She's slightly breathless, her hands on her knees as she leans forward. I signal a right turn, pull to the curb, and stop before her. She doesn't notice my car for a few seconds. I'm glad my taxi lantern is still on the car's roof; otherwise, I would have come out as a creep.

When she looks up and sees my car, she doesn't even flinch.

She's about to knock on the passenger window, but I'm already rolling it down.

Wherever she was supposed to go, it seemed important, and she was late.

"How much to SOKAF?" she asks. Then, a beat later, she breaks into a grin, eyes lighting up with recognition. "Wait a second. I know you! Are you a taxi driver now?"

I nod. "Yep. Thanks to you, actually. You gave me the idea. Congratulations, you were my first-ever customer." I pause for effect. "You just won a free ride."

She chuckles. "Wow. An honour. Do I get a trophy, too?"

"You get a lift. Take it or leave it."

"Oh, I'll take it," she says, pulling open the passenger door and sliding into the seat—her seat. The one she sat in all those weeks ago. Except this time, it's dry.

I glance at her. "What's with you and the bus? How do you keep missing it?"

She exhales dramatically. "I'm not the problem. They are. You saw that, right? That guy could've waited three more seconds."

She's right. But I'm glad they didn't.

I focus back on the road and start driving again. This girl is lucky (or maybe I am), because SOKAF is once again on my way. It's actually very close to my house. Malaza is up on a hill, and SOKAF sits just at the bottom. It's one of the biggest clothing factories in the capital. I pass by it every single day.

"SOKAF is on my way," I say casually. "I was going home anyway, so don't even think about paying me this time."

She scoffs. "It's not even ten o'clock. What kind of taxi driver goes home at this time?"

"I don't know. A lazy one? A rich one? A tired one? Many kinds, actually." I tease.

She smirks. "And which one are you?"

"Not the rich one," I reply.

To my surprise, she thinks I'm funny. She continues with lively conversations during the short ride. I'm not a huge talker. I hate it when people make conversations while I'm driving, but Mystery Girl is obviously different.

"Well, you go home at 10 o'clock, so I can see why you're not the rich kind," she teases.

"Fair enough," I say with a grin. "I just decided to take a day off today. It's quiet out there. Then, I saw you sprinting for the bus and figured you might need a lift. And, as I said, it's on my way. I swear I'm not making that up. I live in Malaza."

"I knew that," she replies simply.

I raise an eyebrow. "Do you work at SOKAF?"

"Yes," she says, then shrugs. "Not exactly the dream, but yeah."

I don't comment on that. I know too well what it's like to do a job I don't love. Instead, I keep things light.

"What kind of person starts at 10 o'clock at SOKAF?"

A factory usually has strict hours, and early ones, too. I assumed workers would be in by 8 am at the latest.

"I'm very late, as you can imagine."

Yeah, I gathered. But more than two hours late?

I don't say it out loud, but the question must be written all over my face because she immediately explains.

"I had an emergency. My little sister had a parents' meeting at school, and my mum couldn't get off work, so I had to go instead. I have four little sisters. Being the oldest comes with parental responsibilities, apparently."

I glance at her while driving and catch her rolling her eyes slightly at that last part. She realises I noticed and quickly corrects herself.

"Sorry, I didn't mean it to sound like that. My parents are wonderful and do everything they can. I'm just a bit tired."

"I wasn't judging you," I reassure her. "I've got six brothers. Luckily, I'm the second youngest. I can't imagine what it's like being the oldest."

"Six brothers?" She leans back, mock-scandalised. "And I thought my mum was crazy to have five girls." She pauses, then smirks. "So... how many kids do you think you'll have?"

I'm so glad I'm not drinking anything, because I would have definitely spat it out.

Even without a drink, I manage to choke on my own spit, coughing uncontrollably. I'm also pretty sure my face has turned a ridiculous colour.

"Oh really? That bad?" she laughs, still playful.

"I just... never thought about that," I say, when I finally manage to breathe.

And that's the truth. I've never thought about having a family. My dreams stopped at being a musician, and when that fell apart, I just... stopped hoping for anything at all.

I no longer have high expectations for my future. As long as there's food on my plate and a roof over my head, I can say I'm okay. That's enough. Or at least, I've convinced myself it is.

Yet, the sight of this woman causes a slight change in my perspective. Perhaps it's fate. She had to attend a parents' meeting today, which made her late for work, and as a result, she missed the bus. And I, for some reason, decided to go home early. If it wasn't fate, what was it? Luck? Coincidence? An unseen power guiding us to the same spot simultaneously?

But if I follow that logic, then I'd have to accept that everything, every setback, every missed opportunity, was leading up to this. That there was some greater reason why I wasn't allowed on that plane when I was eighteen, why my dreams never left the ground.

And I refuse to believe that.

No, meeting this woman isn't fate's way of explaining why my life didn't turn out the way I wanted. If it is, then it's far too late. Too many years have passed since my father's problems derailed everything. Too many years since I've stopped hoping for anything more. If life was going to balance itself out, wouldn't it have done so much sooner? How long after something bad happens can we say the good that follows was "meant to be"? Surely, not nine years. That's too long. Too late. If fate had a plan, I stopped being part of it long ago.

I don't want to expose my negative thoughts to her, though.

Fortunately, I spot the SOKAF sign and immediately signal left, stopping just before the gate.

"Here you go," I say.

Though relieved to end the deep talk, I'm not exactly happy to be parting with her.

"Oh, that was quick. Thank you. I'm Claire, by the way," she says.

"Razaf," I smile back. "Nice to meet you."

She gets out of the car, and just before shutting the door, she says something I never would have expected in a million years.

"I finish at 5 pm. See you later?"

I guess I have a date, then.

Claire is a pretty name. Then again, she's a pretty girl. Though not in a conventional way, which only makes her more intriguing. She wore a white, sleeveless top that was just a bit too short, revealing her belly button at times, paired with blue, elephant-leg trousers. Her short, curly hair, perfectly complementing her light skin, completed the unique look. She's tall, probably an inch taller than me. I know I'm not exactly tall for a guy, but most women are still shorter. Madagascar has the sixth-shortest population worldwide, and I believe the average height is below 160 cm, so Claire already stands out.

Based on our brief conversation, she is also funnier than the average person.

But mostly, she is bold! I mean that in the best way. What kind of woman would get in a car with a stranger, joke around, and then ask for a ride home from work? Many women would likely expect the man to initiate contact. I like that she took the initiative.

I can't believe I'm seeing her again this evening.

I shift into first gear and drive up the hill towards my house. From the outside, it probably looks like I'm just driving, like nothing has changed. But inside, it feels like I've just let out a breath that I held for too long.

***

It's 4:45 pm, time to pick up Claire.

Somehow, my day off has turned into a tiresome, never-ending bore. Normally, I don't experience boredom. Not really. My life may lack joy, but I always find ways to keep busy. Music alone is enough to keep me occupied. But even without music, I know how to fill my time. As a child, I spent a lot of time building houses from my dad's empty cigarette boxes and riding my bike through the forest. I usually find the day too short. And because I'm naturally a pessimist, to me, each day is one less day in our lives, not one more. This is why I rarely look forward to things.

But today is different. I've been counting the hours since I got home.

So that's what anticipation feels like... This is a new experience for me.

I grab my keys and head out. It's a short drive, so I will arrive early, but I'm being cautious. I'm hoping she'll catch sight of my car immediately upon leaving the building. The sight of my car would prevent her from changing her mind.

Putting all the odds in my favour, I park in the same spot where I dropped her off this morning. She won't miss it.

My right leg is bouncing anxiously as I wait. I'm nervous. This girl is making me feel emotions I haven't felt in years, if ever, damn it. I didn't need this. But, somehow, I want it.

About fifteen minutes later, the gate of SOKAF opens, and a wave of workers floods out. Hundreds of them, walking and chatting, a sea of uniforms and tired faces. It's impossible to spot Claire in the crowd, so I can only hope she spots me instead.

And she does.

She waves at me and murmurs something to her coworker. Seconds later, she's back in my car.

"Hi, you're here," she says.

"I'm here," I echo.

"I didn't think you would come."

"Why not?"

"Because... I thought I scared you away."

"You didn't."

She considers it for a moment, then grins widely, her eyes crinkling at the corners. Her eyes are unlike anything I've ever seen. They are the softest shade of brown, but what really strikes me is how rounded they are. The roundness of her eyes, devoid of sharp angles, imparts a feeling of openness and vulnerability.

"Ok, so where to?" I ask.

"Drive towards Tanjombato. I'll guide you."

I nod and drive. The ride will not be very long. I'd estimate a maximum of ten minutes. Fifteen if there's traffic. Strange to wish for traffic. This girl really is turning my world upside down.

A million questions are swirling in my head for her, but my chaotic thoughts make it impossible to figure out where to start.

"So... what's your story?" is all I manage to blurt out.

Talk about being specific.

She hesitates. I don't blame her.

But then, she answers with her usual enthusiasm.

"Funny you should ask, because that crossed my mind recently, too. Like, if my life was a book or a movie, what would its title be?"

I didn't expect this, but I like it. Just when I think I've seen and heard everything, she surprises me again.

"And what would it be?" I ask.

"I don't know. I think that's such a difficult question because it's like summarising your whole life in one or two words. Twenty-three years of existence, boiled down to a title. That's mad, isn't it?"

It is mad. But then again, I have some ideas for mine. As if on cue, she turns the question on me.

"What about you? What would you name a book about your life?"

"Struggle. Failure. Something along those lines," I admit, my shoulders dropping slightly as the words leave me. It feels oddly relieving to say those words out loud.

"Ouch. You're hard on yourself."

"I'm not. Look, I'm a taxi driver. Not exactly a great career."

"First of all," she says, her voice rising with mock indignation, "do not insult taxi drivers. There's no such thing as a bad job."

"Okay, okay," I laugh, holding my hands up in surrender. "I didn't mean to offend anyone. There's nothing wrong with being a taxi driver. But I wanted to be an international musician. It's just... the gap between what I wanted to do and what I'm actually doing is too big. So, failure."

"An international musician? That's amazing!" she says, her eyes lighting up. "But have you ever thought that maybe it's not your fault? Music has to be one of the hardest industries to break into."

I hadn't thought of it that way. She has a point, but still, I can't shake the feeling that I'm drifting further from my dream every day.

"Instead of failure," she says softly, "how about 'resilience'?"

And now, it's my turn to smile. Claire is clearly something out of the ordinary.

"Oh, after the bus stop, turn left," she says, casually pointing ahead.

We've reached the Tanjombato bus stop now, and turning left from here means leaving the main road and heading into Ankady. It's a small neighbourhood, and I don't know it well because it's off the main road. No bus comes this way.

That means Claire has to walk this road home every day. In summer, it's light until 6 pm, but darkness arrives a bit earlier in winter. I can't stop thinking about how unsafe that must be for her, walking alone on unlit streets. It's odd how protective I'm already feeling towards her.

Fortunately, the walk doesn't appear to be very long. We're barely two minutes in when she asks me to stop. That would make it roughly a five-minute walk from the bus stop. I arrive at a large white villa with an imposing black metal gate and look at her with a questioning expression. I wrongly assumed she wasn't wealthy.

"Yes, that's me," she says, as if reading my mind.

"Uh... okay, well, it was good to see you again," I respond, still taking it all in.

"You know where I work and what time I finish," she says with a sly smile, before opening the passenger door and stepping out.

When I'm left alone with my thoughts, I begin to wonder why a woman living in a house like this would want to talk to me, let alone spend time with me.

I wonder what the story of this house is. She mentioned her mum couldn't get off work for her little sister's school meeting. Perhaps her mother has a very lucrative job, like a doctor. She also mentioned having four sisters, so the big house makes sense. That could potentially explain her living in a mansion. But why would she be interested in me at all?

Whatever the reason, I'll have to wait until tomorrow at 5 pm to find out. I'm determined to know more about Claire, so I won't ever miss our daily meeting.

THE EUCALYPTUS TREE

***

I finish my last ride in town at 4 pm and decide to head back so that I can pick up Claire. Today's shift has been uneventful, which doesn't bother me in the slightest. I like it when things become routine. It's when the job gets easier. Back when I was selling junk on the streets, life never settled into a calm routine. There was always pressure to innovate, to discover the most valuable objects, and to attract customers. Those four years remain a terrible memory, except for the friends I gained.

Illegally parked, as always, I half expect Claire to stand me up. It still feels surreal that she wants to spend time with me, and in the back of my mind, I can't shake the thought that one day she'll realise she's making a mistake, and she'll just vanish. That thought has only grown stronger since seeing where she lives.

A short while after, though, she still has the same contagious enthusiasm. Once again, she spots me first. She's practically skipping to my car.

"Hi, you're here," she says.

"You said that yesterday. Of course, I'm here." She seems to wonder why I keep coming as much as I wonder why she keeps wanting me to come.

"Alright, shall we head home, or is there somewhere else you'd prefer to go?" she asks.

That's new. I like the sound of that.

"Somewhere else," I don't hesitate. "Do you have any idea where?"

"Hmm, do you? You're a taxi driver. Surely, you know many interesting places."

"There's a burger place in town," I suggest. "If you're hungry."

"I'm always hungry," she says.

In Madagascar, going out to a burger place for a date is far from common. In fact, the rare times I've been to a restaurant, if you can even call it that, have been while travelling. Journeys from Antananarivo to other provinces can take several hours, which means stopping somewhere for lunch is often necessary. There are specific roadside spots for that, known as *hotely gasy*—Malagasy hotels. These are usually no-frills eateries with the bare essentials, serving traditional Malagasy meals. So, rice. Eating out at all is rare, something reserved for special occasions, and only for those who can afford it. And today, well, this *is* one of those special occasions.

It takes us about forty-five minutes to reach Bons Burgers. I've never been here before but always pass by the place. It's located just a few feet away from the second-hand book market in Ambohijatovo, right at the beginning of Analakely.

We sit on the terrace overlooking the book market.

I'm not much of a reader; books don't really interest me. But somehow, I find myself captivated by the scene below.

The second-hand book market in Ambohijatovo is the go-to place for cheaper books. And I do mean *cheaper*, not cheap. The market spills onto the surrounding pavements, so it's often chaotic down there.

From up here, though, that chaos melts into something more orderly: just people buying and selling books.

I've often wondered where all those books came from. Some are probably from private collections or donations sent in bulk by container ships, but there must also be some questionable sources. Prices fluctuate wildly, depending on how the seller sizes up the customer and how good they are at bargaining. I know how this game works because I've played it myself. Not with books but selling second-hand junk on the streets is a similar process. Most buyers here are parents, drawn by the affordable French school textbooks, dictionaries, and other school supplies. Few can afford to buy them new at a bookshop. There's also a smaller selection of pocket novels, children's books, and, I've heard, the occasional hidden gem. Rare old books or special collections. I wouldn't know, though.

Claire seems impressed by my choice of place, and I decide not to tell her it was purely accidental. I didn't know we'd get this interesting view. I picked this spot because it looked fancy enough for someone like Claire, but not so fancy that someone like me couldn't afford it. And you can't go wrong with burgers. They're a safe bet.

When I think it can't get any better, the sunset adds another layer of magic. Where was all this luck all those years ago?

"I like this place," Claire confirms, her words matching the joy already evident in her expression.

"Me too," I admit.

The moment is self-explanatory; further words are unnecessary.

Okay, it's not exactly perfect. The sunset is objectively beautiful, and the book market below is fascinating in its own chaotic way, but nobody would mistake this place for something out of a fairy tale. Beyond the market, our eyes meet the bustling traffic and the endless line of people queuing for the bus. The air is filled with honking cars and the shouts of street vendors desperately announcing discounts, hoping to sell their last stock of the day, or maybe their first. I remember what that desperation feels like.

But none of that matters now.

"What else can you tell me about yourself?" Claire interrupts my thoughts.

"What do you want to know?"

"Hmm, let's see... I know you have six brothers. I know you're a taxi driver. I know you dream of being a superstar—"

"A drummer," I interrupt now.

"Oh, that's interesting. You're a drummer, then?"

"Yes, I am."

"And why the drums?"

"I play various instruments, but I've grown to love the drums above all others. It's just so... freeing. Also, my fingers are too short and stubby to play the piano."

She laughs at that, but it's not a mocking laugh. "You don't like yourself very much, do you?"

I don't intend to always sound so pessimistic, but I guess it's become my habit.

"I'm sorry."

"No need to be sorry. Just tell me, what's the story?"

At first, I don't understand what she means. But then, she speaks again.

"Something must have happened in your past. I know how it is. I'm sure we have more in common than you think."

I hesitate, unsure whether to say anything at all. But seconds later, the words fly out of my mouth like birds freed from a cage, gush out like water from a burst pipe, and flow like a waterfall. I tell her everything: my misadventures at the airport, the struggles with my father, every twist and turn of the story. I don't hold back.

I pause occasionally, worried I might be boring her, but it's the exact opposite. She's completely invested, her eyes fixed on me, silently urging me to go on.

When I finally finish, she's silent for a moment, and I have no idea what kind of reaction to expect.

But, as always, Claire surprises me. She takes an awkward, vulnerable moment and somehow transforms it into something I'll remember forever, in the best possible way.

"So, what I'm hearing is that your family went through a difficult time, and you sacrificed yourself doing a shitty job for years to save everyone. Well, that's heroic," she says rather nonchalantly, taking a bite of her burger.

No one had ever seen me the way she just had, or if they did, they didn't show it or say it out loud. Claire has this way of saying the most comforting words so naturally, as if she wasn't completely changing my perspective on everything.

The rest of the date—I'm going to call it that—is great. She doesn't share much about herself, not nearly as much as I do, but I don't mind. I feel like I have a lifetime to learn more about her. I drop her off at home at exactly 8 pm, and in an unspoken agreement, we both know we'll see each other again tomorrow at 5 pm. And we do, every single day of the week, except for the weekends.

Every day... Until one day, about three months later, when she doesn't show up. I wait at my usual spot outside SOKAF, watching the familiar crowd of uniforms spill out through the gate. But Claire is nowhere to be seen. I wait a little longer, thinking, *hoping*, something at work just held her back. After staring at the gate for a good half hour without seeing anyone opening it, though, I'm confident she didn't go to work today.

I decide to drive to her house to make sure she's okay. I'm not sure if she's told her family about me, but I hope it won't be too big of a shock when I show up.

Instead, I'm the one who gets the shock of my life.

I press the doorbell of the massive black steel gate guarding the white mansion inside. Its imposing structure makes it feel completely impenetrable. Our house is massive, too, but it's not as well guarded as this one. Our wooden gate looks pathetic.

A grumpy man in his seventies opens the gate, visibly not pleased to see a stranger. He must think I'm a Jehovah's Witness or a beggar. Besides, he was clearly interrupted in whatever fancy thing he was doing in his fancy mansion. I assume it's Claire's dad, even though they look nothing alike.

Maybe he knows who I am and doesn't want me anywhere near his daughter. That happens a lot in movies.

Unfortunately, it happens quite a lot in Madagascar, too. Madagascar is divided into social groups, and there is zero equality between them. The nobles, called the *Andriana*, were once the ruling class, rich landowners who believed their lineage made them superior. My father is from the *Andriana* line.

The *Andriana* were the highest tier in a rigid caste system, where the *Hova*, or free commoners, sat below them, and the *Andevo*, former slaves, occupied the very bottom. The *Andriana* are most commonly associated with the *Fotsy* (literally "white") class and the central highlands of *Imerina*, but this is not always the case. My family is rather dark-skinned, which is why it's always been important to my father to mention our nobility to whoever asks—or doesn't ask—in case our skin colour doesn't immediately make it clear. I never cared much about those titles, which were just imposed on us by history, by a world of rulers and subjects that no longer exist. However, when I stand in front of this imposing man, I begin to wonder whether the colour of my skin bothers him. Claire is much more light-skinned, so it's not impossible that her father would expect someone less... dark? Just the thought of it is ridiculous. And I refuse to tell him where my ancestors are from just to make my presence here more okay.

Besides, I'm still not 100% sure this is Claire's father. Except for the skin tone, I really see nothing in common.

"Hello, sir. I'm here to see Claire," I manage to say in what I hope is a confident tone.

He looks at me, puzzled. "There is no Claire here."

My head is filled with questions, irrational ones at that. Had I imagined the last three months? Was Claire even real? Is this man about to tell me that Claire did live here once, but she died fifty years ago? I don't believe in ghosts or the supernatural. I once walked home alone late at night after a bar crawl with friends, and my biggest fear wasn't spirits or apparitions. It was running into angry stray dogs. So the fact that my mind is jumping to these bizarre scenarios right now says a lot about how confused I am.

Before I can say anything, the man adds, rather impatiently, "There's a Claire in the house next door. Maybe that's who you're looking for."

Oh. Well, that's unexpected, but I suppose it's a more plausible answer.

I thank him and offer the most polite goodbye I can muster, although he doesn't seem to care. All he seems to be interested in is closing his gate and returning to whatever rich 70-year-olds do at 6 pm. I've known a life without money trouble, but wasn't in my seventies. And I won't have the chance to ever live that life again, nor do I think I'll reach 70, so I genuinely wonder what they do.

No time for that now, though. I need to figure out what this house mix-up is about.

I walk to the house next door, and the atmosphere can't be more different. For starters, it's difficult to see that there is a small house there. No wonder I've never seen it. It's tucked behind the imposing white mansion that easily catches the eye. It doesn't help that the other house on its left is also quite big, not as massive as the white mansion on the right, but a decent size. This small house is like a stubborn, bad weed in the middle of a huge garden. The gate is a worn, weather-beaten relic, with wood so aged and splintered that it barely holds together.

There is no doorbell, but it doesn't matter because the panels are unevenly spaced, leaving noticeable gaps wide enough to peer through. I go inside, and there's just a tiny yard to walk through before getting to the house. I knock on yet another door that looks like it's going to collapse anytime.

Moments later, there she is: Claire. Her rounded eyes are open so wide that the shock is written all over her face.

She steps outside and closes the door behind her, and I immediately understand I'm not welcome inside.

"What are you doing here?"

I'm a bit annoyed that she's the one interrogating me when I'm the one with a million unanswered questions, but I reply.

"You were not at work. I just wanted to make sure you were okay."

"How did you find me?"

Really? Another question?

Still, I continue to answer as though my mind wasn't racing.

"I was next door. But it wasn't your house," I say, stating the obvious.

"I... I couldn't go to work. I had to take care of my little sister. She is ill," she says, as if that justifies the rest.

Although the situation is pretty self-explanatory. She was obviously ashamed to reveal who she really was. I wouldn't have judged her based on her house or her financial situation, of course, but I understand the urge to hide this kind of thing.

Still, it stings that she lied, especially after I've opened up to her. She knows I am not rolling in gold either, so she could have come clean then.

Her sisters are peering through the window. If they're trying to be discreet, they're failing miserably. Claire follows my gaze and turns around to see four curious faces at the window. She looks at me, now fully blushing.

"Listen, I'm sorry. I lied, obviously. We're poor. You can go now."

"But why lie? I told you I wasn't exactly a prince either."

"I know, but by then, it was too late. It seemed ridiculous to tell the truth. I never found the right time. But this is it, this is the truth. We're poor," she says it for a second time, making sure I understand.

I do understand, and that doesn't change anything, really. The lie bothers me, not the state of the house.

"Well, show me now. Everything about you. No more lies."

She gives up and throws her hands in the air. "Fine, come in."

The inside of the house matches the outside. As she opens the door, my feet are welcomed by a cemented floor and a patchy wall. There is very little furniture, but they fill the tiny room quite well. One sofa, a dinner table, a few wobbly chairs and a radio airing the news. All Claire's sisters greet me with a huge smile, and all of them are familiar with my name.

So, Claire did talk about me.

I don't know if she used the word "boyfriend," but the way they look at me suggests that they know I'm not just a friend.

"She didn't lie about me being ill," the youngest sister says. "I was ill. I'm better now, but she took care of me all day." She smiles as she says this, and I feel a little guilty for being annoyed earlier.

"Let me show you around," Claire said, pulling me away from her sisters' curious and mocking stares. "It'll be brief, though. There isn't much to see."

It's true, the space is tiny, especially considering seven people live here. They don't have a proper kitchen. Instead, they cook outside, in the tiny backyard, where I can spot the *fatapera*. A *fatapera* is an essential cooking tool in Madagascar. It's a traditional charcoal stove used in almost every household for cooking. It works by placing charcoal in a small central basin, which serves as the heat source. Once lit, the charcoal provides consistent heat for cooking. To maintain the fire, you can gently fan it, ideally with a fan, but cardboard works too, since nobody has an actual fan. A pot of rice is cooking on the *fatapera* while Claire makes me visit the tiny space. Next to the stove are buckets of water, which I assume come from a well. That's the water they use for cooking and washing dishes. That's not uncommon, either. Many people in Madagascar don't have access to a sink or running water.

We go back inside, and she takes me upstairs, where there are two rooms—one for all five sisters. There are five mattresses on the floor, but it might as well be one unique giant mattress, the way they are stuck to each other. The other room is Claire's parents' room, but the door is shut, so she just points at it and lets me know what it is, then hurries me back downstairs.

"That's it. You saw everything. This is the house. My mum works several jobs. She does laundry for some families, babysits when she can, sometimes hauls water for people who can pay. My dad's barely around; he works out of town most of the time," she says once we get back to the living room. There's an edge in her voice, and I don't understand why, since she is the one who lied, and I like to think I've handled it quite well so far.

I decide it's time for me to leave. After all, I only wanted to make sure Claire was okay, and she is, so I can go. There's no need to try to talk to her about this today in front of her family. I know where to find her tomorrow, so I announce my departure.

Her mother comes down the stairs just then.

"Where do you think you're going, young man? We were just about to have dinner." She says.

Unexpectedly, I'm caught between Claire wanting me to leave and her mother wanting me to stay.

"Mum, it's not necessary, he was leaving."

"No, he's staying," her mother says, using the same tone my mum does when a discussion isn't up for debate.

Her father—and, this time, I'm sure it's her father—comes in from upstairs, too, and ends the discussion. "You're staying, Razaf."

Oh, he knows my name.

She told her parents about me. I smile inwardly and comply.

The meal is rice with peanuts. Claire's mother hands each of us a small handful, carefully measured.

During the first part of dinner, Claire, who is sitting opposite me, refuses to look at me.

Setting aside the obvious tension with Claire, though, dinner is great! They're such a happy family. I can see where Claire gets her sense of humour and why, instead of falling into depression like I did when I was in her situation, she always shows a positive attitude. It occurs to me that it takes very little to be happy, yet we as humans always seem to find a way not to be.

Well, except for now. Now, Claire is anything but positive or happy.

As I chat with her family, easing into the conversation and even joking with them, I notice Claire beginning to relax. I steal a glance at her now and then, catching the faint smile on her lips.

By the end of the meal, her guard seems to have dropped entirely, and it's just like a family enjoying a meal together. We could be here or in a Michelin-starred restaurant, we wouldn't feel the difference.

As I'm leaving, I say goodbye to everyone, thanking them for having me for dinner even though I came unannounced. Claire walks me to the gate, and as we step outside, the air is colder and it's completely dark. I definitely lost track of time.

"I'm sorry," Claire says when it's finally just the two of us again.

I nod. And when I say nothing else, she adds, "for the lies... and for everything else. I was embarrassed."

"It's fine. I like your family," I say, trying to be reassuring.

"And they like you," she smiles.

12

Hira

2017

"Trano afindra tsy mitovy zoro."
"A house, once moved, no longer has the same setting."

I'm seeing Leo today for our first official date. *My* first ever official date.

That in itself is enough to make me feel wonderful. But luck seems to be on my side. I woke up to clear skies and sunshine.

I'm not used to seeing blue sky anymore. Three months of grey, dull weather made me appreciate the sun more than ever before. Not until I left home did I realise how lucky I was to grow up somewhere with 2,600 hours of sunshine a year. England's weather made me forget what warmth felt like. Until today.

I know exactly how to spend my morning before meeting Leo.

I skip the underground and take the bus instead. The sunshine's too rare to miss. I sit upstairs, because why not? I'm in this new phase of doing things I've never done before. London finally feels like a fresh start. It doesn't feel like a mistake anymore. Not like when I lived at Mel's, jobless, lonely, and lost in my first school lesson.

Now, I rent a decent room in Wembley. I've got a terrible job, sure, but I'm working. I'm doing well at school. And I have a boyfriend, which is a big fat bonus!

I get off the bus at Waterloo. The air is colder than expected. Even with the sun, it's still under fifteen degrees, especially by the Thames. But none of that matters. I'm already in love. With this city, this day, this new me.

I stroll along the vibrant Southbank, surrounded by street performers, artists, and bursts of music at every turn. I pass hip-hop dancers and then a guy playing an acoustic guitar. I take it all in.

I breathe in like it's the first time I've ever breathed properly. It sounds dramatic, but it's true.

A smile is permanently plastered on my face as I walk.

This city makes me feel like everything's possible. I used to dream about London because of nothing more than movies. Now, I have real reasons to love it. And I haven't even seen much yet!

A short walk later, there it is. Big Ben.

Big Ben rises in front of me, tall and majestic, bathed in golden sunlight. It looks as if the tower is glowing, retaining the warmth of the morning sun. Against the bright blue sky, every detail is crisp: the sharp lines, the arches, and the black and gold clock face. It's magical.

The place is swarming with tourists. I ignore them. My eyes go straight to the tower. Well, technically, Big Ben is the bell, not the tower. Leo told me that.

I try to take pictures, but none capture how it looks or feels, so I give up on my phone and savour the scene with my eyes instead.

This whole morning feels like a celebration. Of me. Of how far I've come. Of this new version of my life I didn't think I'd be brave enough to create.

I think this is the best day of my life.

I keep walking until I somehow find myself at Trafalgar Square. Another place that feels like it's been plucked from a storybook. The massive and majestic bronze lions guarding Nelson's column are impossible to miss; they stand as timeless sentinels.

Once again, the square is alive with street performers, tourists snapping pictures, and pigeons... *so many pigeons*!

They don't really contribute to the fantasy of the location, yet Trafalgar Square wouldn't be the same without them. The street birds are so integrated into the area that people sit on the stairs or benches to feed them. Everything, even something as mundane as pigeons, is beautiful here.

I stay a little longer, taking in the scene and letting the moment settle into me. I feel so relaxed, which is ironic considering how loud, busy, and anything *but* calm the city around me is.

I'm in love with this city.

***

When I finally check the time, I realise it's almost time to see Leo.

I stand up and walk purposefully, even though the nerves quietly eat me alive.

Because yes, I'm nervous. Stupidly nervous.

Leo and I haven't talked about the kiss at all. One moment, his lips were on mine—warm, unexpected—and the next, the train doors slid open, and he had to get off.

There was barely time to plan this date. Sunday. Cinema in Camden. Twelve. That was it.

I have never been to the cinema in my life. Villager all over again.

Back in Madagascar, there were only two cinemas, both with names that sound like dogs: Ritz and Rex. They both closed down in 1996, casualties of the video revolution. They made a brief comeback in 2007 to screen a locally made film, but I was too young to go.

And now, here I am. After hours of walking in busy London and smiling like an idiot (I seem to do that a lot), I'm stepping off the bus, scanning the crowd.

I spot him instantly, leaning against a lamppost, his hands always in his pockets with no care in the world, eyes flicking up just in time to catch mine. He smiles. Effortless. As if nothing has changed. As if my heart isn't hammering.

"Hey," he says.

"Hey," I reply, tucking a strand of hair behind my ear.

He gestures toward the entrance. "Ready?"

I nod.

A thick scent of popcorn and butter hangs in the air inside. My stomach rumbles. I'm so hungry.

Thank goodness Leo doesn't hesitate. The second he's bought our tickets; he rushes to the popcorn counter.

"My favourite thing about the cinema isn't even the movies. It's the popcorn," he jokes.

He orders their biggest bucket without a second thought, his eyes lighting up as he grabs it from the counter. Before we've even turned towards the screening room, he's already reaching in, shoving a handful into his mouth.

I raise an eyebrow. "You're not even going to wait until we sit down?"

He grins. "Why would I?" He holds the bucket out to me. "Go on. You know you want to."

I do.

I grab a handful, and he nods approvingly. The popcorn is warm and salty, a perfect mix of crunchy and buttery.

"You're officially a proper cinema-goer now," he says, like it's some kind of rite of passage.

I roll my eyes, but I can't help smiling.

He leads the way into the room, navigating through the rows until we find our seats somewhere in the middle. I sink into my chair, the seat swallowing me up, the screen already glowing dimly.

There are buttons on the side of my seat. I accidentally press one, and the seat starts reclining, causing me to sink further. The other button lifts the footrest.

"This is crazy," I whisper, pressing another button to bring myself back to normal. "You can just... lie down?"

Leo chuckles, already leaning back with his legs up like he's in his own living room. "Told you, the cinema's the best."

"Duh," I joke.

Around us, people murmur, settling in, but my awareness narrows to the person right beside me.

The lights dim, the cinema falls silent, and the movie begins.

I try to focus. I really do.

But all I can think about is how close he is. How our elbows brush lightly on the armrest.

I barely register what's happening on the screen. Every movement he makes, every slight shift, feels magnified in the dark.

Halfway through the movie, he turns slightly, whispering, "Do you like it?"

I'm not sure if I like it. What is it?

Of course, I don't say that. I just nod, not trusting myself to speak.

He smiles and turns back to the screen. I, on the other hand, am still very distracted.

One thing's certain: I'll remember this date forever. The movie? Not so much.

We don't talk at all for the rest of the movie, but I'm hyper-aware of all his moves next to me. If I moved just a little, our arms would touch. If I leaned in even slightly, our heads would be close enough that I could catch the scent of his shampoo.

But I don't.

I stay perfectly still, my fingers curled in my lap.

It's only when the credits roll and when the lights brighten that he speaks again.

"So? Was it nice?"

"Yes, it was great." It was great for what I've managed to watch, so it's not a complete lie.

But I wouldn't recommend the cinema for a first date. It's torture.

People start shuffling out, but Leo stays put. I glance at him, confused.

"I always wait a little longer," he says. "Sometimes there's an extra scene. And it's easier to leave when the crowd's gone."

"Interesting," I say, amused.

We sit in the quiet while the room empties around us. The screen flickers through the last credits, casting a soft glow over his face. He turns to me, and before I can process it, he leans in.

The kiss is even more intense than the one we shared on the tube. I thought *that* was slow and lingering. Now, it's as if we've been given all the time in the world, and we've chosen to use that time just to kiss.

When we pull apart, he pauses and looks at me for a second with his indescribable blue eyes before standing. "Come on, before they throw us out."

Outside, the air is cool, and the streets are still alive with people. We walk towards the station, falling into step easily.

"It's funny," I say.

Leo looks at me. "What is?"

"This. Walking to the station together. It's becoming a thing."

He smiles. "Not a bad thing to have."

At the entrance, he hesitates. "Up for a second date?"

Inwardly, I scream "Yes, obviously yes!". But I keep my face steady.

I simply nod. "Yeah. Sure."

"When are you free?"

"Now?" I say, because why not? It's only 3 pm, Sunday, and there's no school or work. I hope I don't sound too eager, though.

Leo's eyes light up, and he grabs my arm before I can second-guess myself. "Brilliant. Come on, then."

"Where are we going?"

"The pub," he says, like it's the most obvious thing in the world.

Maybe it is for people here.

I still find it quite unusual. Going for a drink wasn't a casual thing where I grew up. I barely went out at all, let alone for a drink. That's what happens when you grow up with an almost perfect father, save for his alcoholism.

My dad is an objectively good man. I grew up in what people would call an unconventional family, where my dad stayed home while my mum went to work. He cooked, cleaned, took me to school, and played with me. He was the default parent, and that was almost unheard of in Madagascar, especially in the nineties.

His only weakness, the thing that could bring him down, was alcohol. The only thing my parents ever fought over was that. The arguments weren't small; they were major, tension-filled blow-ups that frequently ended in tears and lingered for days. They tried to keep it from me. I don't recall seeing my dad drunk before I was fifteen. But the arguments were too apparent.

Rationally, I know that not every drinker is an addict. Yet, I continue to grapple with the blurry boundary between drinking for enjoyment and drinking as a means to avoid deeper problems.

We go straight to the bar to place our order when we reach the pub.

"Hi mate. Two pints of—"

"Leo," I whisper, tugging his shirt, "just Coke for me, please."

His gaze holds a mixture of confusion and irritation as he looks at me. "What? Why?"

Before I can answer, he turns away and addresses the person behind the bar. "One pint of London Pride, and a glass of Coke," he requests.

Drinks in hand, we find a table in the back corner of the pub. He briefly looks at me. I fake a smile, but my eyes betray my true feelings. My face must clearly show my discomfort. My lips are pressed too tightly, and I feel my shoulders tense. His reaction didn't sit well with me.

Then again, he must be confused, too.

He speaks first.

"Last time, you also ordered a Coke at the pub with the other guys. You don't drink alcohol at all?"

Why does he make it sound like it's a bad thing?

Anyway. I take a deep breath and mumble, "No, it's not really my thing."

It's an understatement, but it's the best I can do.

"It's not exactly my thing either. I only drink socially. You never do that?"

"I've never drunk alcohol in my entire life."

There it is. Now what? I'm angry now.

"Not even one sip? Ever?"

Unbelievable. I honestly don't get the fuss about someone abstaining from alcohol. Is it not the reverse that should be true?

My strained expression must be noticeable, because he immediately softens his voice.

"I'm sorry. I didn't mean to say it like that. It's just... unusual."

I finally relax a little. Culture differences, I mutter to myself. I'm the villager. I'm the weird one. I need to be more understanding and adaptable.

"No need to be sorry. I know it's weird. I'm sorry I let you down by refusing that drink you are so excited about," I joke.

His chuckle concludes the tense conversation.

As soon as his hands are on me, we're back to being lovey-dovey, and that little episode is forgotten. When his lips are on mine, it's not just that little episode I forget about; it's everything in the world. At that moment, it's just us.

And just when I think it can't get any better, he orders food.

Best. Date. Ever.

"Have you ever tried a proper Sunday roast?" he asks.

"Nope," I say.

"Ah, perfect! You're going to have your first roast with me!" He grins, looking genuinely thrilled about this little milestone. At least, food is an offer I won't refuse!

We stand up again and head to the bar to place our order. The bartender gives us two small paper tickets. At first, I think they're receipts, even though they are oddly small, and also, why two? But then, I understand from Leo's instructions that they are, in fact, our food order.

"Alright, so here's how it works," he begins. "This is like a ticket. You just need to take it there, to the carvery."

I raise an eyebrow. "Carvery?"

He grins. "Yeah, that's the station where they serve the roast. You'll see. The chef will slice up the meat for you, and then you load your plate with all the sides you want. Potatoes, Yorkshire puddings, veg, gravy. Anything you want. You can pile it high if you're hungry."

"So, like a buffet?" I say with a little too much enthusiasm, but I can't help it.

I love food. You appreciate it even more when it doesn't reach your plate so easily. We were the kind of family who brought plastic bags to weddings so we could steal away some of the food. So, you can count on me to pile it high. I don't say that out loud, of course. But that's what I plan to do.

The food is good, and I find myself liking the gravy more than I thought. I know it's made of some sort of powder I always see on sale in a supermarket, not appealing. But I'm surprised by how flavourful it is, and how it somehow ties everything on the plate together.

Sunday roasts could become another of my favourite things to do in London, and they're actually pretty affordable, even for me.

But of course, what really makes it special is Leo.

When I get home in the evening, I'm still over the moon. I love London, and today, it feels like London loves me back. I didn't want the day to end.

I am reminded of my father, who views the end of each day with disdain, believing that "each passing day is one less, not one more." I miss my parents. They were a major factor in my almost not coming here, and also a major factor in my decision to actually come. They deserve to see me succeed.

And for the first time, I feel hopeful that I will somehow get there.

Positive thoughts fill my head as I close my eyes and fall into a deep, restful sleep.

13
Razaf
1993

"Toy ny vary sy rano antsaha, tsy mifanary; an-tanety, tsy misaraka."
"Like rice and water in the rice field—they cannot be apart; even on dry land, they remain inseparable."

Things moved quickly between Claire and me. Faster than I could have imagined. We met on a stormy, rain-soaked night in January, and now, just eleven months later, we're preparing to tie the knot. These past months with her have been the happiest of my life.

Right away, it was clear we had a lot in common.

When we met in town that night, Claire came from Ankatso University. She went there to register for medical school. Sadly, she ended up never studying at all. She explained to me later that she'd gone hoping to balance work and studies, but their financial situation meant she needed to work full-time to support her family.

Education, after all, is a privilege in a country like mine, not a right. Actually, anything considered a right in developed countries—a roof over your head, food on the table, access to water—is a privilege here.

Take water, for example. In wealthier places, it's perfectly normal to shower twice a day, and people might even mock those who don't. But access to water isn't a given. Globally, about two billion people lack access to clean water and sanitation. In Madagascar, only a small fraction of the population, those with sufficient means, have access to running water in their homes. For most, water means a daily trip to a shared water access point or a public well, where they fill jerrycans to carry home. It's not free, either. You pay for every drop, so you only take what you can afford. Then comes the choice: do you use it to cook and wash your food or bathe? More often than not, the choice is obvious: you prioritise eating over cleanliness.

Education is no different. It costs money. *Lots of it*.

I'm not just talking about university. If you've made it that far, you're already better off than most. I'm also talking about early childhood education, schooling intended for everyone.

In Madagascar, there are two types of schools: private schools, which require money to attend, and public schools, which are limited in space and, to say the least, questionable in quality. Claire went to a public school.

She's incredibly smart and ambitious. She has always dreamed of becoming a doctor. But after earning her baccalaureate, she had no choice but to set those dreams aside. Her family needed financial support, so she started working. And that was that. Her medical dreams are long gone, replaced by a minimum-wage HR position at SOKAF.

We both had dreams shattered in front of our eyes, so close to the finish line. However, I feel stupid for the way I felt when I couldn't leave the country to become a musician. Some people have real problems. At least, I lived a few years with fortune and fame. Claire has struggled throughout her life, and continues to do so.

I've learned so much about Claire in just a few months, and I like everything about her. She's the first person I've truly opened up to, in ways I never have with anyone else. The only thing I've kept from her is my problem with alcohol. Partly because I've convinced myself it's not such a big issue anymore; it feels manageable now that I have fewer reasons to drink. And partly because I know the truth would drive her away for good. I'm sure she'd leave if she saw the real me. The weak, broken man beneath it all. And I couldn't risk that. It's very selfish, I know.

Claire and I did everything together. I drove her to work in the morning, started my taxi shift, and returned at lunchtime to see her. I worked through the afternoon, then picked her up again in the evening and dropped her off at home.

Saturdays and Sundays were the only days I didn't make any plans with her, because I rehearsed with Dazo. We had officially formed our duet—*The Draz*. We didn't really have any gigs, but we'd made a pact to take music seriously, rehearsing every weekend like something big was just around the corner. Claire never got in the way of that. She knew how much it meant to me, and not once did she try to meet up or suggest I skip a session.

That was one of many quiet clues that made me realise she was the one.

That, and the fact that we went to war together.

I wish I was joking.

***

The Constitution in Madagascar states that the President is elected by direct universal suffrage for a five-year term, renewable only once. I think that's almost everywhere, and it seems fair enough.

However, the President altered the Constitution, increasing the term limit to seven years with the option of two renewals. This means he is now serving a third term, amassing eighteen years in power. For eighteen years, this man has ruled over us, while Madagascar has made no progress since gaining independence in 1960.

And now, we just found out that he was planning another constitutional amendment, to extend his term indefinitely. He wants to stay in power for life.

Finally, the Malagasy people have reached their breaking point. A decade overdue, but it's better late than never. They no longer want him, and rightfully so. We've had eighteen years; that's long enough to judge the country's progress, or lack, thereof.

Firstly, the already fragile education system has fallen apart over the years. One of the President's key education initiatives was *Malgachisation*, which aimed to make Malagasy the primary language of instruction in schools and to replace the French educational system with a Malagasy one.

I understand the basic principles behind this approach. After emerging from colonisation, it's not unreasonable to promote Malagasy as the country's primary language. We learnt more about all the Louis and Henries in France than our own kings and queens, which wasn't very "independent" of us.

After all, we've fought for the *Malgachisation* in 1972. Twelve years after Madagascar had been freed from French colonisation, the French language and culture still dominated the country. The president at the time was a neo-colonialist and was harshly criticised by the people, who accused him of backing French interests. May 1972 was a time of revolution in Madagascar. Young rebels demanded a "second independence". They rebelled against the ongoing French influence, which had been established through cooperation deals signed in 1960. These agreements were meant to define the relationship between the two countries after independence, but in reality, they kept Madagascar tied to its former coloniser. What people wanted was simple: a more equal society.

It all started with a student protest at the Befelatanana School in Antananarivo. Under colonial rule, the school trained what were essentially "second-tier" doctors, just assistants to the French.

It was the medical students who first stood up, demanding an education system that treated all students equally, regardless of background or social class. The morning of 13 May 1972, hundreds of students and teachers gathered at Ankatso University, which was still called Charles de Gaulle University at the time, to organise demonstrations in front of the Town Hall.

But armed forces stormed in and rounded them up to be deported to Nosy Lava, an island off the north-west coast of Madagascar. Nosy Lava had been the site of the country's last penal colony, where Malagasy independence activists were once imprisoned. A few hours later, more than 200,000 students, teachers, parents, and ordinary citizens flooded the streets in front of the Town Hall. They were demanding the release of the 375 deported students and calling for the democratisation of higher education.

It became the largest protest in the country's history. Today, as a reminder of the protest, the square in front of the Town Hall is called the 13 May. The government's crackdown left around fifty people dead, but despite the bloodshed, it marked a victory for the Malagasy people. The movement brought an end to the First Republic and led to the fall of our neo-colonialist president. Power was handed over to the military until 1975, the year this current president was elected, marking the start of the Second Republic. From then on, our country was officially known as the Democratic Republic of Madagascar—which is, of course, ironic now.

So, no, *Malgachisation* is not a bad thing, as such.

In practice, however, it had disastrous consequences. Its failure was due primarily to the fact that the policy was devised solely on ideological grounds, rather than being based on sound pedagogical methods. The outcome was a complete collapse: a reasonably good French-language education was dismantled without any viable Malagasy substitute being established.

I experienced the disastrous effects of *Malgachisation* firsthand. In what is equivalent to Year 10, I was forced to learn mathematics in Malagasy, after having studied it in French throughout my childhood. A year later, the inevitable return to French, though it had never been completely lost, became mandatory. One of the conditions imposed by foreign investors and the development agencies involved in the country's progress was the reintroduction of French.

In Year 11, I was shocked to discover that my mathematics teacher was French. As in a white French man who's unable to speak one word of Malagasy. I was never a smart student, but this upheaval did not serve me well. Admittedly, at that time, I was indifferent, clinging to the naïve dream of becoming a musician. But I know that many of my friends, capable students with genuine ambitions, suffered greatly as a result.

Insecurity also raised in the capital, along with youth unemployment, two problems that went hand in hand. I've said it before: the only thing I feared when walking late at night was running into stray dogs. Now, I had to be wary of people. I wore my backpack on my chest, clung to my wallet in my trouser pocket, and always carried a nunchaku with me. I had no idea how to use a nunchaku, and it's not at all an object that a random Malagasy young lad would commonly own, but it was one of the treasures I found while selling junk. It was so awesome that I kept it. I thought I might as well use it.

I'd always picked up Claire from work, but there was an even bigger reason for me to do so now. No way I was letting her walk that little distance from the bus stop of Tanjombato to her house in Ankady.

So, the country is now clearly under a dictatorship. I mean, we've known it for quite some time now. My dad lost everything just because he was supporting the opposition. We're not the only family who has suffered from that. This President has jailed army members, troops and policemen who support the opposition and are viewed as unfaithful to him. He has more than once ordered his army to use force during pacific protests, taking away the freedom of speech and opinion. He has violated and continues to violate multiple Human rights.

Finally, eighteen years later, long enough for a newborn to reach adulthood, other people can see it too. Protests have been erupting at the iconic 13 May Square, all with one goal: to remove the President from power. Claire and I join the demonstrations as often as we can.

They're mostly peaceful. Well, as peaceful as protests can be. Thousands of people gather to shout, chant, and demand change. Not far off, the armed forces stand like statues, ready to strike. They're imposing men, dressed in bulletproof vests and gripping firearms. Protected, untouchable, prepared for violence if it comes. We, on the other hand, show up with nothing but placards and banners.

Luckily, at the protests I've attended with Claire, there were no gunshots.

Of course, whenever we go, we remain prepared for anything. We never stand too far from a car, just in case we need to duck behind it quickly if the armed forces decide to use force. But, so far, the only counterattacks have been tear gas canisters, fired to scatter the crowds. We would simply put on our masks to protect ourselves.

At least, I can say our dates were never boring. We can tell our future children and grandchildren that we were among the brave people who fought for our country's freedom.

14

Hira

2017

"Ny zavona no manamaizina ny mazava."
"Even the strongest light can be darkened by fog."

Seasons have changed from winter to spring to summer, and I am still in London. I'm amazed I've made it through three seasons. There are only two seasons in Madagascar: the summer, lasting from September to June, and the winter, lasting from June to August. If you're lucky enough to travel to the seaside during the winter, then you get to experience a whole year of summer. It's never cold there. I've never been to a hotter place than Mahajanga, on the west coast, and we've only ever visited during winter.

This year, for the first time ever, I've seen trees as bare as skeletons, slowly dressing themselves in fresh buds of every colour until they stand fully clothed in vibrant green. I'm also experiencing longer days. How is it still light at 9 pm?

I even experienced my first time change, which, honestly, was a bit of a let-down. As a child, I imagined people gathering, counting down to the big moment when everyone would move their clocks at once. I thought it was this huge event, like a celebration for having made it through three months of dreadful weather and endless waves of viruses. But no. In reality, it's just waking up and wondering how it's already 10 am, only to realise it's actually 9 am but the clocks changed, then spending the next two days mildly confused.

My exam results are coming out today, and I'm experiencing a level of anxiety that's far beyond "nervous." I think I did okay. At least, that's what I keep telling myself, but there's always that persistent, nagging voice whispering through worst-case scenarios. Suppose I skipped an entire page? Suppose I aced every subject but media law, the compulsory one? What if my paper got accidentally swapped with a low-scoring one? A whirlwind of increasingly improbable scenarios fills my thoughts, but I can't dismiss any as completely impossible.

Our results are to be emailed, and I get anxious with every phone ping. There's a ping at 8 am and even though I know, realistically, it's too early for the school to send anything yet, I still have a mini heart attack.

It's just the news.

I silence my phone's news notifications. No more useless heart attack today, please.

To cope with the wait for results, I need a distraction; otherwise, I won't be able to function.

I stand up to make breakfast while I wait. I leave my phone in my bedroom, so I won't be tempted to check it constantly. I delude myself into thinking that ignoring the email will make it appear sooner. I decide on hot chocolate. If only I drank coffee; I could simply use the machine and be finished. Besides, coffee smells amazing. Too bad it tastes horrible. Instead, I have to endure the tedious steps of warming milk and stirring cocoa into it. Stirring cocoa is never straightforward either. There's always a defiant clump of powder that refuses to dissolve, fighting for its life rather than sinking gracefully into the milk like it should.

I toast two slices of bread and immediately regret leaving my phone in the bedroom. Now I'm stuck, unsure what to do with my hands while I wait for the toaster to pop. What feels like two seconds when you're texting or watching videos now feels like three working days.

After I eat and clean up, it's only 10 am, and I know it's still too early to hear from the school. But I can't resist. I walk back to my bedroom, every step accompanied by a whispered prayer: *Please God, please God, please God.*

I grew up in a religious family. Well, mostly. My dad never went to church when I was little. He said he'd been forced to go throughout his childhood, and when he finally had the power to say no, he stopped going. Not because he didn't believe in God, but because he didn't agree with many of the religious doctrines. He actually encouraged me to have my own beliefs, as long as they didn't harm anyone. "It's good to believe there's something bigger than us," he used to say, "something or someone with the power to protect us. But also, something or someone to fear, so you're encouraged to do good. It can be God if that's what you choose to believe, but it can also be something else."

I went to church a lot, though. My grandparents took me every Sunday, and it's left me with the habit of speaking naturally to God whenever I'm in trouble or deeply wishing for something. Like now.

The moment I step into my bedroom, I immediately (drumrolls) check my phone. No email, just messages from my parents, who must be as nervous as I am. Worse still, they've been waiting even longer because of the time difference. It's already noon where they are.

I type out a brief message to let them know I'm still waiting. Then, I scroll aimlessly through the internet, trying—and failing—to distract myself from the results. My eyes keep darting to the top of the screen, hoping to see a notification pop.

Nothing.

This is not how I imagined my final results would come through. Movie depictions portray this as a major moment of truth. A family, picture-perfect, sits around the computer, hands clasped, faces aglow with a blend of suspense and hope. When the results are in, expect screams, happy tears, and a group hug. It's dramatic, cathartic, and perfectly choreographed for maximum emotional impact. In my case, it's just me staring at my phone, waiting for an email that will either say I can achieve my dreams or that my life is ruined because I suck. No cinematic soundtrack, no collective celebration. Just silence, broken by the sound of my own overthinking.

I turn on a movie, a last-ditch effort to distract myself, but I'm only half-watching.

My mind momentarily wanders to Leo kissing me at the cinema, providing one single minute of distraction. One minute. Even the kiss lasted longer. I think.

I only receive the email in the afternoon, at around 3 o'clock. I unintentionally open it while attempting to click the search bar for the university's phone number. I was about to call and check on my grades. Thank goodness I didn't need to. If there's one thing I hate more than stirring cocoa into milk, it's making a phone call.

My heart pounds as I realise what I'm reading. I'm only looking for one word.

"CONGRATULATIONS"

A flood of emotions washes over me: happiness, relief, gratitude. No words can fully capture the way I feel. I reread that single word multiple times before forcing myself to move on to the rest of the email, though, at this point, I couldn't care less about it!

> "You successfully completed the General Journalism course. Attached is a scanned copy of your transcript. You can collect the original documents from reception, from 9 am tomorrow."

I scream into my pillow. I dance. I cry.

In that instant, I expertly create a movie-like dramatic and cathartic scene for myself.

Holy shit. I passed.

I'm meeting Gia at school today to collect my transcripts and certificate. Unfortunately, Gia didn't pass. She wasn't too upset, since she didn't need this course as much as I did. She'll simply return to Italy, where she had always planned to go, and continue her studies as though this chapter of her life had never happened. When she told me this, it actually didn't sound as depressing as I expected.

She still wanted to accompany me today. Her flight back is booked for tomorrow, so we don't have much time left together.

Gia is already waiting at the gate when I get there.

She breaks into a wide smile as soon as she spots me and opens her arms for a hug.

"Congratulations again! I'm so happy for you," she says, squeezing me tight.

"Thank you," I say, squeezing her back.

We head inside. It feels strange to see the school this empty. I can't believe it's the same place I walked into six months ago, when my heart nearly stopped at the sight of two hundred students packed into the hall, all staring at me for a good second. The school will remain open for one more week to allow students to collect their certificates, before closing for the holidays.

This morning, only a handful of students are here besides us.

Leo passed too, but he said he'd come later in the week to collect his papers and would let me know when. He had things to take care of. He always has some cool plan or project going on, so I didn't ask too many questions. Besides, today, all I wanted was to see Gia.

It doesn't take long to collect my documents. The same kind lady who handed me my badge on my first day at this school is now handing me my certificate.

"Congratulations, Hira," she says warmly.

"Thank you," I reply.

She glances at Gia. "I'm sorry you didn't pass. Did you get the retake dates?"

"Yes," Gia says, "but I'm not retaking. I'm actually flying back to Italy tomorrow."

The woman looks surprised, like she's about to ask more, but then she just smiles and lets it go.

"There are some professors here today if you'd like to see them one last time," she says as we turn to leave. "They're upstairs."

We pause.

"Is Mr Bramwell here?" I ask.

For some reason, I really want to thank my travel writing professor. His feedback on my assignments was invaluable, and I did well on the exams thanks to him. He made me love writing even more. Now, I just need to work on the travelling part. There's only so much I can write about Madagascar. At some point, I should go see the world.

"Yes, he's here. He's doing some preps. In Classroom five, actually, if I'm not mistaken," the woman says.

It's a shame I don't know her name. She introduced herself on the first day, but I was so focused on trying to understand everything she was saying that I forgot. It's too late to ask now.

"Oh, that's great! Can we go upstairs for just a minute?" I ask Gia.

To say she isn't as enthusiastic as I am is an understatement. We definitely didn't have the same experience with this course. But she nods, and I promise it won't take long.

We make our way upstairs, the quiet hum of the near-empty school making our footsteps sound louder than usual. We go straight to Classroom five. We've walked these corridors so many times that I could get there with my eyes closed. The door is slightly ajar. Mr Bramwell is at his desk, flipping through a stack of papers. I push it open just enough to peek inside. I clear my throat lightly as I step in. He looks up, startled for half a second, before his face brightens.

"Hira! Good to see you. Congratulations."

"Thank you," I say, stepping fully into the room.

Gia doesn't follow. "I'll wait outside," she says quickly, already backing away.

I roll my eyes, amused, but don't argue.

Mr Bramwell sets some papers aside and leans back in his chair. "You should be proud. You've come a long way since the start of the course."

I let out a small laugh. "Yeah, I remember my first essay. You basically told me to rewrite the whole thing."

He chuckles. "I did. But you rewrote it, and you kept improving. That's what matters."

I smile, feeling a mix of gratitude and uncertainty. "Thanks. I still don't really know what's next, though."

He nods like he expected that. "Do you have any plans?"

I hesitate. "Not exactly. I know I want to keep writing, but I feel like I need more experience first."

"And how exactly do you acquire experience?" he asks, raising his eyebrows.

"Hmm, I suppose by writing?"

"You got it!"

We talk for a while, about my strengths, the kind of writing I should explore, whether I should try freelancing or apply for another course. He asks if I've considered pitching articles and suggests a few publications that might be open to new voices.

But more than anything, he reminds me that I can do this.

He gives me one piece of advice. One sentence that will stay with me long after I walk out of this room.

"You've always been a writer. You know it. All you've got to do now is let the world know it too."

I walk out of the room feeling like someone else entirely. I'm still unsure about what comes next, but at least I know what I want.

I rejoin Gia, who doesn't even try to hide her boredom. "So?" she asks.

"Let's go see Mr Anderson now," I joke.

She *hates* the sports journalism professor.

She rolls her eyes so hard I'm surprised they don't get stuck. To drive the point home, she even makes a gesture like she's going to shoot herself.

"Let's get out of here before you injure yourself from too much eye-rolling," I say, and we head down the stairs.

And that's when I see him.

My heart stops. Or it breaks. I'm not sure which.

***

Leo is at the end of the corridor, blatantly flirting with a girl from the Creative Writing course.

The moment my brain registers the scene, all the colour drains from my face.

Right. We never explicitly said we were exclusive. Apparently, in this part of the world, you need to talk about it before you can call yourselves boyfriend and girlfriend. I'm not entirely sure about the rules, but I think that means he's technically in the clear.

But what the hell? This hurts.

I feel Gia's gaze on me, but I keep my eyes fixed ahead, refusing to look at her. I know she's watching for my reaction, but the truth is all I want at this moment is to disappear.

What are you supposed to do when you feel betrayed by someone who technically hasn't betrayed you?

But then again... isn't this still a kind of betrayal?

Oh my God, I don't know what this is.

From my limited knowledge of relationships, we are together (*were together?*) so this is cheating. But maybe, here, it's not? Or is it?

Jesus, I need to sit down.

However long I stay frozen on the stairs, it's long enough for Leo to notice us.

Thank God for Gia's arm, which I cling to for dear life because my legs have completely given up on me. The humiliation is bad enough, I don't need to literally fall down the stairs to make it worse. My body somehow keeps moving, one shaky step after another, thanks to Gia practically dragging me.

But my face betrays me entirely. My expression must be an open book. Confusion, humiliation, shock.

I want to cover my eyes like a child, to avoid facing Leo and his *girlfriend* as we walk past. But curiosity wins. I have to look at him.

I glance at his face, searching for something, anything. Guilt, regret, hesitation. Is he sorry? And if he is, is it because he got caught, or because he actually regrets it?

Or maybe he's not sorry at all, because in his mind, there's nothing to be sorry for.

The uncertainty is excruciating.

It doesn't matter, though. I didn't imagine it. We were together, but we were clearly never on the same page. What I want is the kind of romance I'd write for a character in one of my future books. That's not Leo.

As much as it hurts, I need to refocus. I'm here for something far more significant than romance. Not even Leo's distracting antics should derail that.

When we're finally at a safe distance, I glance at Gia for the first time, and to my surprise, she bursts out laughing. That's when I realise, I've finally let go of her arm, which is now red and imprinted with the shape of my fingers. I laugh at the sight, horrified that I've essentially massacred her skin.

"Sorry," I manage between laughs.

"Don't worry about my arm. But seriously, what the hell just happened?" she asks, as baffled as I am.

"Yeah, what the hell?" I echo, because I genuinely don't have any smarter words to describe what we just saw. "Did you notice anything in his face? I couldn't tell what he was thinking when we walked past." His face had been unreadable. He smiled... I think. But then again, I also managed to contort my lips into something that resembled a smile while I was dying inside, so a smile doesn't really mean much.

"I think he was embarrassed. He definitely didn't want us to see them," Gia says, though I'm not sure if that's comforting.

"Well, the school corridor isn't exactly the most private place if he was trying to hide," I point out.

"Yeah, but maybe he's just not that bright," she says with a shrug, and I reluctantly agree.

We walk in silence for a minute, before Gia speaks again.

"So, what now?"

"I don't know. It's stupid. I feel like I need a good cry," I'm only half-joking. I know I'll be crying and breaking down as soon as I'm alone in my room.

"It's not stupid," she says firmly. "And just so you know, this was not a cultural thing. That was a jerk move in every culture. Come on, let's go."

I take one last look behind me before stepping out into the open air.

Leo is still talking to that girl like nothing happened.

That's the last time I'll ever see him.

My first heartbreak in London. Not the kind of "first" anyone wants to celebrate.

15
Razaf
1993

"Izay mitambatra vato, fa izay misaraka fasika."
"Together, we're as strong as stone; apart, we're as fragile as sand."

Today, the 7th of December, I'm setting up the living room with the help of Dazo, my parents, Lala, and Rado. We're hosting Claire's family for our *vodiondry*, the official engagement ceremony in its traditional form. My parents were surprised when I told them I wanted to marry Claire. They thought I'd never marry at all. Truth be told, I didn't think I would either.

Mum is especially overjoyed. This will be the first engagement party for one of her sons that she can physically attend. My brothers, who are all settled in France now, have long since got married. I even have two nieces and a nephew, though I've never met them. And yet, strangely, I know I love them deeply.

It's odd, isn't it? Me, the guy who once claimed not to know anything about love, finding myself capable of loving people I've never met, and loving a woman enough to know I want to spend the rest of my life with her.

It's exhilarating, but also terrifying. Loving someone feels a bit like lowering my defences, like letting the walls I've built around myself crumble. Allowing myself to be happy now means opening myself up to the possibility of greater heartbreak later. If every hardship in life is a key to some greater understanding, then isn't it also true that every joy carries the shadow of future pain?

Sometimes, though, today's joy is totally worth tomorrow's pain, so I'll let it happen.

This is also the first *vodiondry* in our family. My brothers have got engaged, but since they live in France, none of their ceremonies followed Malagasy traditions. One of my brothers isn't actually married at all. He just lives happily with his fiancée. My parents weren't thrilled about it, but they didn't push further.

In Madagascar, marriage is sacred, deeply rooted in both tradition and religion. Couples aren't allowed to live together until they're married. And by "married," I mean that they've completed every step: the *fisehoana*, the *vodiondry*, the civil wedding, and the religious wedding.

Ah, the *fisehoana*! I haven't mentioned this yet, but it's the first step for a couple. Essentially, it's about introducing the two families to each other, but in Madagascar, it's elevated into a major event. It's like a point of no return. The moment your families meet, you're practically betrothed.

In practice, it's just the man's family visiting the woman's family to get acquainted... So it happens at the woman's place, traditionally.

Claire was so stressed out about my parents coming to her place and seeing the state of her house. I got used to this small house, its cracked walls and its old furniture, but I admit I was a little shocked when I first saw it. Then again, I wouldn't have been shocked if I hadn't been made to expect the interior of the huge white villa next door.

So we didn't want to risk any judgment from my family, which is why I got to work and improvised myself a handyman, about two weeks before the *fisehoana*.

Every day, I drove Claire to work, bought some materials in town and went back to Ankady to fix something in their house. I changed the curtains, painted the walls and window frames, removed the old, worn-out sofa cover and replaced it with a fresh one, and fixed the wobbly table.

At least, the house was one less thing to worry about, because the *fisehoana* could be a seriously stressful process. There was the whole noble versus non-noble issue, which I absolutely despised.

Of course, during our *fisehoana*, my father was going to ask where Claire's ancestors were from. There were different ways this could be approached. Sometimes it was a simple "Where do you come from?" Other times, it was as bizarre as "Where is the family tomb?"

You see, the *andevo* or slaves were historically forbidden from owning land and, by extension, from having family tombs. So knowing there *was* a family tomb confirmed that the lineage was noble. My father could even deduce their ancestors' identity based on the tomb's location. Personally, I found it all ridiculous. I'd never even thought about where Claire's family came from and IF they had somewhere to bury their dead relatives.

But my father needed the information, obviously. I was just relieved they passed his test. My family didn't seem bothered by Claire's modest background as soon as they knew they were noble. Although it's sad how discriminatory it is, that they'd prefer a poor noble over a wealthy slave.

Okay, it wouldn't be much better in reverse.

I didn't care anymore. I just wanted everyone to be happy and for us to move on. The less drama, the better.

Except, there was a drama I couldn't have predicted in a million years during our *fisehoana*. In this process, we usually only had to worry about the parents getting along. Even that was a difficult enough task. But Claire's family apparently had a guest of honour that everyone respected and from whom I needed an approval as well. Her uncle.

Because of his extensive help and close bond, her dad's brother was like a second father, a crucial figure in their family. So naturally, she explained, he would be there for the *fisehoana* and he would need to give his approval.

Now, a random uncle did not seem too difficult to please. If Claire's father and my dad got along, what kind of reason could there be for an uncle to interfere?

Well, turns out, a pretty *big* reason.

The famous uncle was late. He came after all the talks about cast and ancestors. He basically came when everything already appeared to be locked in and I had a foot out of Claire's house, ready to go home and prepare for the next step of our union.

As soon as I set my eyes on the mysterious uncle, he was no longer mysterious at all. In fact, I remembered that man so well that he still appeared in my nightmares. My whole world shattered the day I saw him for the first time, and I couldn't believe he could ruin my life a second time.

He was easy to recognise. Hard to forget, in fact. His face was square and uncompromising. He was broad-shouldered and built like a stone monument. His dark and thick eyebrows were angled downward, exactly the same way they were the first time I saw him. Made me wonder whether they were naturally shaped like that. He could easily be in command of an army or leading a high-stakes security operation, because he was. It was the man who asked us to step out of the queue at the airport all those years ago: "The Ministry of Finance has ordered an investigation against your father regarding a suspicion of money laundering".

Fuck.

I hated that man before, but that hatred was nothing compared to what I felt that day I was supposed to make my relationship official with Claire. It took my dad only seconds to react. I didn't even have time to hope he would make an effort not to ruin my day. He was already marching towards the man who was physically much taller and much stronger, but in determination, much less imposing.

"I know you," my dad said, pointing his finger at Claire's uncle, just a few centimetres away from his nose.

There was a silence in the room. It was like someone had died. I kinda wished I *had* died.

There were only a few seconds before the uncle spoke, but they were very uncomfortable seconds.

"And I know you," he said matter-of-factly, not breaking eye contact.

Oh shit, I immediately thought. Claire glanced at me, as if asking whether we should do something, but I was just as petrified as she was. My mum and Claire's parents didn't move a muscle either. It's as if everyone was holding their breath, waiting for the confrontation to end. Another really uncomfortably long moment passed before somebody talked again. It was my dad.

"This is my son's day," he simply said.

The uncle, whom I later knew was called Jean-Paul, replied. "Your son seems alright. I trust my Claire in her choice. I won't be in their way."

"Good. The wedding will be held at my house. I think you'd understand that I don't want you anywhere near my property," my father then continued.

Claire's father seemed like he wanted to protest, but Claire's widened eyes begged him not to.

"I did not intend to," he answered reasonably.

As sad as it was for Claire that her uncle couldn't be part of the wedding, we were both relieved it was over and didn't do too much damage. It was bad, but it could have been worse.

Once everyone was satisfied, the *fisehoana* was deemed a success (although success was a stretch in our case).

From there, traditionally, the couple can move on to the next step: the *vodiondry*. And that's where we are now.

***

Claire's family is set to arrive at 8 am. Traditionally, the bride's family hosts the *vodiondry* since it's technically the groom's family asking for her hand in marriage, but we decided to hold it here, as our house is bigger. While we're following tradition for the most part, a bit of modernity doesn't hurt when it's practical. In truth, we're not exactly in a position to adhere to tradition perfectly. There's a rather important detail we haven't disclosed to the family yet, for obvious reasons.

Claire is pregnant.

For us, it's great news, and I know the rest of the family will feel the same, eventually. But right now, we need to get through the *vodiondry* and the wedding without stirring the waters.

The pregnancy wasn't planned, though we all know it's always a possibility when you're not actively preventing it. When Claire told me, it was a shock, but a good one. I searched for even a hint of negativity—something I'm particularly skilled at—but I couldn't find a single reason to see this pregnancy as anything but a blessing.

She was nervous when she broke the news, which made sense, considering how I'd reacted when she first asked if I ever wanted kids. But the first thing I did after her announcement was propose. No ring, no grand gesture, no preparation. Just me, fumbling my way through it. And she said yes.

No one questioned why we were rushing to get married. If anyone had suspicions, they didn't let them show. My parents were just thrilled that I was moving forward in life after what felt like years of one step forward, two steps back. Claire's parents were relieved she was finally getting married, too. At 24, she was considered "late" for marriage by Malagasy standards.

We've been setting up since early this morning, arranging chairs in two rows facing each other, perfect for the impending battle of speeches. Her family will sit on the right, mine on the left. Claire's father has hired a professional speaker to represent her family in the speeches, but I chose not to.

My father offered to handle our side. He's just as good as any professional, if not better. I say it often, but he really is a brilliant man.

There will be no real battle anyways. It's just for the form of it, because usually, if we get to the engagement step, it means both families are already happy to be joined. It's all about showing off now, especially if the other speaker is as competitive as my father. Sometimes, it can get really serious. Claire and I do not care much about it. Oftentimes, the *vodiondry* is more for the family than for the couple. We just want to get it done and start our lives.

For food, everything is homemade. My mum and Lala have been cooking since 5 am, preparing canapés, petits fours, and, of course, my mum's legendary *cuisse-dame*. These are elongated, donut-like pastries whose name translates to "ladies' thighs" thanks to their shape. I love my mum's version because they're never too sweet. None of us in this family are big fans of sugary things. Maybe it's because we're all a little bitter, which is funny, if you think about it.

As for the guest list, if it were up to me, it would be just Dazo and my parents. But, of course, it's not up to me. I keep having to remind myself that the ceremony is for the family and not for me.

My mum wanted to invite, with no compromise, the whole family, including aunts, uncles, grandaunts, granduncles and cousins I had never heard of. Bear in mind that *vodiondry* is even more important than the wedding itself for some Malagasy families. Besides, Claire and I have decided to complete all the steps in one day. The civil wedding and the religious wedding will follow in the afternoon. It's not uncommon that couples decide to combine all three in a day. It's mostly for financial and practical reasons. Other people who have the means to, hold the *vodiondry* and the wedding a week apart. But we are not those people, so we have to gather everyone in just this one day.

Claire told me it was the same for her. Her parents were so proud of her marrying someone "wealthy" and "honourable" that they wanted to show me off to the whole family. They know we are not as wealthy, but our house tells a different story, and it's the only one the guests need to know.

Everything is a bit on a budget. I can't exactly afford a grand ceremony with a taxi driver's income. I only have to thank the house for making it look grand enough to impress Claire's extended family. Other details shouldn't matter as much, as most people do judge a book by its cover.

I remember the day I showed Claire this house. She couldn't believe it. She told me she'd passed by it countless times, always wondering who lived in the eucalyptus villa. She used to say that one day, she'd have a house just like it.

Now, she's not just going to live in a house like this one. She's going to live in *this* one. There are plenty of rooms for us two, so I don't plan to move out. Financially, it's the smart thing to do. We, however, plan to build a floor up one day so we can fully have a space of our own. I also think it's a great idea for our child to grow up with their grandparents around. Not to mention how great it will also be for the grandparents to have a child around.

The ceremony starts at 9 am.

Only one hour later than the planned schedule, which is a record considering the average lateness for an event like this must be around three hours in this country. We couldn't afford to be too late, because our civil wedding was going to be held at the Tanjombato city hall at 11 am, immediately followed by our wedding at church at 1 pm.

By 9:30 am, we're done with the speeches and the reversed dowry rituals, and it's finally time for Claire to show up.

During the speeches, the bride hides in another room. She only comes out when the two families have reached an "agreement". Now the coming out is a fun part, and not just for me who had been dying to see Claire, but for everyone. To make it entertaining, all the single women in the bride's family would come out one by one, while the speaker asks, "is this the one?"

For them, it's a moment of fame. They march with determination, showcasing their beautiful dresses and hairstyles. The engagement is an occasion for everyone to get special outfits and visit the hairdresser.

The actual bride comes out last.

Everyone stands up and applauds, and it's chaos. Chaos I completely ignore, because, as Claire steps in the room, everything else fades into the background. Her dress is a vibrant, off-the-shoulder gown that blends traditional Malagasy style with contemporary elegance. It was made by my mum so it's stunning, but no offence to Mum, it's Claire wearing it that makes it especially beautiful. Its dominant colour is a bold and rich red, Claire's favourite, but it's accentuated by delicate white floral embroidery that runs vertically along one side of the skirt. The dress flows into a long, A-line skirt that cascades to the floor, moving with a quiet grace as she walks. Claire wears it with confidence, her smile radiant and warm, as if she knows the effect she's having on everyone in the room, especially me. It's a vision I'll never forget.

Once Claire is here, we proceed to the next part of the *vodiondry*, which is the ring.

The ring is hidden in a flower bouquet given to the bride and she has to search for it, while everyone observes, smiles and talks about how beautiful the couple is.

After a few minutes, Claire finds the ring and shows it up in the air and everyone applauds once again. I put the ring on her finger and that's it, we're officially engaged. This same finger will receive a wedding band in a few hours, and it will be done.

The whole ceremony is nerve-wracking, I can't wait for it to be over.

The rest of the day is as great as can be. No hiccups except a few delays here and there, which means that the guests were back here from church for the real party two hours later than initially planned, and they were starving. Again, this happens all the time, so it's not shocking.

A few of the aunts are just going to point it out when they go home and present a whole report of our wedding to their other family members, but that's okay. They will criticise things like the food being served cold or the cake being too sweet, and they will also say nice things like the wedding dress being beautiful or the venue being nice. It will be as if they'd been asked to review the wedding like Michelin inspectors. It's almost like you didn't have a wedding at all if nobody talked about it afterwards.

The party is so busy, with everyone wanting to talk and congratulate us, that I barely see Claire. We didn't hire an orchestra or a DJ. We only put our instruments out and invited anybody who wanted to come and sing. This means that I am behind the piano or the drums a lot, and Dazo is behind his bass or the guitar. Everybody appears to be happy. Whenever I spot Claire, she greets me with a genuine smile that crinkles her eyes, or a hearty laugh.

The only moment I really share with her alone is the first dance. Well, not really alone, but it's so emotional that I feel like it is ours alone. We've decided to sing our wedding song, while dancing. Dazo is on the piano this time. We rehearsed for days in the basement studio before the wedding, but now that we're here on the dance floor, we don't care much about sounding good any more. We sing and dance as if we weren't being watched by our one hundred something guests (we even ignore the nosy aunts).

At the end of the celebration, always marked by the cake cutting, the guests line up at our table to congratulate us once again, offer their best wishes, and give the wedding presents. Usually, it's money in an envelope, unless the couple has stated otherwise. We haven't stated otherwise because we do need the money, let's be honest.

When everyone's gone, we each find a chair to collapse and sigh in unison, before bursting to laugh.

We're married.

16
Hira
2017

"Indray mandeha ve no manta-vary dia handevi-tsotrobe."
"Don't bury the ladle just because the rice was undercooked once."

Gia is back in Italy. Leo went completely silent. My messages all went unanswered; he didn't even offer an explanation. I'm alone again, back where I started with no friends, feeling overwhelmed by London's vastness and loneliness.

I am also searching for a job again. I was foolish to think it would be easier with a degree. Looking for a job at a newspaper or magazine makes finding one in a restaurant seem like child's play. I started sending applications with confidence, but each rejection chipped away at it, inch by inch, until now, I have none left.

We are in the midst of summer. Catherine is in Lisbon with her boyfriend. Eli is in Turkey with her friends. Everyone seems to have exciting plans, and I'm stuck looking for a job. When I'm not sending applications, I'm wondering where Leo is and who he's spending the holidays with. I don't know which stings more—the job rejections or that. Leo isn't a social media guy. The last picture of him online is from 2015. That's it. No updates, no posts, nothing. It's super frustrating that I can't even stalk him. In the future, I'll be very wary of guys who don't do social media and claim they don't like texting.

Just for a day, I'm taking a break from applying and deciding to enjoy some London summer sun. British weather isn't as straightforward as in other countries. Summer here can mean rain, cold, or a heatwave. But today is one of those stifling hot days, which some people may find uncomfortable, but not for the tropical island girl I am. I like this.

I'm not sure whether I've changed since I arrived in the middle of the winter, or if it's the Londoners who have switched to a whole different vibe since being hit by the sun's rays, as if the sun cast a spell over them. Or a bit of both.

But what I know for sure is that it's not the same London I stepped foot in all these months ago. The city moves more slowly. It seems that everyone is less busy and rushed now (well, the days are longer).

The parks burst into life. Londoners love a walk in the park. Never in a million-year will you hear someone in Madagascar say they want to "go for a walk", as in walking nowhere in particular and with no purpose. Walking to school, walking to work, walking to the next bus stop, walking to the shop... sure, but not *taking a walk*.

Here, they just walk and enjoy the fresh air. The enjoyment of breathing never crossed my mind.

They also walk their dogs, which is another really odd concept to me. In my country, dogs walk themselves. My two dogs in Madagascar are always out socialising with the neighbourhood dogs, only returning home to eat and sleep, just like teenagers. But I see dogs being walked constantly around here. I know I've seen it in movies, but movies have plenty of other absurd moments, like when a character pours a drink and never touches it.

So, to me, it didn't seem real. But apparently it very much is. People in London take many walks, either alone or with their dogs, and they have a great time doing it.

For my first time "taking a walk", I go to Regent's Park. This park's beauty is beyond words, so I'll borrow Sylvia Plath's term: a "wonderland".

The lawns are dotted with picnic blankets, as music, laughter and loud conversations fill the air. Sunglasses perch on every face, bright dresses flutter like petals, linen shirts ripple in the breeze, business suits loosen, sleeves are rolled up...

Oh, and all the colours.

I almost forgot there were more than three colours in this world as London has got me used to black or beige coats, and grey sky. Trust the twelve thousand roses of Regent's Park to remind you of the beauty of colours.

It's also quite central, so the lively London life is never too far. What a perfect location.

I send a picture to Gia, as promised. With nothing new to report on the job front, the park will have to do.

"So cool, here's one from home." She texts back with a beautiful picture of a park in Rome.

The word *home* twists something inside me, like the opposite of butterflies. I realise I miss home too.

But I can't imagine myself going back home empty-handed.

My parents made immense sacrifices for my future, a future they were denied, and I won't disappoint them.

Like many Malagasy people, they endured incredibly hard times. Madagascar's history is unfortunately that of political challenges. It was hit by political crises in the 1970s, the 1980s, the 1990s and a big one not long ago, in 2009. A bloodshed. Fifty deaths reported at least.

Each political crisis had a huge impact on an already fragile economy.

When you look at the world, as in globally, you can clearly notice change, *progress*. In The Great Surge, Steven Radelet wrote: "The number of people living in extreme poverty (with less than $1.25 per day) shrank from almost two billion in 1993 to a little more than one billion in 2011." Several studies show that. And it will get better from here, with expectedly three or four percent of all humans living in extreme poverty by 2030.

There is real progress, even though we don't really see it.

Unfortunately, the exceptions to that, and probably those who will remain in the three or four percent of people living in poverty, are people in Africa... Malagasy people are obviously among them.

In fact, Madagascar seemed to have done the opposite of progress. The United Nations established the Millennium Development Goals (MDG) in 2000 with goals to achieve worldwide by 2015, in sectors like education and health. One of the goals was to half the number of people living in hunger and extreme poverty. The goal was reached well before 2015 in many countries. In Madagascar, not only have we not reached the goal, but we have also regressed. In 1993, 67.5% of Malagasy people lived in extreme poverty. 80% in 2010.

Hunger is not the only problem there. The country also has one of the highest numbers of out-of-school children in the world. It's just generations of struggling people.

My parents wanted to end the cycle with me. I started with more privileges than most Malagasy people, thanks to them. They prioritised my education, enrolling me in a private school regardless of the cost. Knowing that, giving up is not an option.

I need a plan. Not just a plan B. A plan from A to Z, at this point.

I sink onto an empty bench, the warmth of the sun seeping through my clothes. I can almost hear my mum say, "Natural vitamin D, at last!" Through the cold months here, she kept reminding me to take vitamin D supplements.

My thoughts are tangled, looping endlessly around the same uncertainty. I don't know what to do. I *still* don't know what to do.

The park is alive with people who all seem so sure of their place in the world. I watch an old man walking slowly with his dog, pausing now and then to let it sniff the grass. A child squeals with delight as her father lifts her onto his shoulders. People stretch out on the grass, eyes closed, soaking in the sun as if they have no worries at all. Or if they do, it doesn't show.

This city brings out the best in people.

I belong here.

I have to stay.

I just need to keep applying. Be more open. Cast a wider net. There's a way in. I just have to find it.

***

"Dear Hira,
Thank you for applying for the Staff Writer position at Northbridge Magazine. We were incredibly impressed by the quality of applicants, and making a decision was difficult. While we won't be moving forward with your application on this occasion, we truly appreciate the time and effort you put into it. We hope you'll keep an eye on future opportunities with us, as we would love to consider

you for another role.
Wishing you the best in your career journey."

"Dear Hira,
Thank you for your interest in the Junior Writer position at Harbor Press. We enjoyed reviewing your application and learning more about your background.
After much consideration, we have decided to move forward with another candidate whose experience and skills are a better fit for this role. However, we truly appreciate the time you took to apply and hope you will consider applying for future opportunities with us.
We wish you the best of luck in your job search."

"Dear Hira,
Thank you for your interest in the Junior Reporter role at The London Post. We appreciate the time and effort you put into your application.

At this time, we are unable to proceed with your application.
We wish you the best of luck in your job search."

"Dear Hira,
Thank you for your application for the Editorial Assistant position at EchoPoint Media. We received a high volume of applications, and after careful consideration, we have decided to proceed with candidates whose experience more closely aligns with the role. Unfortunately—"

Nope, not reading this one. I think I've seen enough.

***

"Attached is a short story I wrote when I was seven. Please do not hesitate to reach out if you have any questions. I'm looking forward to hearing from you. Kind regards, Hira".

I sent my fifth job application of the week. This one to Nomad Note, a magazine for remote workers, digital nomads, and travellers.

This time, I did things differently.

When I first applied, I wasn't as careful. I didn't even know that including a photo on a CV in the UK was discouraged because of anti-discrimination laws. I must've looked stupid to the other companies.

But now, for Nomad Note, I pulled out all the stops. I didn't just polish my CV (what I should have done before, duh), I attached something extra, something personal: a story I wrote when I was seven. *"You've always been a writer. You know it. All you've got to do now is let the world know it, too"*. Mr Bramwell's words.

The story was titled "Why Do We Always Have to Move Out?" It followed a teenage girl who was tired of relocating every time her dad got a new job.

It was entirely fictional, of course. I've lived in the same house my whole life. While some of my friends changed schools because they had to relocate, I always stayed in the same place. Same house, same school. I used to wonder what it felt like to leave a home behind. That curiosity is what led me to write the story in the first place.

I asked my parents to retrieve it. It was still saved somewhere on the old family computer, so I sent it along with my application.

Of course, now I know exactly what it's like to move away. Not just to a new house, but to a whole new country, thousands of miles away from home. I hope Nomad Note can see the journey. That little girl who once imagined what it meant to be uprooted has now lived it and grown from it. And I hope they will like me for that.

In any case, I at least have a better chance here than with Globetrekker, a magazine for adventure seekers that features extreme travel experiences and rugged hiking trails. I was desperate when I applied for that one. That rejection was the easiest in the history of rejections. I always stretch the truth a little on my CV, but there's only so much you can invent about hiking trails, when you have never been on one.

Now, with Nomad Note, all I have to do is pray and cross all my ten fingers and toes.

17

Razaf

1994

"Hasambarana tsy miohatra ny mionona."
"There is no greater happiness than contentment."

If you went outside now, you would see war. The air would be thick with acrid smoke, stinging the eyes and burning the throat with every breath. Shouts would rise above the chaos, blending with the sharp cracks of shattering glass and the distant thud of something heavy falling. The streets would be a blur of motion, people surging from nowhere and everywhere, some running in panic, others with determination.

Today is the day people have given up on peaceful manifestations. There's been no peace, to speak of, from the military anyway. They've thrown tear gas bombs like a first-time flower girl at a wedding. This time, though, the protesters retaliate with violence. Manifestations started this morning at the 13 May place. But the protesters are now heading to the Iavoloha Palace, the official residence of the President of Madagascar. The distance between the 13 May and the palace is approximately nine miles. These people are on a nine-mile trek to call for the President's removal.

They've reached our gate, leaving 3.1 miles to their destination. With Claire heavily pregnant, we're staying indoors for safety. As safe as it's possible to be. Our gate is not exactly made of steel. It's just a flimsy wooden barrier made of faded planks of brittle wood leaning against each other, held together more by habit than strength. A gentle shove and it would likely splinter.

The voices outside are loud and determined. The ground trembles faintly with the rhythmic pounding of boots. I stay in the living room with Claire, Dazo, Mum and Dad. Their expressions are unreadable, but I suppose we're all a little worried. It's not the protesters we are scared of. In fact, we share their motivation, and we would probably be one of them if Claire wasn't pregnant. It's the armed forces' reaction that makes us fearful.

They can fire at any time.

Sure enough, screams, no more defiant but filled with raw fear and desperation send a surge of panic through us.

Then, through the noise, a flying object with smoke and a hissing sound comes into view. Tear gas. There it is.

The police are trying to scatter the crowd. One canister flies over the gate, landing in our yard with a dull, metallic thud.

Best-case scenario, it is a tear gas canister. Worst-case scenario, it's a grenade.

Let's not think about that one.

Claire, clutching her belly to shield our unborn child, and I dive behind the old wooden cabinet where Mum keeps her creepy porcelain dolls. As Dazo crawls under the dining table, Mum and Dad fall to the floor, partially beneath the sofa. We all cover our mouths with our clothes to avoid inhaling the toxic smoke.

Seconds stretch unbearably. No explosion. No shrapnel ripping through the air. Just silence, until the acrid sting of gas seeps in.

Tear gas. Just tear gas.

The sheer number of protesters—thousands—means it takes several minutes for them to pass by. But it may as well be hours. It feels like an eternity. None of us speak the entire time. Dad just turns on the TV, and we watch the protest unfold on the news, the sounds outside blending with the ones on the screen.

It's Dazo who breaks the silence first. "Imagine if that was a grenade."

"Or imagine if they broke into the house. And they killed us or something," Claire adds.

"Or imagine if they fired actual guns, and the bullets came through the windows," I say.

And on and on we go, stacking worst-case scenarios on top of each other, while feeling incredibly lucky that nothing worse had happened.

Especially since, several minutes later, when the protesters finally reach their destination, the armed forces fire real bullets. No warning shots. *Real* bullets. They shoot into the crowd.

It's a bloodbath.

We're silent again.

One hundred deaths and over two hundred injuries are announced in the news. Although we never know the accuracy of these numbers. This President has been accused of ordering his army to hide bodies in previous "peaceful" protests.

The news coverage looks like something out of a war zone. Reporters wear gas masks, their voices muffled, trying to stay composed as chaos erupts around them. The red ticker scrolls relentlessly at the bottom, updating the number of injured and dead like it's part of the weather forecast.

And finally...

Finally...

It reads the words we've all been waiting for:

"THE PRESIDENT HAS FLED."

He left. The people won.

***

The days after that big event are the most incredible.

The President fled to France, and the country is now under military rule until new elections can be held.

Meanwhile—and this is the incredible part—most people who were wronged by the previous government receive compensation. My dad receives a substantial amount of money and is informed that he's allowed to work again. He decides not to. Instead, he takes early retirement to claim his pension.

Fair enough.

I'm just sitting here, thinking about this rollercoaster of a life. When I was eighteen, we lost everything. Today, over eighteen years later, we've got it all back. Well, not exactly everything, because you can't reclaim the years spent drowning in alcohol, battling depression, and struggling to survive; and it's not like we got eighteen years' worth of my dad's salary. But still.

The fight we gave up on long ago was suddenly over, just like that.

In a matter of a week, my dad is a different man. It's as if there was a switch somewhere that got turned on, and now he's back. The distant look he always had in his eyes fades away. He's not even the same way he used to be before the incident. He's better. And for the first time in years, I don't feel like I'm holding my breath around him.

But you know what? That's not even the best part of this year. What makes this year really *really* special is that I'm going to be a father.

***

It's Wednesday, the 27th of April, and the day starts like any normal morning. I take my coffee. Black, with no milk or sugar, as usual. I make bread and butter for Claire, and we enjoy breakfast at the table with Mum, Dad and Dazo.

Since Claire and I remain in the family home, we continue to share the kitchen and living room with the others. It is a common practice in Madagascar for the bride to live with her husband's family. Couples don't always move into their own home, mostly because they can't afford it.

Claire gets on very well with my family. She calls my mum "Ma", and my mum treats her like an actual daughter. That's not surprising from my mum. Her kindness is well-known, and having always longed for daughters, she vowed to treat her seven sons' wives as if they were her own.

We eat, we laugh and we talk.

With all my dad's troubles now behind us, eating together has a different sense.

Claire gets up to bring her empty plate back to the kitchen.

And then... water.

It's all over the floor. She freezes mid-step, her plate still in her right hand. Slowly, she turns to face us, her expression oddly calm for what's clearly happening.

"Did I just pee myself?" she asks, her voice steady, almost curious.

We all stare—at her, at the spreading puddle on the floor—, unsure which deserves more attention.

"Claire, the baby's coming," Mum says quietly, her words slicing through the confusion like a bell.

And just like that, we're all in motion, as if we've been rehearsing this moment in secret.

My mum runs to our bedroom to make sure the room is set. Claire wants a home birth, which, again, is very common here.

My dad guides Claire back into the chair so she can sit and relax. Dazo just hands me the phone and pats my shoulder as if to say "This is it. You're going to be a father". Always supportive, this guy.

I call the midwife and tell her about the broken water. She tells me what to do. I grip the phone tightly, my heart hammering in my chest. The midwife's voice is calm, reassuring, thank God for that.

"Alright," she says. "First, check the fluid. Is it clear?"

I glance at Claire, then at my mum who's already wiping up the small puddle on the floor with a towel. She looks up at me and nods. "Clear."

"Good. That's what we want," the midwife says. "Now, how's Claire feeling? Any contractions yet?"

I crouch in front of her. "Are you feeling anything? Contractions?"

"Yeah. A little."

A little? This moment in most movies usually features a woman screaming in agonising pain.

Anyway, I relay the message to the midwife.

She hums. "Okay. This is totally normal; they will get more frequent and more painful. You need to time them. When they're close together, say under five minutes apart, that's when you need me there. If they're still spaced out, we've got time. Either way, keep her hydrated. Small sips of water. And she should empty her bladder often."

I relay the message again while Mum rushes off to grab a glass of water. Claire takes a slow breath, her fingers gripping the arms of the chair.

"Make sure the birth space is warm and quiet," the midwife continues. "Dim lighting, soft voices. It helps keep the oxytocin flowing. And have towels and clean sheets ready."

I hear my mum in the bedroom, muttering about fresh sheets as she fluffs pillows. My dad stands by, hands on his hips, looking around as if searching for a job to do. Dazo nudges him and says, "Boil some water. That's a thing, right?"

The midwife chuckles on the other end. "Hot water's good for wash cloths if she needs comfort. Also, have a bowl or a bucket nearby, just in case she feels nauseous."

I squeeze Claire's hand. "You got this."

She nods.

"What else?" I ask the midwife.

"Just keep her moving if she can. Upright positions help things progress. And call me back if anything feels off."

"Okay."

This is happening.

Another four hours pass before the contractions get close enough to each other. Claire's earlier calm demeanour has completely vanished. She's tired and just seems fed up.

Four hours of pain *does* sound excessive.

Dazo is on a mission to bring the midwife here, so he grabs the car keys and is on his way in a flash. In the meantime, we wait and try to reassure Claire as much as we can. Fifteen minutes later, the midwife is here, courtesy of Dazo's remarkable illegal racing experience. Then, it's just me, Claire and the midwife in the room. One hour—and what must've been every swear word in Claire's vocabulary—later, the baby is here.

Nothing prepares you for the moment you meet your child for the first time. You obviously know you will love the child with all your heart. You know you will be so happy that there will undoubtedly be tears of joy, and it will even be the happiest you've ever felt. While everything you know is accurate, the actual experience is far more intense than you expect.

It's like watching fireworks. You know the fireworks are about to go off at the end of the countdown, and you're prepared for the loud explosion. Yet, when the sky erupts in bright colours and booming noise, you still flinch and feel a surge of awe.

Holding my daughter, seeing her small red face for the first time, makes all my previous dreams seem silly. Becoming a musician, going abroad, building a career, all of it seems so trivial now. This, right here, is real happiness, real purpose. I have never known love as strong as this.

My trembling hands make me fear dropping her, so I think about putting her back on the bed. But I can't bring myself to let her go either. I don't think I can stand being away from her. I take time to examine her little face, her little eyes, her little nose. This is unconditional love.

"Does she have a name yet?" my dad asks.

I look at Claire who, God knows how, doesn't at all look like she just pushed an eight-pound baby out of her. The woman is strong. She smiles and I smile back.

"It's Hira," I say.

Hira, in Malagasy, means "song". The name fits her perfectly. She is music itself, a song that was always waiting to be written. I can't rewrite my own tune, but hers— hers will be different.

18

Hira

2017

*"Aleo mahantra an-tanindrazana, toy izay
malahelo any an-tanin' olona."*
"Better to endure poverty in your homeland
than sorrow in a land of strangers."

Sometimes I wonder why I came to London. I could have chosen anywhere else in this world. France, for instance, would have been a much more strategic choice. I would have had a better shot thanks to my native-level of French. I would have been a really good French-speaking writer. I wouldn't even have had to apply for any job. I'm sure Joanna would have given me my writing job back, this time as a real employee in the office and with a real salary, as opposed to being an underpaid freelancer. Besides, I have five uncles in France. *Five!* I would have lived rent-free. Can you imagine?

Not only that, but French people wouldn't be so surprised every time they saw a Malagasy person. They know about Madagascar. The agents in the airport wouldn't have examined my passport like a detective searching for clues. They wouldn't have said "I have never met anyone from Madagascar" and I would have just been one of the many foreigners they encountered in their daily work. Not like some kind of phenomenon the agents were going to tell their families over Christmas dinner.

Madagascar was a French colony from 1896 to 1960, so we are part of their history as much as they are of ours. Although, I don't expect French people to know our cultures as much as we know theirs. For instance, I'm fairly certain that they're unaware Madagascar has its own New Year's Day which differs from the European New Year. And that's because we didn't use to follow the same calendar.

Up until 1810, each region of Madagascar had its own calendar. Then, there was the standardised calendar under the Kingdom of Madagascar, whose kings reigned from 1810 to 1896. It was a lunar calendar with thirteen lunar months consisting of twenty eight days.

With the lunar calendar, the New Year's Day is the first day of *Alahamady,* the first lunar month. The *Alahamady* month typically falls at the end of the rainy season and the rice harvest, which takes place around March compared to the Gregorian calendar. The first full moon of the year, so the first full moon around March, is the night before New Year's Day.

The whole month of *Alahamady* used to be a huge celebration, when Malagasy people would also congratulate themselves on having emerged victorious from the violent winds, the torrential rains, landslides, devastating fires. Unfortunately, the celebrations were viewed as pagan by the French colonisers, so they were abolished around 1897.

It was only in the 1990s that the Malagasy people started to celebrate it again, but only as a resurgence. The official New Year's Day remains the 1st of January.

So no, they don't really know Malagasy people. Not like I know about all the Henries and the Louis. But they know more than most, who've only ever heard of Madagascar because of the movie.

The movie is, by the way, far from the truth. There are no giraffes, zebras, hippos or lions there.

But, in all fairness, the island had been full of confusion since its discovery. The name Madagascar was given by mistake by the explorer Marco Polo, who thought he had landed in Mogadishu, Somalia, which is approximately 1,200 miles away from Madagascar.

He misread and misspelled Mogadishu and that's how it became Madagascar. The letter 'C' doesn't even exist in the Malagasy alphabet. That is why we, natives, write it "Madagasikara". The population's name itself is a major source of conflict, sparking endless debates. The French-speaking nations call us "Malgache", the English-speaking nations call us "Madagascans" and we call ourselves the Malagasy.

Why I sit here thinking about an alternative city to London is simply because I have finally found a job. But I fricking hate it.

The job description was pretty straightforward: Communication and marketing intern in charge of content for the website and newsletter. The reality is far from that. It's a senior position with intern-level pay. The intern's salary being so tiny, I still work at the restaurant on the weekends.

I expected more guidance on my missions as an intern. That's why I applied for it. My job applications were unsuccessful, leading me to believe that an internship would provide valuable experience.

Nope.

THE EUCALYPTUS TREE

***

This is my first *first* day at a job, so I'm not sure if it's supposed to be this hard, but this *is* hard.

When I came in this morning, I was met by my boss and one coworker. That's it. There are three of us in the office. The founder, a business developer and I, the intern.

The first thing my boss showed me how to do was how to use their payroll and HR software. There is no HR, so this is my job too.

Awesome.

I thought today would be about onboarding. You know, reading documents and guidelines, and getting to know the team. Though now that I know there are only two other people working with me, that would've been very quick.

But nope. The founder and the business developer left me here on my own, and I have to figure out what to do.

"I gave you access to the website. Just text me if you need anything else. Otherwise, we'll see you later."

Then, they were off to a very important meeting.

Luckily, I'm not completely alone. Quite the opposite. Like you would expect from a startup, it only has a desk in a massive coworking space. The space is actually really inspiring. The air is thick with creativity. It's more like a fun place than a workplace.

There's a hammock, first of all.

Employees can also take naps in a designated room during their breaks. There's a bottomless supply of coffee and tea, and small private rooms are available for confidential calls.

Nothing here screams business, yet everyone is busy doing something and talking to others. It's hard to tell who's working with whom amongst the many startups because everyone is mingling.

Then again, this is my first day.

It feels like my first day at school all over again—trying to slip into a group that's already fully formed.

Gosh, it seems like that was ages ago, when it's only been seven months.

I still loathe socialising. This is why, today, I am drinking my first cup of coffee.

Trying to be a grown-up here. I don't want to be the villager anymore.

I've always loved the smell of coffee. It's the taste I can't stand. I secretly add an unhealthy amount of sugar to make it drinkable. I'm hoping drinking it might serve as an icebreaker.

Sure enough, a few people gather, mugs in hand. The conversation begins with the weather—of course. I've got used to that one. I do it too. There's surprisingly a lot to say about the weather here.

Then it shifts to tea. How they take it—some with milk and sugar, some without sugar, some with nothing at all. It's riveting.

And then, another debate around coffee.

"This coffee machine is brilliant. Beans to cup, mate. You can't beat that," one says, nodding with satisfaction.

"I actually prefer capsules," another chimes in.

"What?" they all cry out, almost in unison, before launching into protests.

"All that plastic."

"Terrible for the planet."

A few variations of the same argument.

"My favourite is instant coffee," says Marion, the only person whose name I know so far. She introduced herself earlier, when it was just the two of us in the hallway.

"Ew, instant coffee is the fast food of coffee!" someone exclaims, horrified.

Of course, I don't mention how I like mine.

These people are fascinating. I can't imagine talking about coffee with this much passion. My grandfather could. But when it comes to this, I take after my dad, completely indifferent.

Though, now that I think about it, I *could* write about coffee. Writing is a whole other thing.

Unfortunately, the short break and the interesting chat aren't enough to help me find a friend. There's no Gia here. Not that anyone could ever replace Gia.

I go back to my desk, alone, and the solitude feels sharper now. Mine is the only desk with just one person at it. The others are grouped in small teams—at least two, maybe up to five people each.

I don't actually mind being alone. I just don't like *looking* lonely.

And worst of all, I have no clue what I'm supposed to do. Nobody's here to train me.

I'm pretending to be busy, just like I used to at the restaurant. Faking productivity, so I wouldn't get sent outside to hand out flyers in the middle of a grey February.

But keeping busy in a restaurant is fine. There's always a glass to wipe. It doesn't matter if it has been wiped a thousand times before. Staring at a screen, however, is an entirely different level of pretending. I click everywhere on my empty screen. I open a Notepad and type things that I then delete. And after all that, three minutes have passed.

Long. Day.

***

The job isn't glorious, but what's worse is the London tube after a long day of work. How could I have loved this a few months ago? Oh, I know... there was the novelty of it at first, then, there was fricking Leo.

Oh no, not thinking about him.

And this is rush hour. I have seen busy tubes. I even have busy tubes to thank for helping me have my first kiss.

No, not thinking about him...

But that was not the real rush hour. School was always over at 3 pm, much before the workers finish their day. And when my shift was over at the restaurant, it was between 11 pm and 1 am.

This, though... what I'm seeing now, this is it.

And damn, it's ugly. This, coming from someone who's fought for a seat on a bus in Madagascar, a full-on *mêlée* of elbows and urgency.

Every time the train stops, its doors rattle open, releasing a wave of commuters onto the platform while another surges in. Another crowd that is clearly not going to fit, yet they push through. The doors can't even close until we all shuffle and squeeze more than is possible.

Inside the train is a slow-moving crush of bodies. The air is thick with fatigue, boredom etched into every face, including mine.

I don't get tired of the diversity of London, though. The train rattles on, and with every stop, the crowd shifts, morphs, rearranges—an ever-changing mosaic of cultures, backgrounds, and lives intersecting for just a few minutes before scattering again. That makes me smile. Only a brief second. Before I'm reminded once again of the horror I am in.

Despite my first day not going exactly as I had hoped, and despite the train ride—now a confirmed part of my daily routine, rush hour both ways—I am still determined to make London a place where I thrive. Tomorrow will be better.

It just has to be.

***

I didn't get much sleep, as the two bags under my eyes are proudly making it known to everyone. All kinds of unpleasant thoughts kept me awake. So much for trying to stay determined. I kept wondering what the hell I'm doing. I'm 24, and I have nothing figured out. No relationship, no real job, no money.

Before dragging myself out of bed this morning, I read a post on social media that made me laugh. A girl complained about how hard it was to be a young adult.

> "I'm still figuring out how to 'adult', but today I went grocery shopping and froze meat for the first time ever. That's a very adult thing to do, right?"

I nodded along as I read it, reassured that I wasn't alone in navigating this wildly confusing phase of life.

Then I made the mistake of checking the comments. Someone asked her age.

Nineteen.

Shit. That girl was nineteen.

I'm not a young adult. I'm an aged and mature adult. And I'm clueless.

***

With a not-so-determined spirit, I push open the door of the coworking space, bracing myself for my second day. After yesterday's shaky start, I can't help but feel a little apprehensive.

But the moment I glance up and see my boss and coworker already at our desk, a wave of relief washes over me. Today will be better. They'll guide me, show me the ropes, and we'll actually work as a team.

After all, this startup has an incredible purpose.

They restore and resell old furniture, giving discarded pieces a second life instead of letting them go to waste. The idea is simple: take something others have thrown away, repair it with eco-friendly materials, and turn it into something people will love again. A scratched coffee table, a faded wooden chair, a dresser missing a handle—nothing is beyond saving. And in doing so, they're not just reducing waste; they're challenging the mindset that everything has to be new to be valuable.

That's the speech I prepared for my interview. The one that got me this job.

It's also the speech I was eager to spread—through blog posts, newsletters, and media outreach. I pictured myself representing this startup, using the power of writing for something meaningful.

This is my chance. And I'm not going to mess it up.

"Hello," I say as I get to our designated desk.

"Oh, hello! How was your first day yesterday? Did you get a chance to figure out how everything works?" My boss smiles at me, but his eyes flicker back to his screen almost immediately.

"I logged into the website," I say, hesitating for a second before continuing. "I think it would be good to update our blog. The last article is from months ago. I believe we have images and—"

"Yes, that's great," he cuts in. "Ahmed, give her access to the drive so she can find all the images she needs."

Ahmed nods without looking up.

Okay. That's... not too bad. They're not unkind. They just seem busy—too busy to properly onboard an intern.

"Do you need anything else?" my boss asks, glancing away from his laptop briefly.

I need everything, I want to say. A proper introduction to the company, clear tasks, and some sort of structure. But instead, I force a polite smile and say, "Nothing. But do you need anything in particular? What should I start with today?"

"No, no. Just go with your own planning," he says. "We have an important fitting today. Two big bookshelves for a café in Wandsworth. This contract is what's going to pay us this month." He exchanges a grin with Ahmed, both of them laughing, proud of their work. "We're leaving in about fifteen minutes. I just wanted to make sure you had everything you needed first."

So much for hoping for guidance.

I nod. "I'll be okay."

The words come out too quickly, too forced.

This job is not going to be easy. I know many would appreciate this much freedom, but it's not my nature. I completely lack self-confidence. Professionally, I'm a complete novice. That's why I wanted to start with an internship: for guidance, feedback, and a gradual entry into the workplace.

Instead, I feel like I've been thrown into deep water without knowing how to swim.

This is a six-month internship that could lead to a permanent contract. That means I don't just have to survive six months—I have to impress them. And as things stand, I have no chance of that happening.

The days blur together.

Some mornings, I convince myself to push through. I write blog posts, draft newsletters, and even tag along for a furniture fitting, hoping that by throwing myself into different tasks, I'll finally feel like I belong here.

But the reality is... no one is paying much attention.

Other days, I sit at my desk, clicking between tabs, pretending to be busy. I take multiple coffee and tea breaks just to make the hours pass, stretching out whatever task I can think of. No one checks in. No one asks about my progress. I've definitely overdosed on caffeine more than once: shaky hands, frantic typing, and a racing heart — all the classic symptoms. I mistook them for productivity at first.

Some weeks, I see Ahmed and my boss twice. Other weeks, they don't show up at all.

In terms of growth, there's nothing. They haven't read my articles, much less offered any feedback. I don't have the skills to measure the impact of my newsletters or blog posts beyond the basic reports on how many people have opened them.

Six months of this? And then what?

If they barely acknowledge my existence now, how am I supposed to impress them enough to get a permanent contract?

The thought makes my stomach turn.

This whole thing feels wrong.

I made it through journalism school without fully speaking English. I found a job that paid my rent. I had a friend. I even had a boyfriend. I had a favourite place, a routine, a sense of belonging.

Now, all I have is a lump in my throat and a wave of uncertainty.

19

Razaf

1990

"Miady fo toy ny oran-ko ritra."
"Fighting in vain, like rain falling onto parched ground."

I'm stuck in Mahajanga, on the west coast of Madagascar, and there is no way of getting back home. At least, Dazo is here with me so I'm not alone, but there's, of course, somewhere else I'd rather be. Home, with Claire and Hira.

We've been stuck here for six days. It was supposed to be a quick trip.

But now, I'm in a city that isn't mine, wondering how on earth I got into this situation.

Life was good. I'm not one to brag, but life really was good. After Dad received that big lump of money, he offered each of his sons a portion, encouraging us to invest it. Instead of taking it individually, we decided to pool it together and start a family business.

My brothers, now well established in France, didn't want the money directly. They've come a long way, from broke students to (in order of age) a maths teacher, an electrician, a store manager, an accountant, and a real estate broker. On the side, they still played or even taught music. They used to have a jazz band called *The Big Five*—which is what Dazo and I always called them. We've since realised it was very close to The Jackson 5, but they didn't change the name. The band eventually faded out as they moved to different cities for work and family, but the music never really left them.

It's thanks to them that Dazo and I have created *The Draz*, our super badass bass and drums duet. We, too, have finally managed to perform a few times at a jazz festival and at a bar nearby. During *The Draz*'s first performance, we were a mix of nerves and adrenaline. The crowd was small, but that didn't make it less terrifying. That's the thing about jazz, at least in Madagascar. It doesn't draw large audiences, but the ones it does are deeply passionate, which somehow makes it even more daunting.

But that first time was all it took—I was hooked on performing.

From then on, *The Draz* was invited back every year for each edition of the Malagasy Jazz Festival. Unpaid, of course, but that doesn't matter. Artistic pursuits, including music, are rarely chosen for their financial rewards.

My dad thinks Hira will be a writer because she's already showing an interest in making up stories. She writes songs and poems. Naturally, I am impressed by my daughter's intelligence, but also worried about the tough realities of the creative industry, especially in Madagascar.

My brothers and I agreed to open a printing company. None of us had any expertise in printing—none of us had even been near a printing machine before. The idea came from the accountant in the family, who handled the finances for a printing company in France. They were upgrading their equipment and giving away their old machines, so, we took one.

We had to pay for the shipment, which was still far cheaper than buying new. A printing business also made sense because, while we lacked experience, we had something else: the advantage of novelty. There was no competition. We became the only printing company in town.

Dazo and I were the printers. Dad used his connections—at least the ones he hadn't lost, or the ones he managed to rebuild after regaining his dignity—to find our first clients.

It took a month to ship the machine from France to Madagascar. Once it arrived at the port in Tamatave, we had to rent a truck to bring it home. We cleared out one of the rooms in our house, set it up as our office, and moved the machine in.

Well, moved isn't quite the right word. We dumped it in the middle of the room, and it's stayed there ever since.

The thing weighs two tons. It's not moving. Not today, not ever.

It looks like a beast of metal and gears, impossible to miss, if not for its size, then for its smell. A faint scent of oil, paper dust, and ink lingers in the air, clinging to the hands and clothes of anyone who steps inside that room.

Our biggest client is a local biweekly newspaper. That contract alone keeps us afloat, along with occasional one-time clients.

Just a year after we started, Claire and I had saved enough to build our own space. Not quite enough to buy land, but enough to add a new floor to the family house, just as we had planned from the start.

It's good for Hira, having her grandparents just downstairs, along with her uncle and aunt. Dazo got married. He and his wife now live in the room Claire and I vacated.

So, business has been good. Family life has been perfect. Even music has been, well, something.

And now? Now, it's a nightmare.

Maybe when things are good, we shouldn't try to make them better.

Good is good.

Better is overrated.

Lesson learned.

***

We're in Mahajanga to bring back two cars home—another idea from my brothers in France, who convinced us that buying cars there then shipping them over was far cheaper than purchasing them directly in Madagascar.

And they are right. A car in Madagascar will always cost more than the same car in France because you're paying for both the price of a brand-new car and the cost of shipment. Now, by buying second-hand in France, we're cutting a huge portion of that cost.

Buying these cars seemed like a great idea when we first made the decision. Now, though, excuse me if I'm struggling to see what was so great about it.

The plan was simple enough: my brothers in France would buy the cars, ship them over to the port of Mahajanga, and we'd drive them home. Once in Antananarivo, we'd rent them out, turning a profit, a way to avoid our past mistakes in business. We had spent too long playing it safe, never investing, never daring to do more than the bare minimum. This was supposed to be different.

We arrived in Mahajanga by *taxi-brousse*, which literally translates to "bush taxi"—a name that makes sense given that it barrels through the countryside, racing down dirt roads and village paths at speeds that would make anyone question their survival. It's essentially a bus connecting Antananarivo to the provinces.

We didn't even bother with a hotel. The plan was to pick up the cars and drive straight back, stopping along the road if we needed to rest. If we got too tired, we could just sleep in the cars.

Simple.

Except nothing is ever simple in Madagascar.

Our plan, once again, has been derailed by Mister President.

The one and only. The man who was exiled to France. The same man the people had forced out of power in 1993, only for him to return in 1996 and reclaim his place at the top. Three years. That's how long it took for the country to forget why it removed him in the first place.

His replacement had been a university professor, a man deemed too democratic for Malagasy politics. Of all our past leaders, the university professor remains the only one who actually upheld democratic principles, the kind the country claims to stand for. Above all, he championed freedom of expression. His presidency saw the emergence of private radio and television stations, after years of censorship under the socialist regime. Civil society found its voice again. People spoke out without fear.

But in the end, his tenure was short-lived.

He clashed with his own prime ministers. His political career crumbled beneath him. And just like that, he was gone—no negotiations, no second chances.

And Mister President waltzed back in.

His re-election shocked many, yet at the same time, it didn't. Malagasy people have never had strong political guidance. The cycle repeats itself over and over again. It's like a toxic relationship. One we know is bad for us, yet we just can't seem to leave.

At first, his return didn't affect us much. It's not like we had any power to stop it, so life carried on as usual. Or, as normal as life can be under a dictator.

But now?

Six years later, the cracks are impossible to ignore.

Another opposition party has emerged, challenging the President's grip on power. It took six years. *Six years*.

Not eighteen, thank God. But still, six years is a long time.

In six years, Hira has learned to talk, walk, use the toilet, write, and read. An entire childhood milestone in the time it took for an opposition to rise.

And, of course, history is repeating itself.

Instead of a peaceful election, instead of civil debate, the country is being dragged into another political crisis. And this time, it's deeper, uglier, and more divisive than before.

We're at its peak now. Or at least, I hope this is the peak. Otherwise, we're fucked.

The country is split into two: the coastal provinces against the central highlands. Antananarivo versus the rest. The *Imerina* versus the other ethnicities.

Mister President is from the South Coast, which secures him the unwavering support of the coastal populations—the *Sakalava, Betsimisaraka, Antakarana, Antandroy*, and others.

The opposition leader is *Imerina*.

And just like that, this has become more than politics.

It's become an ethnic war.

Just what we needed.

This war is no joke to the *Sakalava* of Mahajanga. They've made it clear: no vehicles from the capital will enter the city, and no car heading towards the capital will be allowed to leave.

Dazo and I had no idea the situation was this bad. We got in without trouble, but that's only because *taxi-brousses* are an exception. Their passengers are mostly locals, and they weren't about to block their own people from coming home. All personal vehicles, though, have to go through the roadblock they've created.

When I say roadblock, I don't mean a flimsy barricade of debris or a few men standing in the way. I mean a wall of people—fierce, determined, armed. A human blockade, shoulder to shoulder, ready to use force without hesitation.

Among them, gendarmes—not with riot shields or rubber bullets, but with real guns strapped to their chests, fingers resting near the trigger. Around them, civilians gripping thick wooden clubs, some clutching knives that glint under the burning Mahajanga sun.

They are not here to negotiate. They are not here to talk.

This is our sixth day stuck here.

Every morning, we try. Every hour of the day, we hope.

We tried at dawn, thinking they might not be there. They were.

We tried late at night. Still there.

Lunchtime, mid-afternoon, random attempts throughout the day—always there.

War doesn't pause, apparently.

THE EUCALYPTUS TREE

Yesterday morning, a car in front of us tried to force its way through. The protesters didn't hesitate—they burned it down with the driver still inside.

He was lucky. He managed to escape before the flames consumed everything.

His car, though? Now just a charred skeleton on the side of the road.

Well, we won't be trying that.

Every day, the same scene repeats itself—lines of cars waiting, trying, then giving up and turning back to their hotels.

Dazo and I ended up getting a motel too. The first two nights, we slept in the cars, still hoping this wouldn't drag on.

But eventually, we had to accept that we needed a better place to sleep.

For a tourist, spending six days in Mahajanga would be a dream. For us? Stuck here, unable to leave, waiting for a roadblock to lift—it's anything but. And we're definitely not in a resort.

Our motel is the kind of place you only stay in because there's no other choice.

The rooms are small—just four walls and two single beds, the kind with thin, sagging mattresses and mismatched sheets that smell faintly of soap and dust. A single wooden chair sits in the corner, its paint chipped and peeling. A mosquito net, full of tiny holes, hangs loosely from the ceiling, more of a suggestion than actual protection.

There's no private bathroom, just a communal squat toilet at the end of the hallway, with a bucket of water beside it for flushing. The shower? A cement stall with a plastic barrel of cold water and a small cup to pour it over yourself.

It's not shocking to us.

Despite being raised in comfort, we were never blind to how most Malagasy people live. Growing up in Toliara, we had friends from small villages, visited their homes, and learned to adapt. We knew what it was like to sit on woven mats instead of chairs, fetch water from a communal well, and live without luxury.

And later, when we lost everything, we learned to live with nothing—no electricity, no running water, barely enough food.

So this motel, with its thin walls and the constant hum of mosquitoes, doesn't shake us.

Besides, none of that matters.

Villa or motel, I just need to get home.

My heart clenches at the thought of Claire, at how she tries to sound calm on the phone, even though I know she's panicking.

She told me she'd been taking Hira into our bed. Claire hates sleeping alone. She never has.

Growing up, Claire shared a small room with her four sisters, all packed together. Then we got married, and I was always there.

Now, I'm not. And she can't stand it.

God, I need to get home.

Cigarettes in hand and two beers on the table, Dazo and I sit in the motel's so-called restaurant. If this were a proper hotel, it might deserve the name. But here, it's nothing more than a collection of mismatched tables and chairs, a worn-out wooden bar, and an air so thick with smoke that we're only adding to it.

"We need a plan to get out of here. These human walls aren't breaking anytime soon," Dazo says, his voice low but firm.

"I know. But what the fuck can we do?" I mutter.

We're both good at keeping our emotions in check, but I know my brother well enough to sense his fear. And he has every reason to be scared. Right now, the protesters are only blocking the roads, but that could change at any moment.

All it would take is one shift in mood—one spark of rage—and suddenly, we're not just trapped. We're targets.

For now, they just block the road. But who knows—maybe next, they'll kill every *Imerina* they come across.

I hate that we're divided by ethnicities when we're supposed to be one country. Divide and conquer. That's what our leaders want, and it's working.

Dazo exhales a long stream of smoke. "I don't fucking know. I was hoping you'd have an idea."

I hesitate before answering. "I think we need to sell one of the cars."

It's the only way. There's no chance we're getting both out of here. If we're lucky, we'll escape with just one.

Dazo doesn't argue. He nods. It's the beginning of a plan.

"Now, which car are we selling?" I ask.

It's not an easy choice. After six days of driving them around and sleeping in them, they don't feel like just cars any more. Dazo has been driving the Renault Express and I've had the Renault 5. Without even realising it, we've each claimed them as our own.

Not that it would matter once we get home. They were always meant to be rentals.

But right now, choosing between them feels heavier than it should.

"I don't think it matters," Dazo finally says. "We put a sale sign on both, and we let go of the first one that gets a buyer."

And that's what we do. The next day, the two cars are parked on the street, just outside the motel. Both with the sign "*AMIDY*"—for sale—and a phone number. It only takes half a day for someone to make an offer on the Renault Express.

The buyer is a wealthy man with a massive house in Mahajanga. When he comes to check the car, we chat for a bit.

"Why are you selling?"

A standard question from a potential buyer. We answer truthfully, explaining our situation.

He listens and seems friendly and easy-going. He doesn't even try to bargain, just takes a quick look at the car, nods again, and agrees to the price.

Then, just as he's about to leave, he surprises us.

"If you need a place to stay until you figure out how to get home, you're welcome at my house."

It takes me a second to process his words. A complete stranger, offering us a place to stay. In the middle of all this chaos.

And that's what makes this war so senseless.

The people of Mahajanga are good and welcoming. This division isn't natural. It's created—fed by those in power who want to keep us apart. Back in Toliara, there was never tension between the *Vezo* and the *Imerina*. We grew up together, ate at each other's houses, and celebrated the same things. No one cared where you were from.

At least, not in my experience.

We accept his offer and drive the cars back to his house—where one of them will now stay forever.

Our house is massive, but it would probably shrink in intimidation next to this one. No wonder he offered for us to stay here. This place is so big we could live here for years and never bump into each other.

"Well, just settle in any room, gentlemen. Thanks for the car. If you need anything, ask Toto."

Toto must be the janitor. He smiles and lets us in.

The owner disappears minutes later, and we don't see him again for the rest of our stay.

"You need to get back to Antananarivo?" Toto asks, his Mahajanga accent thick.

This is something most people don't know—Madagascar has dozens of dialects and just as many accents.

"Yes," we answer in unison.

He nods, like he already has a plan. "I have to go as well. I'll help you if you drive me. Well, technically I'll drive. But we'll use your car."

Our eyes widen.

Hope.

They would let a local through, wouldn't they?

This is our escape.

Absolutely fucking yes, I think. But it comes out much softer.

"Yes, sure, that should work."

***

The next day, we're on the road.

Toto is driving the Renault 5, I'm in the passenger seat, and Dazo is in the back.

Toto used to be a taxi driver here and still has his taxi licence. That's our cover.

As we approach the roadblock, my heart pounds so hard I swear it's about to break through my ribs and fling itself onto the dashboard. If not for the noise outside, I'm pretty sure everyone in this car would hear it.

The car stops.

An armed man approaches the passenger side.

I roll down the window, and just like that, his gun is in my face.

Not intentionally, not as a direct threat, but from the way he's standing and the way I'm seated, it just lands there. About ten inches away. Close enough to see every scratch on the metal. Close enough to imagine the worst.

"Hello, boss," Toto says smoothly.

Dazo and I just smile—tight-lipped, forced—and do our best to look casual.

Toto had warned us they'd probably clock us as *Imerina* right away, but our darker skin tone might help us pass as locals. "We're not going to pretend you're from here," he explained yesterday, "but if they assume you are, we'll have better chances. So, don't say a word. Your accent will give you away."

So that's what we do.

We say nothing.

"What's this? Where are you going?" the armed man asks, still standing there, still unaware that my soul has left my body.

"I'm a taxi driver. Just taking these clients to Berivotra," Toto answers in their dialect.

Berivotra is a city outside Mahajanga. Safer to mention than Antananarivo. We just have to pray there's no other roadblock once we're out.

The man stares directly at me.

It takes every ounce of willpower to stay still. My pulse throbs in my ears, drowning out everything else. My throat tightens, dry and useless, as if even swallowing might give me away.

Other men gather around the car, all armed, peering inside.

Toto hands over his taxi licence, and my heart somehow beats even faster.

It's expired. It's not even registered to this vehicle.

If they check properly, we're done.

A few minutes pass. Or maybe an hour. Time has lost all meaning.

Finally, the man nods.

He gestures for the protesters to let us through.

They shift just enough to create a passage, barely wide enough for the Renault 5 to squeeze through. Not an inch more.

Toto eases forward. Slowly. Carefully. Not drawing attention.

As soon as our rear bumper clears the barricade, the human wall closes behind us.

And then, Toto slams the accelerator.

He drives fast. No glancing back. We just go, go, go.

For the first forty miles, nobody speaks.

Nobody moves.

We just drive.

When the adrenaline finally fades, when we can breathe normally again, when we're sure there won't be another roadblock, Toto pulls over.

We exhale together.

And then, we burst into laughter.

"I have never been that scared in my entire life," Toto says first. "I didn't think we'd pull it off. When he looked at the licence... fucking hell!"

Dazo shakes his head, still catching his breath. "I almost shat myself."

I let out a shaky laugh. "That gun... shiiit! So close to my face!"

And we can't stop laughing.

The laughter lingers as Toto restarts the engine, and even as we roll back onto the road.

In about twelve hours, I'll see Hira and Claire again.

Life will be normal again.

I'll sleep in my own bed tonight. I'll wake up, take Hira to school, drop Claire off at work, then head to our printing space and get to work.

All. Normal.

20

Hira

2017

"Izay tsy mahay sobika mahay fatam-bary."
*"He who doesn't know how to weave a basket
knows how to carry rice husks."*

The dizziness hits me out of nowhere. One second, I'm gripping the metal pole on the tube, trying to stay steady as it jerks forward. The next, my vision tilts, black spots creeping at the edges. My body feels light, as if I might just tip over and collapse right here, between a man scrolling on his phone and a woman staring blankly at the doors, earbuds in her ears.

Breathe.

I close my eyes for a second.

Shit. I don't feel good.

I didn't have breakfast this morning. How can my stomach be empty, yet still threaten to empty itself?

It's been two months at this startup, and it hasn't got any better. I feel the opposite of useful and do the opposite of learning. If that's possible.

I clench my jaw, using the last of my energy just to stay upright. My stop is two minutes away. I just need to hold on for two more minutes. If I just keep breathing, I should be fine. I breathe in, hold it for three seconds, and breathe out again. I'll be fine. I have to be. Passing out on the tube is definitely not something I plan to tick off my London bucket list.

The tube finally lurches into the station, and I stumble out onto the platform, barely registering the surrounding sounds. People rush past, their footsteps a blur against the floor. My legs feel weak.

But then, I see it.

A vending machine.

I almost laugh. Thank God. Something sweet will help. Just enough sugar to get me through the ten-minute walk to the office. I look for a one-pound coin in my bag.

It's a hard task because there are many coins (along with rubbish and flyers) in this bag and the dizziness doesn't help, but I finally fish out what I need and push it into the slot before selecting a number for a chocolate bar.

The machine whirs, the coil twists... I feel better just knowing my body will have the sugar it needs in just a few seconds.

Then, it stops. It fucking stops.

The chocolate bar doesn't fall. It's right there, barely hanging on, just one little nudge away from dropping into the tray. But it won't move. I press the button again, as if that will change anything.

Nothing.

I can only stare at it, stunned, disbelieving. I rest my forehead against the cool glass, breathing hard, fighting back the sting of tears. I just spent my only coin and my last bit of energy on a chocolate bar that won't fall.

What now? How much worse can it get?

It's not just about the chocolate bar. And it's not London. London is a wonderful city and has been very welcoming. The problem isn't the city. It's me. This moment, this stupid vending machine, this useless fight for something just out of reach—they're just a perfect analogy for my failure.

I try my best to reach the office without passing out. I focus on walking straight, placing one foot in front of the other, inhaling deeply, exhaling slowly, willing my heartbeat to steady.

It's not the first time this has happened to me. I had these exact symptoms just before my first flight. The days leading up to my departure were overwhelming. Applying to the school, waiting for the results, applying for the visa, gathering the money to pay for the ticket, looking for a place to stay...

The whole process felt like climbing a downward-moving escalator. Each step forward only dragged me three steps back. On my way back from the visa centre, after I collected my passport, I took a bus and felt exactly like this.

It started with the dizziness, then came the black spots, and finally the sudden feeling that my lungs could hardly get air in. I was lucky I was not too far from home when it happened.

When I got off the bus, my hands were trembling, but I made it home safe, practically floating from the bus stop to the gate. I felt lightheaded; I don't remember my feet touching the ground at all. I blamed the heat then. Besides, with all the stress I'd endured, I may have skipped a few meals back then, too.

It also happened to me when I was sixteen, just before my baccalaureate.

Now that I think about it, this might just be anxiety. My body handles stress as well as a cheap umbrella in a storm, making me want to punch it. We—this body and I—don't exactly have the luxury of falling apart. We don't get to be fragile. We don't get to buckle under pressure. And yet, here we are, teetering on the edge of collapse.

This is a reminder that I can't keep pushing my body to the edge of a breakdown. My grandma once said to me that if I didn't listen to my body, it would find other ways to be heard. And that comes from a woman who birthed and took care of seven kids, while running her own business for eighteen years. If that woman found time to rest and listen to her body, what's my excuse? Then again, it's also the woman who always tells me feeling ill is a good thing. As a child, whenever I was poorly, my grandma would walk into my room and say "It's good to be poorly. It means you're alive. You don't feel poorly when you're dead."

I can do this. I'm not going to faint. I'm strong. I'm resilient.

I repeat those words over and over again until I believe them.

By the time I get to the office, I barely register what's happening around me. I need sugar.

I head straight to the coffee and tea station. Tea and sugar will help.

As I pour hot water into a random mug, I hear a voice behind me. At first, I don't realise it's directed at me, but it's so close that I instinctively turn around.

"Are you alright?"

I hesitate, blinking an embarrassing number of times before answering.

"Yes. I'm fine. I think."

"You don't look fine."

"Thanks. Just what every woman wants to hear on a Wednesday morning."

His face twists in horror as he realises how that sounded. "That's not what I meant."

I let out a small laugh. "It's okay, don't worry. I know what you meant. Honestly, I wasn't feeling great, but I think I'm fine now."

And it's true. This anxiety thing is strange. The second I stop thinking about it, it vanishes. And right now, my mind is fully occupied with the beautiful man standing in front of—

Nope. Not doing that.

I had a terrible experience with Leo. I still don't understand how relationships work here. I don't want it. Not now. Not again.

"Which startup are you with? I don't think I've seen you around before." He shifts the conversation, and I'm relieved. Talking about how unwell I look isn't exactly fun.

"ReForma. I'm fairly new. Just started two months ago."

His eyebrows lift. "Wait, you're the new girl?"

What? Who is this guy?

"I'm one of the fitters," he continues. "You don't see us much; we're always in the factory."

That makes sense. I barely even see the two people who are supposed to be in the office, let alone the ones in the workshop.

"Oh. So why are you here today?" I ask.

"Actually, I came to see you." He pauses. "Well, I didn't know it was you, but I was here to talk to whoever handled our last payment. There was a mistake in the amount you paid me."

Brilliant.

The boss dumped the invoices on me, and told me to sort out the payments, so I did my best to guess my way through it. Apparently, I guessed wrong.

I sigh. "I'm sorry. I've got no clue what I'm doing when it comes to payments. Not even sure I can help you." The boredom in my voice is hard to hide.

He smirks. "You look like you love it here."

I don't even bother to hide it this time. I roll my eyes. "Come on, let's take a look."

I lead the way to my desk. He follows me up the stairs, and suddenly, I'm hyper-aware of his presence.

I can sense him close by as his footsteps maintain a steady pace behind me. I try to focus on the stairs, on walking like a normal human being, but somehow, I become conscious of every movement—how I'm holding my shoulders, where I'm placing my hands, whether my stride is too fast or too slow.

For goodness' sake, what is it with London that makes me so horny?

Considering my last heartbreak, this doesn't seem rational.

I subtly shift my gaze to the side, catching a glimpse of him from the corner of my eye. I think he's looking at me.

Obviously, I'm right in front of him. Where else would he look?

Yet, my rapid heartbeat makes it feel like something deeper.

Focus on the desk. One step after the other.

I reach my desk and lower myself into the chair, trying to shake off whatever strange energy just followed us up the stairs.

He pulls out the chair opposite mine and sits down, leaning back slightly like he has all the time in the world.

I wiggle the mouse to wake up my screen, hands moving with purpose—like I actually know what I'm doing.

"Right, let's sort this out." My voice comes out steady and professional.

Good. This is a work conversation. No need to focus on how broad his shoulders are or how green his eyes are.

He slides a folded invoice across the desk towards me. "It's the last payment. There was an error in the amount."

I unfold it, scanning the numbers, and feel my stomach sink.

Shit.

A typo. A very unfortunate typo. Instead of £2,800, I'd transferred £280.

I resist the urge to slam my forehead onto the desk. "Oh."

He lets out a low chuckle. "Yeah. Oh."

I glance up, expecting him to be annoyed, but he just looks amused.

"Look, I'm really sorry about this—"

He waves a hand. "It happens. I figured it was a mistake."

"Yeah, definitely a mistake." I exhale, rubbing my temple before opening the payment system. "I'll fix this now. Should go through by the end of the day."

He leans forward slightly, resting his elbows on the desk. "I mean, I wouldn't mind if you made another mistake and added another zero or two there."

I shoot him a dry look. "I wouldn't push your luck."

He grins, like this is all very entertaining to him.

I click through the system, making sure I don't mess up the numbers again. I double-check and triple-check. I am not making this mistake twice.

Finally, I press submit.

"Done." I lean back, relieved. "You'll have the full amount soon."

"Appreciate it." He stands, stretching slightly.

"Sorry again."

"Don't worry about it."

I nod.

There's a brief second when we just stare at each other, not sure what to say next. Then he breaks the silence.

"Well, cool, thanks. I'll leave you to it."

He turns to leave but stops just before stepping away.

"See you around, new girl."

There it is again. That look. That tone.

And as much as I try to ignore it, I can't help but think...

Yeah. I probably will see him around.

And there's my idiotic smile. What is wrong with me? I'm not even over Leo yet.

When I get home, I collapse onto my bed, kicking off my shoes with a sigh. Given how the day started, it could've easily turned into a disaster—but somehow, meeting Alex balanced it out. I only know his name because I caught it on the invoice. I'm more interested in him than I'd like to admit.

He's done nothing but exist so far, and yet, thanks to him, I'm starting to think a little more positively, for the first time in a long time.

I think about my dad; what he would do in my situation.

Well, for one, he would look for another job.

My dad had done just about every job imaginable. He used to say that, without a degree or a specialised skill, he was never tied down to one thing, which forced him to try a bit of everything. No expertise, he explained, equals the possibility of all expertise. Or without one path to follow, every path was open—something along those lines.

Though, I'm not as resourceful as he is.

I know I won't be jumping from being a mechanic to a printer anytime soon. Writing is all I have.

Of course, he didn't mean that I literally should explore all sorts of expertise. What he meant was that there are always other paths. I just need to find mine.

But until then, I just have to keep going.

So every day, I wake up, get ready, take the tube from Wembley to Finchley Road, and go to work—or at least, pretend to. I take coffee breaks because that's what people do.

I go, I don't give up, and by the end of the month, I make my modest £500. Somehow, I even manage to send fifty back to my parents. £50 equals Ar300,000, which sounds like a lot but really isn't. The loan they took out to pay for my ticket to London still weighs on them.

Three weeks pass.

I function like a machine. Wake up. Work. Go home. Repeat.

I write blog posts about sustainability, post pictures on the company's social media, sort through emails—the boss gave me access to his inbox—flag the ones I think he should reply to, and handle the freelancers' invoices.

The boss has never once told me whether he's happy with my work.

But he hasn't complained, either.

So I count that as a win.

Not sure what that says about me.

But I've made my peace with it.

And just when I've settled into my routine, I see him again.

When I spot him in the hall, at the coffee station, just like the first time, I stop so abruptly that the lukewarm coffee in my mug sloshes dangerously close to the rim.

He spots me too and looks just a little surprised.

I, on the other hand, have lost the ability to act normally.

"Oh hey." It's all I manage to say.

He smirks. "Oh?"

"I didn't know you'd be here today."

"Neither did I."

I frown. "What do you mean?"

He chuckles. "Last-minute thing. Boss needed something, so here I am."

Of course. The boss actually communicates with him. Must be nice.

I nod, willing my heart to settle. "Right. Well. I should—"

"You still underpaying people, or have you sorted that out?"

I roll my eyes, but I can't stop the small smile that creeps onto my face. "That was one time."

He raises an eyebrow, unconvinced. "If you say so."

A small pause and a minute of awkward silence later.

"So, how's it going? Enjoying your time here?" He asks.

I let out a breath, shaking my head. "Not even a little."

He laughs. "Yeah, figured."

I raise an eyebrow. "Oh? And what gave it away?"

He grins, taking a step closer—not close enough to be inappropriate, but close enough that I feel it.

"The eye-rolling. That, and you look like you'd rather be anywhere else."

Beautiful and observant I see.

"Yeah, don't tell the boss."

He smirks again. I have to look away, because that smile will be the end of me. I don't have time for this.

"Do you want company for lunch?" he asks. "It looks like I'll be here all day. We're making some changes on one design, and I can't go until that's done."

A little voice tells me not to go because this guarantees another heartbreak. I shouldn't do this until I figure out what to do with my career. But another stronger voice, the troublemaker in my head that made me fall for Leo, tells me to say yes. And once again, that's the one I listen to.

Lunch with the fitter, it is.

We end up at a small sandwich place. It's nowhere near as fancy as the Italian restaurant I went to with Leo, but I'm genuinely happy to be here. The atmosphere is relaxed, and the conversation flows easily. It's different, in a way that I really like.

Alex is from Romania but has lived in London for seven years. He talks about Romania a lot, and calls it "home", which I think is very sweet. He doesn't say "back in Romania", he says "back home". He doesn't say "I'm going to Romania for summer", he says "I'm going home". I don't recall referring to Madagascar as home when I talked about it. At best, I might have said home country, which was just a practical way to call it rather than an ode to my motherland.

It also turns out Alex is very smart. He has a master's degree in Wood Technology. I had no idea what that was, and I still don't think I fully understand, but hearing him talk with so much passion, I can only assume it's a really interesting topic.

"Basically, it's all about using wood in construction. Like, designing buildings and structures with wood, testing wood-based materials, and even creating new, innovative ones for construction. We aim to create wood that's as strong and effective as steel or concrete, but in a more environmentally friendly manner," he explains rapidly. Like this was a sentence stored somewhere in his brain and ready to come out whenever someone asked.

He also happens to know many interesting facts about trees. He can name all the trees he spots, which I consider a superpower, since I know absolutely nothing about them.

To contribute to the conversation, I bring up the eucalyptus tree in my yard back in Madagascar. When I mention Madagascar, he doesn't say, "Oh wow, I've never met anyone from there."

Instead, he tells me the first time he heard about Madagascar was when a former mayor in Romania fled there to escape persecution.

His knowledge of Madagascar is about as good as mine of trees—or of Romania, for that matter—so I'd say we're even.

Honestly, I'm just happy trees exist because I learned in school that they give us oxygen. That's the extent of my expertise.

When I say that to Alex, he tells me that pine trees produce the least oxygen because of their thin needles, and maple trees are among the top oxygen producers.

Interesting.

If this was somebody else or said differently, I would have probably hated it. Trees are cool, and we do need them, but there's only so much we can say about them without falling into boredom. But with Alex, I find it really charming. It's the sparkle in his eyes when he talks about it.

He then admits his dream has always been to open his own furniture factory in Romania. I want to ask him why he doesn't do that, especially when he clearly has so much knowledge and passion for it. But I decide against it. The sparkle in his eyes when he talks about it must be matched—if not overshadowed—by the pain or disappointment of why he had to give it up, whatever the reason may be. I'm not unfamiliar with the concept. I come from a long line of broken dreams.

My grandfather's career was taken from him. My father's dream of becoming a musician remained just that—a dream. My mum always wanted to be a doctor but never had the chance to study. I'm here to try to break that cycle.

So, there's no point in asking Alex a question that could reopen a wound. I don't want to see that effortlessly charming, happy face clouded by sadness and grief.

"What about you?" he asks, just as I'm mid-thought about how disarmingly charming he is.

"What about me? What do you mean?"

"Well, I know you hate this job. What do you really want to do?"

I'm caught off guard. Apparently, human interaction involves me speaking too, not just listening. But I reply honestly.

"I want to be a writer."

"That's incredible," he says, genuinely impressed. "Like... writing a book?"

"Ultimately, yeah. But really, any job that involves writing to start with. Magazines, newspapers, blogs, whatever I can get."

"That sounds very achievable for someone like you. You're smart," he adds, then smirks, "as long as you don't have to pay people."

I roll my eyes, but it's hard not to laugh.

"It's not that easy, though." I say.

"I didn't say it was easy," he says. "I said 'achievable.'"

That makes me smile.

"Why a writer? Is there a story behind it?"

Funny. I wanted to spare his feelings, and now he's the one pulling mine into the spotlight.

"I just love writing. Always have. I've always been better with words on a page than words out loud. When I was a kid, I kept a journal and poured everything into it. I wrote it in English, so if my parents ever read it, they wouldn't understand."

He grins, and I think the conversation is winding down. But then he asks again.

"Are your parents not here?"

Guess I'm still talking, then.

What's strange is... it doesn't feel uncomfortable. It feels natural.

"No. But I hope they'll come. One day."

THE EUCALYPTUS TREE

"To live here?"

"Oh, no way. They'd hate living here. I just want them to visit, at least once. They've worked so hard their whole lives and never really gone anywhere. My dad wanted to study abroad, but he never got the chance. Having them here wouldn't change any of that, but... it would mean something. Like, after everything, we finally made it."

There's a short silence while he processes what I just said. I'm a little lost in my own thoughts, too.

Then he says something I didn't know I needed to hear.

"Did you know eucalyptus trees have really high survival adaptations?"

Huh?

He laughs at my puzzled look.

"Yeah. They can grow in nutrient-poor, sandy, even rocky soil. Places where most trees wouldn't survive. It's because of their deep root systems. They're kind of a symbol of resilience and adaptability."

"Resilience and adaptability," I repeat, smiling to myself. That sums up everything.

This guy is going to be a problem.

In the best way possible.

I already liked what I saw. Now I like what I hear.

Oh, to hell with it. What's the worst that could happen? I fall for him, and one day I catch him flirting with someone else?

Meh. Been there, done that. I'll survive.

21

Razaf

2004

"Tanora ratsy fihary, antitra vao ratsy laoka."
*"A youth who gathers poorly will, in old age,
suffer bad meals."*

Another president, another fucking political crisis. There appears to be a pattern in Madagascar: one leader toppled by an angry population, only to be replaced by another who meets the same fate—because he's simply no better.

In 2002, after the ethnic war we so graciously managed to get ourselves tangled in, Mister President fell once more, and was swiftly replaced by the Mayor of Antananarivo, who was leading the opposition party.

Hooray? Sure. But only briefly.

Two years in, and the new president's leadership has brought back chaos.

He, much like the last, needed a crash course in democracy.

He was a businessman. A good one at that. So good, in fact, that all the other businesses that were not his... were slowly dying. Ours included.

While his story was inspiring, his greed prevented him from being the brilliant president he could have been. The story of the young milkman pedalling through the streets before rising to become Madagascar's king of yogurt is well-known across the island. He was a modest man whose entrepreneurial adventure began in 1977. His business took off five years later, thanks to a $2 million loan from the bank. With the success of his milk and yogurt business, he founded a political movement in the late nineties, which led him to become the Mayor of Antananarivo.

After his time as Mayor of Antananarivo, he ran for president in 2001 and assumed office in 2002, bringing an end to the ethnic conflicts, socialism, and the dictatorship. Or so we hoped.

His company founded the country's largest supermarket chain. It exclusively sold its own products. Any food you wanted to buy, outside the fresh vegetables and fruits in the market, was branded with "Mada Mart". Claire lost her job at the Solo Market because it had to shut down.

She went back to work when Hira was 3 years old. She felt terrible guilt and anxiety about not being the one to take Hira to school and look after her. I'm the one who had that chance, as the printing company is here, at home. And my hours are flexible.

"You should only go if you feel ready," I advised, but she countered.

"I'll never feel ready, but I need to return to work. It's not for me. It's for her. I want her to see I fought for her, and I want her to be inspired by me and be proud of me".

I *am* definitely proud of her.

Her job applications yielded no results during the initial months. Her chances were slim, with a three-year employment gap after the baby's birth, and no degree. Her talent is undeniable to me, but companies dismissed her potential because of her insufficient education and work history. My dad used his influence to get her the job at the Solo Market. A small, self-owned grocery store in the neighbourhood. My dad's an old friend of the director.

The fact that she needed to pull strings to get hired didn't bother Claire. "Sometimes you have to accept help," she said. Plus, it wasn't solely my father's influence that got her the position. My dad only got her the interview. She aced the interview and began her new job the following Monday.

She woke before sunrise each morning, preparing banana beignets—what we Malagasy call *mofo akondro*—for Hira and me before heading to work. Then she was gone from 6.30 am to 4.30 pm.

Each day following school, Hira's gaze remained glued to the bus stop from the balcony as she waited for her mum. Each bus brought a flicker of hope to her face, dashed when Claire wasn't there. As another bus neared, her eyes gleamed with renewed hope. When Claire finally stepped off, they exchanged a long-awaited, excited wave.

I always watched the emotional scene unfold from the window, overlooking both the balcony and the bus stop. Whenever Claire arrived at the gate, the funniest thing would happen. Hira would greet her with the question, "What did you bring for me today?" Claire, predictably ready, would then give Hira a bag of plums—Hira's favourite.

But now, everything changed since Claire lost her job. It was bad enough that we were now down to one single income, but worse was the fact that Claire lost one thing she truly enjoyed.

That wasn't the end of it.

Initially focused on agribusiness and retail, the president's company had grown into a vast conglomerate encompassing various sectors.

First, the media sector. He established the Malagasy National Broadcasting—a radio station, TV channel, and newspaper—all under his team's complete authority. Talk about freedom of expression.

He later founded Malagasy BTP, gaining exclusive rights for all road surfacing contracts in the capital. Didn't stop there. He ventured into aviation with Sky Mada, then the petroleum industry with Madagascar Energy Solutions.

And finally... publishing, printing and paper manufacturing with Blueprint Press. That destroyed us.

Our printing company was doing well, with a client base large enough to keep it running. But we were definitely too small. Dazo and I took care of the printing; Dazo's wife, and a few cousins needing extra money handled quality control and packaging.

Deliveries were another task I handled, with the car we unexpectedly retrieved from Mahajanga—a car that we didn't use as a rental after all. My Simca conked out upon the Renault 5's arrival, as if it sensed its retirement after years of use; hence, we exclusively relied on the new car for everything.

Blueprint Press was bigger and faster, with equipment shifting towards digital printing, making traditional offset printing, and our beast of an iron machine, as efficient as a horse in a car race. Blueprint Press provided rapid order fulfilment with customisation options, short print runs, and quick turnaround times.

Our clients left one by one, starting with our biggest one. They were considerate about it. Following their departure, we received a letter of apology and gratitude for our years of service. While heartwarming, that letter was not financially helpful, so we shut down.

Once again, the years of effort were reduced to dust. Tossed in the trash.

And once again, we were down to zero income.

Fuck. This.

THE EUCALYPTUS TREE

Hira and Claire are in bed. It's Tuesday, 11 pm. I sit in the dark in our living room. We practically built this room ourselves. We laid the floor and painted the walls. Little by little, with every job the printing business brought in, we added to it. It dawns on me that I really had something good with that printing company. It was something I was proud of and something I thought I'd be doing all my life. The loss feels much heavier than ever before, heavier than when I lost the garage—not even mentioning the junk dealing or whatever we call that. That was hardly a loss.

This one is not easy to take.

And my dad... Shit.

He invested in us and lost everything in this, too. I couldn't bear it if he went down that road again. Luckily, this time, he won't struggle too much, thanks to his retirement.

There is no fighting the urge.

I pick up my glass, and drain the whisky it contains, hating myself a little more with each gulp, but also feeling a little lighter.

I've significantly improved my drinking habits since getting married to Claire and having Hira.

Let me be clear. I continued to drink. Never went a day without it. But I never let myself go too far.

Never came home drunk.

It was easy to hide, since Claire was at work and Hira was at school all day.

To meet deadlines, Dazo and I worked nights, and I'd increase my alcohol intake on those nights. But that's all.

I felt I'd finally balanced things and gained control over my arch-nemesis.

The fuck I did.

I lack any control whatsoever regarding alcohol. Sure, it hasn't consumed every waking hour of my life lately, and it's been a while since I've jolted awake to the relentless pounding in my skull and the bitter taste of self-hatred coating my tongue. But it never truly left me. It stayed hidden, waiting patiently in the dark corners of my mind, ready to strike the moment I stumbled. And all it took was one slip, one treacherous step down that familiar, slippery road, for it to return with devastating strength. Now, it feels unstoppable, and I despise myself for letting it take hold once more.

***

Claire wasn't concerned the first time I got drunk. Or if she was, she didn't show it. One time could be a mistake. I had a hard time with the company shutting down. I felt bad for all the things we've lost, and I felt guilty for failing my dad.

It seemed reasonable for anyone to drink excessively, given the circumstances.

The next day, it still seemed normal to her. A rough patch. A man needing to take the edge off.

By day three, she was surprised, yet not entirely bewildered.

Surprise gave way to worry on the fourth day.

She was always aware of my drinking; she's far too perceptive not to have noticed. But I'd kept it so carefully hidden, so meticulously "controlled," that it never crossed her mind it had once been a problem, let alone that it's *still* a problem. To her, I was just someone who occasionally enjoyed a drink. Oh, I wish.

I hate myself for it. I always have, but now that self-loathing runs deeper, cuts sharper, because it's hurting Claire—and if I'm not careful, it might harm Hira too. At least I always manage to remain sober until she sleeps. But the minute Claire tucks her into bed, the glass is already halfway to my lips.

***

It's been a little over three months now and I've been drunk every single night. I saw the shift in Claire's eyes. She's worried, sad and heavily disappointed.

Disappointed that I hid this from her?

Disappointed that I'm not making more effort for our family?

All of it?

I don't know, but they're not the same eyes that used to look at me with admiration.

Then again, my own self-disappointment could be distorting my perception.

She tried everything: helping me feel better, talking sense into me, reasoning gently, giving me space, staying close, showing compassion. She tried anger and tears, pleading and threatening, ultimatums. She left me alone, held me tight, shouted, whispered, and waited quietly.

Nothing worked.

Now, she's reached the point where she simply ignores it. It painfully reminds me of how we dealt with my father's drinking, ignoring it, acting like it wasn't happening, as if refusing to see it could somehow make it less real. There's a word for that: denial. But sometimes denial is easier to bear than facing the raw, unbearable pain of the truth.

"I got another rejection," Claire says

I'm sitting in the living room. God, it seems to be the only place I sit these days. The TV is on, but I'm not sure I was watching.

Hira is at school, so I suppose this is a good time to talk. I briefly meet her eyes when she sits next to me on the sofa, but her sorrowful expression forces me to look away quickly.

"I'm sorry. I'm sure you'll find something." I say. She's been sending out job applications.

"The thing is, there is not much time. We need to find a solution. We have to pay for Hira's tuition. Tomorrow, we're meeting at the school office to discuss an extension on our payment deadline."

Shit.

It hurts to hear Claire say "we", because she's been single-handedly addressing problems around here for months.

The trouble came much faster than I anticipated. We saved a small amount of money. I expected it to last more than three months.

"I'm so sorry. I'll think of something."

I mean it.

If I was waiting for something to shake me, this is it. My daughter's future can't be fucked over my everlasting self-loathing.

I considered driving a taxi again, but regulations have tightened. During my time as a taxi driver, I'd go out, find and pick up passengers. No paperwork necessary.

Nowadays, taxi licenses are required, and all taxis in Antananarivo must be beige. Because they're yellow in New York and black in London, we also had to make up our own "identity". Like that's what's going to save the country. All of that was going to require some investment.

With a shaky voice, Claire confides, "I've talked to Perle, and I may have a plan."

Perle is a former colleague of Claire's. With visible surprise, I look up at her once more. She carries on.

"She found a job, you know?" She says.

Yes, I know that, because she told me a few days before. I wonder if she repeats herself just to make sure I pay attention and haven't completely lost it. It stings a bit, but I'm not going to blame her for something that is entirely my fault. It also stings that everyone seems to have bounced back. Claire is sending job applications, her friend has secured a new job, and even Dazo is now a supervisor at a garage in town. All those years spent running a garage in the yard finally paid off. I'm happy for them, especially for my little bro. He deserves it. But let's be honest, it just makes me an even bigger loser.

"Yes, I know. I remember," is all I can say.

Perle secured a position with a firm specialising in offshore outsourcing, providing diverse digital services to

French businesses. Claire applied too, but her French wasn't good enough, so her application was rejected.

"She gave me an interesting piece of information."

My eyebrow instantly goes up in intrigued curiosity.

"Her main point was that the workers have nowhere to eat during their breaks. The closest shop is too far for a quick break, and preparing lunch beforehand isn't convenient for everyone. Most of them are in their twenties and don't cook at all," she explains, then adds, "a few start as early as 6 am, leaving no time to cook before work."

I listen carefully because I still don't see where she's going with this.

She goes on, "They break at 9:30 am and noon," seemingly expecting it to explain her point.

"I see. So, what—"

"I'm going to sell sandwiches there. In front of their workplace. I've thought about it. I don't need anything fancy. Just a table and some trays to put the food on. And you... You can drive me there."

The firmness in her voice mirrors my mother's when she declared she'd get a job to help the family. This also implies that there's no room for debate. She is going to do it.

I can't spare the time to calculate the costs and potential profits. I'm just going to trust her here.

It's not like we have other choices. I've worked as a junk dealer, mechanic, taxi driver, and printer—what's another job to add to the list? Provided it supports my family and keeps my daughter in school.

"Let's do it!" I say.

And for the first time in three months, I see my wife smile.

***

It's 8 am, and my hands are tired from the rhythmic motions, scooping mayo, spreading it evenly, stacking lettuce and tomato, layering slices of mortadella and cheese, only to repeat the process over and over. We're like machines. Claire made the mayonnaise, washed the salad, and sliced the mortadella and the cheese as thinly as possible so we can get more sandwiches out of them. I put the sandwiches together, carefully letting the ingredients peek just beyond the bread, making them look as tempting as possible.

Twenty-six sandwiches in total. That's a pretty good start. I think.

As I box the sandwiches, Claire is squeezing lemons. With today's heat, we thought selling lemonade would be a good idea.

We need to act fast to catch the workers' 9:30 am break. The drive is usually twenty minutes, but traffic is unpredictable. We also need to allot some time to set up our small "shop".

Arriving precisely at 9:22 am, we position ourselves directly across from Optima Outsourcing's gate, perfectly aligned with the entrance. Setting the table, I arrange two trays of sandwiches, a 'Ar600' price tag, three bottles of lemonade, and ten plastic cups.

In case we sold more cups, we brought a bucket of water on hand for cleaning. We have no idea how many people, if any, will show up.

9:30 am: A wave of workers pours out of the gate like ants emerging from a tiny hole.

There are far more than I could possibly imagine. Fifty or more people rush forward, their eyes shining with excitement at the sight of the food stall.

They spot the limited supply and immediately understand there won't be nearly enough for everyone. They actually race to get to us. Claire's hands are full, handing out sandwiches, taking money, and giving change. I'm on lemonade duty, pouring cups, collecting empties, rinsing them in the bucket, then serving the next.

It's madness.

In less than ten minutes, we're completely sold out!

"Wow, what a fantastic idea!" Perle shouts as she approaches us when we finally get a minute to sit down. "Make sure you bring more next time, okay? They're hungry teens. You'll need to triple your stock," she grins.

"I can't believe it. You didn't tell me there were so many people in there!" Claire tells her friend.

"You didn't tell me you were going to open a food stall right in front of the gate; I would have given you a heads-up," she teases. "The next break is at 12 pm. Bring lunch! We'll be even hungrier. And good to see you Razaf!" She winks at Claire and is already on her way back to her office.

A hopeful look passes between Claire and me.

Holy shit.

There's a chance this will work.

22

Hira

2017

"Toy ny sambotra valala main'andro, raha tsy azoko anio, azoko rahampitso."
"Just like catching grasshoppers in the dry season—if I don't catch them today, I'll catch them tomorrow."

November's cold is nothing like February's. Sure, the cold air feels sharp and crisp against my cheeks, causing me to bury my hands deeper into my pockets as I walk, but the atmosphere has changed.

It is far from dull and colourless. Oxford Street is a spectacle. A thousand tiny stars, reflected in the pavement's glassy puddles, seem to stretch overhead in strings of golden light. Shop windows are dressed to impress, and giant nutcrackers stand guard outside department stores.

It's only mid-November, but the city has already given itself over to Christmas.

London doesn't wait.

London never waits.

I move through the crowd, past shoppers juggling bags, past couples huddled close, past street performers singing *Last Christmas* for what is probably the hundredth time today.

It should feel overwhelming, but it doesn't. It feels alive. It feels like I'm exactly where I'm supposed to be, while I'm headed to my favourite place in the world... The Paper Lantern.

As soon as I enter, the street's clamour fades, overtaken by the rich, welcoming smell of books and coffee. The Paper Lantern always feels enchanting, but with Christmas approaching, it's transformed into a holiday postcard. Wooden bookshelves are strung with fairy lights, and a small Christmas tree with book-themed ornaments and paper stars stands by the cash register. Glowing lanterns in a pine and berry garland draped over the counter bathe the room in golden light. Near the entrance, a table displays perfectly wrapped books labelled "Blind Date with a Book / Christmas Edition". They're all wrapped in brown paper, each with handwritten story clues. It feels like a place where time slows down. A refuge from the outside world's cold, rush, and noise.

After I take in every little detail, I close my eyes for a beat. I inhale deeply, letting the delicious smell fill my lungs. This is my happy place. I'm finally where I'm meant to be, both literally and metaphorically.

The news came unexpectedly, to say the least. I was in my bed, lost in my usual thoughts, wandering between a love life and a career that didn't really exist.

When my phone vibrated at 8 pm one night, I didn't jump to look at what it was.

I assumed it was unimportant. It couldn't be my parents, because they were asleep at that time. They wake up every day at 5 am.

It couldn't be Alex because, well, stupid me didn't give him my number. I would have if he had asked, but he hadn't.

Whoever it was, I didn't expect it to lift my mood.

But I reached for my phone anyway—if not for curiosity, then just out of boredom.

An email.

> "Dear Hira,
> Thank you for your application for the Content Writer position at Nomad Note. I sin-

cerely apologise for the delay in getting back to you.

The position has now been filled; however, we were very impressed with your application and would love to offer you an alternative opportunity. We have recently opened a Junior Writer position, and we believe you would be a great fit for the role.

If you're interested, we'd love to discuss the details with you. Please let us know your availability for a quick call or meeting at your convenience.

Looking forward to hearing from you.

Best regards,

Ada

Nomad Note"

Nomad Note!

I stared at the email, rereading it twice, three times, four times just to convince my brain that it was not hallucinating.

This position had been filled. No surprise there.

I sent that application months ago but have never heard back. I had already written it off as another dead end.

I double-checked the sender. Legit.

I scanned the wording for some kind of hidden trap. None.

It was real.

I was being offered a job.

I blinked. My brain short-circuited.

I screamed. Not a dignified, restrained sound—a full-on, oh-my-God-this-is-happening scream.

My body vibrated with adrenaline, legs pumping under the covers in a frantic, childlike tantrum.

The reality hit me like a wave. The past three months had been filled with doubts, feeling stuck, thinking I had no future here. And now, out of nowhere, this email?

I laughed. Or sobbed. I didn't even know. My body didn't know how to process it.

One week later, I left ReForma.

I didn't make a big deal out of leaving the startup. No dramatic goodbyes, no sentimental last looks at work. Just paperwork, and an exit as unremarkable as my time there had been.

I knew there was no permanent contract waiting for me at the end of that internship, and honestly, I didn't think I even wanted one.

I emailed the boss, keeping it short and professional. His reply was just as brief: a simple "Good luck". There were no questions, no follow-ups, nothing to suggest he was particularly bothered by my departure.

Which, honestly, was fine with me.

Before I logged out of my work email for the last time, I did one more thing.

I searched for Alex's email address.

I typed one out to him, too. It was quick and casual. Nothing dramatic. I sent a short message saying goodbye, that it was nice meeting him, and that he could text me if he wanted to get coffee sometime.

I added my phone number at the end.

Then I hit send.

Instantly, my heart thudded violently against my ribs.

That was a bold move, but for the first time in months, I felt bold. I felt invincible.

Because I had just secured a job at Nomad Note.

***

I still can't quite believe it, but here I am, officially one of the writers for Nomad Note magazine. Suddenly, I'm one of those magical beings downstairs at The Paper Lantern, endlessly tapping away at their laptops. Earphones gently humming my favourite music, I'm passionately weaving together an article about a courageous 30-year-old woman who swapped Manchester's grey skies for Malaga's golden sun, embarking on a new life with her spirited seven-year-old daughter.

The job is amazing. It involves travel writing, practical guides, and the occasional deep dive into remote work culture.

My work varies widely; one day I might be comparing the cost of living between Mexico City and Bangkok, and the next interviewing a successful camper van business owner. A lot of it is research-heavy: digging into visa policies, finding the best coworking spaces, and comparing internet speeds in different cities. But the part I love most is the storytelling. When I get to interview people, I'm so invested in their stories.

More than just the numbers, it's about conveying the experience of living and working abroad. They talk about the unexpected hardships, and the truths that surface once the initial charm diminishes. And somehow, through those people's stories, I learn things about myself that I haven't realised before.

I'm also a foreigner. A woman who left home to find a home elsewhere. The stories about belonging and the unique difficulties of making a new place feel like home resonate with me the strongest.

Almost one year ago, I moved from Madagascar to London, so I've experienced that unsettling feeling of outgrowing my childhood home. I realise that the longer I'm away, the more foreign my home starts to feel, even as it stays stitched into the fabric of who I am.

Through the stories I write, I see my own experiences reflected back at me in different ways. Someone talks about how they carry pieces of their home country with them, in the way they cook or the music they listen to, and I realise I do the same.

Someone else describes the guilt of feeling more at ease in their new country than the one they were born in, and I know exactly what they mean. This job is about writing other people's stories, but in the process, I keep finding pieces of my own.

I love it. I think I'm meant to do this.

And I'm doing my parents and my grandparents proud with this job. When I told them I found a job, albeit as a Junior, they all had their way of showing me how happy they were. My mum cried on the phone, my grandma said a little prayer, my dad, ever practical and ever careful not to be too happy in case something went wrong, asked if it could lead to a Senior position. When I said it could, he was the happiest I'd ever seen him.

THE EUCALYPTUS TREE

But what stuck with me the most was what my grandpa said: "This is it, from here, there's nothing you can't do".

He didn't just mean the job. He meant my future. In his eyes, the hardest part was already behind me—I'd left. I'd broken the cycle. Poverty and political instability kept my family from moving forward, trapping us in destructive patterns.

But I had done what my dad couldn't.

My grandpa still considers that his biggest failure today, the fact that, because of him, my dad could never leave the country and do what he wanted to do. So, this is also for my grandfather.

I had left Madagascar and built a life elsewhere. With this job, I was finally setting down roots in a career that meant something to me. Now, everything else was just a matter of time.

"This is it, from here, there's nothing I can't do," I say to myself. I don't know if I believe that as fully as my grandfather does. London isn't exactly easy, and making a living as a writer isn't either. But when he said it, there was so much certainty in his voice, so much pride, that I let myself believe it too, for a moment.

The road is still long. But hey, we're through the tunnel now.

23
Razaf
2017

"Ny hery tsy mahaleo ny fanahy."
"The strength of the spirit is mightier than physical power."

While Optima Outsourcing's employees come and go, we're still here. This is the longest job I've ever held. It's also the only one that wasn't shaken by political turmoil.

In 2009, Madagascar was once again plunged into chaos. A large part of the population rose up against *Monsieur le Président laitier*—the milkman president—and the crisis reached a devastating climax when security forces opened fire on protesters. At least forty bodies were left lying in the streets, that we know of.

My interest in politics had waned by that point. I stopped protesting. All that mattered was our business's survival. Work and food were always unavoidable for everyone. So, thankfully, our food stall was spared.

Setting aside the political upheaval, the past thirteen years have been relatively uneventful. I'm definitely starting to feel my age, though. I'm nowhere near as motivated to fight as I used to be. Honestly, if it weren't for Hira, I'd probably have given up long ago.

Hira is clever, *really* clever. We've never had trouble with her at school. Teachers always praised her intelligence during parents' evenings, congratulating us as if I had anything to do with it. Maybe Claire did, but me? Not a chance.

After finishing high school at sixteen, Hira started freelancing straight away, knowing she'd have to earn money herself to attend university. Paying for a private school in Madagascar is already a challenge, but paying for a private university is something else entirely. She had no interest in the public university, and I can't blame her. With only one overcrowded public university regularly disrupted by teacher or student strikes, there's barely any proper learning going on.

Eventually, Hira realised that if she genuinely wanted a shot at becoming a writer, she'd need to go abroad. I couldn't fault her for wanting to leave. I myself had those same dreams when I realised just how messed up this country was. And sadly, things haven't got any better since then.

People say the grass isn't always greener on the other side. Sure. But, bloody hell, it's got to be at least a little greener than it is here, hasn't it?

Don't get me wrong. I love my country. I'm proud to be Malagasy. Our culture is rich and distinctive; I genuinely believe we've got the best music, the tastiest food, and the most beautiful language. Where else do you find words like *sotro rovitra* for fork, literally meaning "ripped spoon", or *solosaina* for computer, translating beautifully as "replacement for the brain"? Poetic, clever, brilliant.

But I'm also realistic. And the reality is that this isn't a country where dreams easily come true.

The queue is as long as the list of promises politicians never keep. It doesn't help calm my nerves. It's incredibly crowded at the bank. In my fifty-three years on this plentiful earth, this is the first time I've been to the bank. I can't imagine what all of these people need to do here.

Claire and I are here to apply for a loan. Hira was accepted at the London School of Journalism. As in, a school of Journalism in London.

London. England. Great Britain.

For real.

There's no way we can afford to send her there. Not with the little money we earn from our food stall.

We started out small: just a simple table with two trays of sandwiches and three bottles of lemonade. Since then, we've expanded steadily. While not yet a fully-fledged shop, our stall is now a proper wooden structure offering an extended menu, including sandwiches, beignets, and pasta salads. We still don't have walls or a roof, relying instead on a large yellow umbrella to shield our food from the sun. But despite this progress, we barely earn enough to cover food costs and bills.

There's simply nothing left over. No extra. 7th December, our wedding anniversary, is the one day of the year we allow ourselves a little indulgence. We always celebrate by taking Hira to Bons Burgers, making it a special family tradition. But that's it. Just once a year. Nothing more, nothing extravagant. Just that single day for the last thirteen years.

We also started without a name or registration for our food stall. Like many small businesses here, it just existed. No paperwork, no official recognition. Taxes in Madagascar aren't very strict, at least not for businesses like ours. No one comes knocking to check if we're paying, and honestly, most of us aren't. It's good for us, of course. One less expense, one less thing to worry about when every *ariary* counts.

We know it's not good for the country. No taxes means no proper roads, no decent hospitals, no support when things go wrong. But that's the thing about living in a poor country. It's *chacun pour soi*—every man for himself. You do what you have to do to survive, even if it means playing a part in the very system that keeps things broken.

However, to be able to get a loan, Claire and I needed to prove that we had enough income to pay the loan back. Registering the business and income was the only way to achieve that, so we're now the proud owners of Le Parasol Jaune food stall. Hira named it after the yellow umbrella.

We have all the documents we need for the loan, but the wait is excruciating. I'm as nervous as the first time I went on stage to perform with Dazo, minus the adrenaline.

In fact, it is the opposite of adrenaline. Dread. Lethargy. Deflation. I don't know, something like that.

When we arrived, we were given a number. 245. That must mean we are the 245th customer today.

With 232 showing on the screen, we're thirteenth in line. Figuring ten minutes a customer, the wait will be at least another two hours.

What the fuck?

As predicted, about two hours later, an agent finally calls us in.

The small office contains a desk that seems too big and a dusty fan that hums quietly in the corner. The agent, a middle-aged man in a neatly pressed shirt, greets us with a polite but practiced smile, the kind that says he's done this a hundred times before. Just another boring day for this man, when our daughter's fate is in his hands.

He asks for our documents first. We hand them over, watching him flip through each page with slow, deliberate movements. Identity cards, business registration, income proof—everything we scrambled to gather—he scans them, and starts typing into his computer, the rhythmic clacking of the keyboard filling the silence.

Then come the questions.

What kind of business do we run?

How long have we been operating?

How much do we earn monthly?

We maintain a steady pace in our responses, even while he hesitates, his expression showing slight confusion.

Next, he explains the terms: the interest rate, the repayment period, and the penalties for late payments. He tells us how much we qualify for, a figure that seems hopeful.

The whole time, my mind screams, "Give us the money already". And something in Claire's expression tells me she's losing her patience, too.

More typing. More waiting.

Then he prints out a stack of papers, sliding them across the desk with a pen.

That's a good sign, right?

He wouldn't print papers if it was rejected.

"Read carefully before signing," he says.

Yes, that's definitely a good sign. I've never heard of anyone needing to sign a rejected loan. We sign the papers one by one.

Signing papers always feels like something important, like a moment that shifts the course of things. It's been 24 years since I last signed something—my wedding certificate.

As I sign the final page today, my grip tightens just a little.

The bank agent reviews the documents one last time, tapping each sheet against the desk to align them neatly. Then he looks up and nods.

"Congratulations," he says, sliding a copy toward me. "Your loan is approved."

The agent leans back in his chair.

"The funds will be transferred within three business days. Your first repayment is due in thirty days. If you have any questions, you know where to find us."

I nod, but my mind is already racing ahead. We shake hands politely and formally. We step out of the office, back into the heat, back into the world where nothing has changed yet—but everything will soon.

24

Hira

2024

"Kodiaran-tsarety ny fiainana ka mifandimby ambony sy ambany."
"Life is like a cartwheel: you may be low today, but you'll always be lifted back up."

This is it. After seven years of hard work, this is the day I've been waiting for. The airport looks different from here. It's the same airport I landed in seven years ago, but standing at arrivals is an entirely different feeling.

Back then, I was the one stepping through those doors, suitcase in hand, eyes scanning unfamiliar signs, heart pounding with the weight of everything I was leaving behind. I remember the cold air that hit me as I stepped outside, the hum of a city that didn't yet feel like mine. That day, I was the foreigner, the newcomer, the one adjusting.

Seven years. That's how long it took for me to go from an uncertain student to a Senior writer, and finally turn my promises into reality.

25

Razaf

2024

"Ny tiana tsy mahalavi-tany."
"Love knows no distance."

The airport is bigger than I expected—bigger than what Hira has prepared us for. She told us about the long hallways, the endless signs, and the moving walkways that pull people along as if walking isn't fast enough. But being here, *actually here*, is different.

Claire clings to my arm. Out of fear or out of habit, I don't know.

We keep walking, one step at a time, swallowed by the crowd spilling through the arrival gates. Everything here feels different. The air, the lights, the endless movement.

Voices echo from every direction, in languages I barely recognise. The sharp beep of scanners, the rolling of suitcases against polished floors—it all blurs together, like a place that doesn't stop, that doesn't wait for anyone.

To think, seven years ago, Hira walked through these same gates, alone, carrying all her fears and hopes in a single suitcase.

And years before that, it could have been me. Not exactly this airport, but still. Forty-two years have passed since I was supposed to board a plane and pursue my dreams. Gosh, it's been so long, it's like it never happened.

Mum and Dad took us to the airport. As we got there, there was an uncomfortable air of déjà vu. It didn't help that the airport in Antananarivo looked exactly the same. There has been no improvement since then.

Before boarding the plane, I expected someone would stop us.

But we checked in. Nobody stopped us.

We hugged goodbye. Nobody stopped us.

We walked to our gate. Nobody stopped us.

We boarded the plane, and still, nobody stopped us.

And now, we're here.

We walk for what feels like forever. The airport stretches endlessly ahead.

Claire and I move forward, unsure of where we're going but going anyway, following the current of people who seem to know exactly where they're headed. We don't speak. We walk on, suitcases trailing, our hearts pounding with a feeling that is neither fear nor comfort.

And then, there she is. Standing just beyond the barrier, waiting. Hira.

As I spot her, her promises echo in my mind: *"I'm not leaving you behind. I'm moving us forward."*

THE END

Acknowledgements

I've always said I wanted to publish a novel when I turned 30. Exactly one week from today, the day I'm writing this, I will celebrate my 31st birthday. I'm slightly late on my deadline, but this book is still being published before I officially leave my 30th year, albeit at the very last minute. And for this achievement, I have some very important people to thank.

First and foremost, I want to thank my daughter. Being a writer has been my dream for as long as I can remember, yet for years I did little to make it a reality. It was simply an aspiration I carried quietly. My daughter inspired me to finally take action. She dreams of becoming a ballerina, an artist, a singer, and sometimes even a ballerina police officer. I wanted her to know she can truly be anything she wants, so I finally took my first step toward becoming a writer. After all, showing her is better than simply telling her.

I also owe deep thanks to my incredibly supportive family, who encourage me endlessly. At the forefront are my parents and my husband, whose unwavering support means more than words can express. A special shout-out to my sister, who's not nearly as into books as I am and yet still powered through my draft in two nights, fuelled by sibling duty, and provided brilliant feedbacks! And to my brother, who's always ready with the wildest ideas, including the suggestion to turn this book into a podcast or something. Who knows? Maybe it will happen.

And finally, I wouldn't be a writer without readers. So my heartfelt gratitude goes out to you, dear reader, for making me not only a published author but an author whose work is genuinely read. I've always said that if even one person outside my circle of family and friends read my first book, I would consider it a success. You've made this a success. So, from the bottom of my heart, thank you!

Printed in Great Britain
by Amazon